Ship of Tears

Ship of Tears

A novel of WWII
by

Timothy Cole

www.penmorepress.com

Ship of Tears by Timothy Cole

Copyright © 2025 Timothy Cole

ISBN-13: 978-1-957851-96-1(Paperback)
ISBN -978-1-957851-85-95-2(e-book)

BISAC Subject Headings:
FIC002000FICTION / Action & Adventure
FIC014000FICTION / Historical
FIC032000FICTION / War & Military
FIC047000FICTION / Sea Stories

Cover work by Emilija Rakić PR Emily's World of Design

Please send all correspondence to:
Penmore Press LLC
920 N Javelina Pl
Tucson AZ 85748

Dedication

Ship of Tears is dedicated to all the hometown heroes in the Finger Lakes region of New York State, who wore the uniform and answered the call.

Prologue
Man Overboard

The day of our man-overboard incident began like any other and I was up, showered, and dressed by four-thirty a.m. My overly sumptuous cabin aboard the *U.S.S. James F. Bridger* had a small wardroom for taking meetings, a sitting area with club chairs, a head with a shower, and a double bed in a compartment behind a sliding pocket door. *Bridger* was a converted ocean liner, so certain officers on the upper decks had to put up with this kind of sinful comfort.

As I walked toward the bridge, I passed by the radio shack and could hear coded Morse signals reach out to find us in mid-Pacific. I stuck my head in the door of our navigation section, and I saw our quartermaster team putting the finishing touches on three intersecting lines that would define our position on this watery planet. I glanced at the fix on our dead reckoning plot and saw we were about a hundred miles west-southwest of our last position, right where we wanted to be.

Up in our big wheelhouse, someone shouted, "Commander on the bridge!" and my team came to attention. I never cared for this sort of puffery. I was a reservist and a country lawyer. I prided myself on being able to relate to all walks and all stations. But little acts like this helped burnish the chain of command and fostered good relations. When we were at action stations, the crew depended on its leadership, and the leadership depended on the crew. The ship's formalities helped maintain this primordial order.

I told them "At ease" as I walked over to my elevated chair on the port side. The bridge was bathed in an ethereal crimson from our night lamps. I glanced over to the man at the helm and saw one of our young seamen etched in the glow of the binnacle light. The officer of the deck was standing next to the engine room telegraph, maintaining an instantaneous synapse between the wheelhouse and the throttle panel belowdecks near the boiler room. I had a sound-powered phone within reach to my left, a nearby holster for my binoculars, and a small folding desk where I could sign reports. A steward from the officers' mess had my coffee and a blueberry muffin still warm from the oven.

We were at darken ship, and a sliver of moon was sinking over the bow, adding relief to the fantastic dome of stars that enfolded us. First light would be coming in a few minutes, but right then, we were lone voyagers on a tranquil sea and the perfection of this solitary instant was belied by a world war that had touched nearly every continent. We were a tool to be fed, watered, and harnessed in this global catastrophe. But right then we were sailing through a blissful calm. I sipped my coffee and was struck anew at how lucky I was to be at this rare time and sacred place...on the bridge of a mighty ship at sunrise.

That's when the klaxon sounded, and the words "man overboard, port stern quarter, B deck" came out of the shipboard public-address system, which we called the 1MC for "one marine channel." I put my muffin down on my folding desk and walked out on the port bridge wing. There was a small enclosure at the outboard end and I could stand inside and look all the way aft to the scene of this morning's emergency. Now, there was a siren added to the klaxon, and as I looked aft, I could see the sun's orange glow painting a limitless horizon. It was early, but there was enough light to see down the majestic flanks of our troopship. I could see a party down on B deck where the person apparently went in. The space was devoted to our after mooring tackle. I knew we had plenty of talent concentrating on the problem back there. I wanted to get to our deck officer and our chief petty officer, who would guide our neophyte bridge team through the drill.

We needed to turn ninety degrees northwest, perpendicular from our present heading, then perform a sweeping turn to port through two hundred seventy degrees relative so we could take up a bearing on the reciprocal track. We needed to get our lookouts forward and we needed to phone up to our crows' nests fore and aft to keep a sharp eye. Today's officer of the deck and the CPO were way ahead of me and I could see a deck party moving forward as we made our turn northwest, and then west, southwest, and finally northeast into a sun just breaking over the fiery lip of the horizon.

I grabbed my binoculars and walked back out to the bridge wing so I could see what was going on astern. I discerned a lot of milling and pointing, and I knew I'd have to get back there in a few minutes as soon as our bridge party had the situation in hand. The good news: it was an agreeable day. There was a light breeze out of the east creating a slight roll in the sea state. The bad news: finding a man on these soft swells wouldn't be easy. Imagine trying to find a tiny coconut on a vast ocean. The OD telegraphed the All Slow to the engine room and I could feel *Bridger* settle as we found the reciprocal of our outbound heading and started to backtrack. I would have to report all this to the captain, who kept our schedules. He was not going to be happy. I also needed to get down to the scene and I needed to be ready to call off the search when the time came. It was a tough and unforgiving business, but the loss of one person could not disrupt this giant, crawling, pulsing organism pushing relentlessly toward the Solomon Islands and the battle for Guadalcanal.

The traditions of the Navy dictated that I must make my way aft and down along the port side. Moving forward meant walking starboard side and up. We were a crowded ship and this small piece of traffic management meant we could maintain an orderly flow, particularly important during general quarters. Soon, I was standing on B deck and I was peering at a large blood stain. I was accompanied by my chief of security, Lieutenant-Commander Nathan Haggerty, and my damage control assistant, an unrated seaman named Salvatore "Sal" Marchionda, who, quite correctly, called in the man overboard alarm when he spotted the stain.

"Let's be clear, Seaman Marchionda, you didn't actually see a person go overboard."

"No sir, I didn't," said Marchionda. "But the blood stain on deck near the gate in the rail told me somebody went through there. Seemed like a man overboard call was the right thing to do."

"I'd do the same thing, Sal," I told him, and he relaxed a bit. Sal made the discovery near the fantail. It's a lovely term we use for the more severe "stern" when it came to defining a point at the after extremity of our ship. The space was an extension of B Deck, and it was open all around except for A Deck over our heads. B Deck was where we kept *Bridger's* after mooring tackle. Casual visitors out for a smoke would have to maneuver around the big windlasses and bollards we used to attach our ship to a pier. We used the gate in the rail so we could come and go if we were rafted up to another ship. It was a place to step through if circumstances permitted, but it was also a long way down to the foamy wash kicked up by *Bridger's* twin propellers. Haggerty had his head over the side and offered an opinion.

"The guy stayed in the gate with the door open," he told us. "There's a good bit of blood running down the topsides."

"Holy crap," offered Marchionda, whose limited yet colorful expressions belied an insightful mind. Marchionda was a thief, and I'd fished him out of the brig early in *Bridger's* travels so I could employ his highly irregular talents.

"What are these two streaks back here?" Marchionda wondered aloud, and that got Haggerty's attention.

"Looks familiar," he ruminated, scratching his chin.

"Drag marks?" I asked him.

"Looks like it." Haggerty closed the gate in the rail and we continued our huddle around the blood. The streaks pointed in the direction of a big horizontal winch we used for hauling in cables. We walked back in that direction and stopped when we saw more blood streaks.

"Two of them," said Marchionda, articulating what our eyes could plainly see. Marchionda had moved deeper into the small forest of gear. "This way," he told us, popping up from behind a big windlass drum.

Haggerty and I eased in that direction. Soon we were standing over a prodigious pool of deep, red blood, browning around the edges in the morning heat.

"Guy got knifed right here," said Haggerty. "And not a

little nick either. I'd say by the spray, he got it in the neck."

"There's blood all the way out here," said Marchionda.

"Careful Sal," I told him. "We need to maintain the hygiene of what looks like a crime scene."

"Quite correct, Commander Pratt," Haggerty said. He and I sometimes reverted to the formal, especially when in company with other members of the ship's crew. I saw two or three clear footprints in the blood, plus a partial that might have belonged to another boot or shoe.

Haggerty was tall, beefy, and looked like he'd been chiseled out of a piece of granite...just what you'd want in your chief of security. He'd been with *Bridger* since her first cruise right after Pearl Harbor. There was a time when Haggerty and I didn't see eye to eye. I was hoping the war would paper over any grudges, but there were days it looked like it was going to be a long wait. The crew had given Haggerty a nickname—'Hit 'Em Hard' Haggerty—and that about summed it up.

"Well," I said. "We have no body. We have no murder weapon. We can't make an ID, form associations, contact next of kin, sift evidence."

"Only thing we can do is wait for someone to turn up missing," said Haggerty, an insight that later proved correct. "What's the size of our complement Mr. Pratt?"

"Almost seven thousand, give or take," I told him. "Plus, ninety-three Navy officers and four-hundred thirteen Navy enlisted." *Bridger* was a moving, floating city, with food, drink, sanitation, berthing, barbershops, a theater, three hospitals, a swimming pool, now dry and filled with boxes of consumables, especially Lucky Strikes. The nurses in the medical department had assembled a dance troupe, and we had a barber-shop quartet. But, as we discovered on our first cruise, our big ship was not immune from the kind of criminal activity that could afflict any small society. Still, we couldn't let lawbreakers distract us from our primary mission: delivering man and machine, the tip of America's spear, to the battlefront. It was an awesome responsibility and I would not have traded my job for anything—except perhaps a chance to drive a battleship and fire those big shells into Yokohama. But that was for the Annapolis crowd. I was a small-town lawyer and a reservist, and I told myself putting our people into the fight was just as important as delivering fire and brimstone to the enemy's doorstep.

"We need to get the word out to all our Marine units to check for missing personnel," I told Marchionda and Haggerty. I turned to Marchionda and offered the next logical step.

"Sal, get yourself to the after medical department on D Deck. Find a vial, some rubber gloves, a tongue depressor and try to get a blood sample," I told him. "And swing by the Master at Arms department for a camera. We need shots of these footprints."

Haggerty was our lawman—an FBI special agent in civilian life—and he nodded in agreement. Haggerty had come aboard as a lieutenant commander and he'd remained at that rank, while I had been elevated to full commander and *Bridger's* executive officer, number two after our overlord, Captain Aldous Kelly, Jr. I was responsible for the ship and all her functions. Captain Kelly and our leadership in Admiral Nimitz's office at CINCPAC had been tasked with setting up the schedules according to where and when they needed to put America's finest into battle. The captain took care of the big picture. My job was to position *Bridger's* 783-foot length, 90-foot beam and 32-foot draft where the captain told me to. She needed to function at high speed, keep her crew and guests safe, and, if necessary, wield her deck guns to smite the enemy. We'd yet to bump into any hostiles on this cruise.

Could *Bridger's* enemies be coming from within?

"And Sal, see if you can pull some strings to expedite the serology," I said. Haggerty gave me a wink, conceding when it came to forensic science this Ivy League lawyer might occasionally have a good idea. Out here, there was no room for resentments. We had a busy ship to run. Marchionda trotted off to perform his errands and Haggerty and I kicked around ideas.

"Our victim was lured in," I observed. "There's no other reason to come out here unless you're on the boiler team and you're having a smoke." I had given our engine room chief Elvis Foster and his team of Caymanian contractors free run of this space so they could take the air. They'd run *Bridger's* massive boilers when she was *Majestic*. The Navy had had the good sense to hire them back. Elvis and his team were keeping *Bridger's* propulsion in a keen state of readiness.

"We will need to start counting heads in Elvis's department," said Haggerty.

"If anyone's missing, he would have called me," I told him. "But we've got more than seven thousand other options. Our victim probably knew his attacker, Nate. Assailant proposes a quiet meeting. Guy shows up without a clue. The deed is done. Over he goes."

"A grudge?" speculated Haggerty. "Fighting over the same girl?"

"Maybe," I responded. "But right now, I don't think our victim could survive this blood loss." Marchionda returned with a corpsman and a blood kit. They got to work taking a sample and shooting pictures. Haggerty and I stood next to the rail.

"Nope, our guy sank out of sight," Haggerty concluded. I nodded and walked over to Marchionda and his assistant.

Hygiene be damned.

"When you get your sample and your shots, open up that

raw-water hydrant and wash this deck down," I told him. "No way our guy is going to make it after this blood loss. I have to get the ship turned around."

Haggerty and I left Marchionda to his labors and we followed those bloody footprints inside and forward on the ship's gray steel deck plate. They seemed less distinct with every yard, and petered out altogether after about thirty feet, as if our killer had simply vanished. But the ghostly footprints told me whoever did this was still among us. Haggerty went back to the scene to assign Marchionda to mop the passageway and I made my way starboard, forward, and up, stopping by the Master at Arms Department.

Bridger's police force was operated by a Navy chief named Donahue, who came from a family of Boston cops. I informed him of our findings and let him know the odds of recovering our victim in all this ocean were simply impossible. I let him know we would be resuming our journey to the west-southwest. I would keep him advised regarding how we'd inform the Marine Corps section leaders, from Vandegrift, the general in charge of the First Marine Division, all the way down to the squads and the fire teams. The Marines needed to take attendance. It was the only way we'd find out who our victim was so we could notify next of kin. The victim's identity would also tell me who his buddies were—and if he had any enemies.

I made it to the bridge and ordered the officer of the deck to change course.

We had a schedule to keep, and the war wouldn't wait.

Chapter One
Bad Blood

Our man-overboard event sparked the beginning of some grim, dark days in the summer and fall of 1942. I am writing this account more than three decades later from the comfort of my law office in the thriving village of Bath, New York. Our village is the seat for the county of Steuben, in what the geography books call The Southern Tier. I am now the elder partner of Pratt and Pratt, the law firm started by my grandfather back in the last century. We still occupy the little brick building that fronts on Pulteney Park across from the courthouse. The office is next door to the National Hotel, where I join a few of our burghers each morning for coffee. I am dialing back my schedule, as I am ably assisted by my son Bart, who toils on behalf of clients near and far. He's a better lawyer than I'll ever be—efficient, productive, reassuring—and he's reached his full height. He understands the rigid, purified facts in the ancient tomes that line our bookshelves—along with the subtle subtexts where good lawyers seek advantage. He has a deft, gracious touch when clients arrive with their grievances and their outpourings.

Bart's labors give me time to attend to my quest. I am getting around to writing my war diary, to set down at last the great pitch and moment that attended my time as executive officer, then captain, of the great troopship *U.S.S. James F. Bridger*, a converted ocean liner that delivered more than three-hundred thousand of this country's fighting men and women to the far shores of World War II.

She was called "The Gray Ghost" because she could pour on her thirty-knot speed generated by her six Babcock and Wilcox boilers. Cranking up her steam turbines, she could outrun German U-boats, Japanese I-boats, and any surface threats the Axis Powers could throw her way. Early in the war she shed her lumbering destroyer escorts to sprint for the horizon, her massive silhouette broken up by her camouflage. She was made spare and lean, fixed with makeshift gun batteries, and sent across the seas to deliver America's best—her people—to the forward edge of battle. My job was to keep her functioning, from her bilge to her masthead, so Captain Kelly could set the schedules in step with War Department planning.

At this stage of my waning life, I am also shackled to hard fact—no excuses and no shading. I have to get it all down, and that means subjecting this writer to a searing scrutiny. I project an outward confidence, but I know that's all veneer. I have been tested, and I have made mistakes.

Now, in my twilight, I have some time to examine those deadly days of 1942. Through some accident of fate, I too entered the trenches and fighting holes on Guadalcanal as the Allies began their conquest of the Pacific. But the tale began when a passenger went overboard that brilliant morning and ended with a pursuit to the death of the most evil person I've ever known. As I take up my pen, my older brother and law partner Josiah—who became senior U.S. senator from the State of New York and ranking member of the Senate Armed Services Committee—is looking down on me from a photo on the wall. Josiah knew the story. He would want me to get this right.

Timothy Cole

The sun was up and nicely inclined as I took my seat back up on the bridge. Our emissary from the officer's mess had returned with fresh, hot coffee. I asked the yeoman to deliver a note to Captain Kelly begging his indulgence for a meeting, and I got the word he'd receive me for breakfast at seven. It gave me an hour to check in with my sections, and I sat above it all working the phone. Damage control was quiet, vigilant, and ready. My gunnery teams were locked and loaded, but we didn't expect any contact with the enemy this far east. We carried three-inch and five-inch guns in tactically positioned tubs fore and aft. We had .50-caliber machine guns for air and surface threats, and a bevy of fully automatic twenty-millimeter Oerlikon anti-aircraft machine cannon. As we learned off Okinawa later in the war, these armaments weren't enough, but they were all we had.

As I scanned the horizon with my Bausch & Lomb binoculars, the quartermaster group was engaged with maintaining our dead reckoning position every quarter hour. I reminded our Officer of the Deck, or OD, that Captain Kelly liked to oversee the noon sight. He needed to round up a few young ensigns to sit at the captain's knee.

I rang up Elvis in the boiler room and inquired as to the health of his men and his machinery. He returned in that lovely Caymanian lilt, "Right as rain, Mr. Pratt." Signaling was a bit sleepy this far out, but in the pre-dawn hours we had received a message from Pearl our code teams were deciphering. I had a quick word with supply and I learned there'd been a worrisome cargo shift in the forward hold on C Deck, probably due to a loading error. It would take the rest of the morning to unpack, repack, and get things sorted. I worried about the various munitions we had stored belowdecks, from .30-caliber armor-piercing rifle rounds to hand grenades to flame throwers. I finally got around to culinary—more important than our gun emplacements if you asked our Marine guests or ordinary seamen. I learned from our master chief that, except for the long lines, the morning's meal delivery was proceeding apace, and he was particularly pleased with the raspberry scones his team had whipped up in the quiet hours after mid-rats, or midnight rations. Our contingent operated on their stomachs, and getting this precious national resource fed, watered, and rested was all a part of *Bridger's* warfighting acumen.

Before stepping aft to the captain's quarters, I placed a call to Donahue in the Master at Arms Department. I was about to get into the weeds.

"I think, if our assailant hasn't chucked his clothing overboard, we're looking for some blood-stained utilities," I told him.

"Utilities" is the word the Marines use for their green twill dungarees and blouses worn in the field. *Bridger's* naval officers were in their summer khakis, but our Marines were ready to hit the ground running. Maybe I was a bit preoccupied and I had started to over think it. In my mind, I heard Captain Kelly's not infrequent admonition 'Delegate, Commander Pratt.'

"I'll put the word out," Donahue said, tolerating my intrusion. "When will you inform our Marine section leaders?"

"I have a meeting with the captain," I told him. "Making notifications will be the priority directly afterward. I'll start at the top."

At two minutes before seven I stepped aft to the companionway that led down the centerline away from the bridge. Navigation was to my left, the radio shack to my right, followed by our combat information center and intelligence group. The captain's quarters were on the starboard side, and my smaller cabin was to port. I lightly rapped on his door and he opened it briskly, as if he were standing on the other side. The captain was smoking his first pipe of the day, and I could see the mess had arranged breakfast for just the two of us. Eggs and bacon were arranged under a pair of domed silver warmers. There was toast, marmalade, a pot of coffee, and a small fruit bowl. The Waldorf-Astoria couldn't have done better. I knew the captain was just as embarrassed as I was with all the privilege that rank afforded. But we had to do it the Navy way.

"Incident to report, Captain Kelly," I told him as I removed my napkin from the silver ring and covered my lap.

"I heard the klaxon," said the captain. "Did we recover our guest?"

"Unfortunately, no," I told him. "Sal Marchionda...you remember him?"

"Marchionda? Of course. Our artful dodger."

"He discovered a substantial blood stain on B Deck aft, near our mooring tackle. It was right in the middle of the boarding gate through the rail."

"Oh my," said the captain, a grizzled mariner nearing the end of a 40-year career. Even though he'd probably seen it all, he still seemed touched by the gravity of a murder this close.

"We cast a wider net and found the place where our victim was stabbed. Lots of blood loss and drag marks over to the gate from where the initial assault took place."

"So, it's a murder," said the captain, growing pensive.

"I estimated the blood loss was not survivable, so I turned us around."

"I would have done the same thing," said the captain.

"Chester Nimitz has high expectations for *Bridger*. We don't have a minute to lose."

"Still...we have no murder weapon, no corpse...just a lot of blood in all the wrong places," I told him.

"Are you sure the corpse went overboard?" the captain asked, a devilish postulation. But that's why he was the captain. He had a reputation for being able to see around corners.

"It can't be confirmed," I told him. "No one witnessed our victim go overboard. But we had a lot of blood running down the topsides. Not sure where you might stuff a bleeding body if the victim is still aboard. Marchionda cleaned it up with a raw-water hydrant."

"Next steps?" asked the captain.

"I will speak with Major General Vandegrift and ask him to assemble his regimental commanders," I suggested. "We'll need to get the units to take a head count.

"Helps we're hosting the CO of First Marine Division, but you should know he doesn't have all his regimental commanders with him. He's got units scattered on ships all over the Pacific, converging on our rally point off Fiji. And some of his people on board answer to other division commanders. It's a bit of a cock-up."

"Well, we've been at this for less than a year after Pearl," I said in support. "It'll take us a while to get it right."

"There's more. Training's been foreshortened. And we've had to scrounge for smaller transports for the close-in work. There's a huge rush for landing craft," said the captain.

"Throw in the usual rivalries, jealousies, squabbles and politics," I mused. "There's always a bit of jockeying for position, isn't there?"

"All the way up the chain," said the captain. "Admiral

Nimitz and General MacArthur are in a pissing contest over who gets the privilege of conquering the Solomons."

"Admiral Nimitz and the Marines have won this one," I responded.

"This round at least," said the captain. "The Solomons will be an all Navy/Marine Corps show. MacArthur can twiddle his thumbs in Australia."

"No doubt *Bridger* will be hosting the Army in her customary style when the time comes," I said with a smile.

"It will be a high honor, and we will be just as hospitable," said the captain, the quintessence of inter-service diplomacy.

"Any update on the strategic picture?"

"No change since we left San Francisco," said the captain. "The Japanese are using their base at Rabaul on New Britain to stage for a southerly incursion down the Solomon Island chain, which runs the risk of disrupting our lines of communication and supply to Australia. Chester has decided to stop them in the vicinity of Guadalcanal, with our first raids on nearby Tulagi and Florida, plus a few more outcroppings the Japanese use for their seaplane bases."

"Did you know a lot of our guys are still carrying the old 1903 Springfield?" I asked

"Not the worst," said the captain, taking a bite of toast. He was schooled in Naval gunnery but he was still something of a small-arms connoisseur. Somebody said he had gunpowder in his veins.

"The old 'Aught-Three' is a real sharpshooter's rifle," he said. "Big .30-06 caliber, able to field armor piercing ammo for stopping power. A bolt-action that demands mindful shooting. The new eight-shot M1 Garand offers semi-auto for faster cycling, but accuracy isn't worth a damn."

Ship of Tears

We spent the remainder of our breakfast time together discussing ship's systems, personnel changes, re-enlistment ceremonies, and captain's mast. We wrapped up with another swing at our morning murder.

"I will pay a call to General Vandegrift and see what we can do about identifying our victim," I told Captain Kelly.

"Don't start a panic," the captain said. "See if he can get a head count without a lot of hoo-ha."

"I think I will be able to get the general to buy into that," I offered.

"And let Haggerty investigate the murder, Jonas," said the captain. "You've got a ship to run."

"I'll do my best to stay out of it," I told him, and we spent the rest of our morning touring the horizon. It had become apparent *Bridger* was best served by shedding her slower escorts and traversing the world's oceans alone. We'd already demonstrated Hitler's U-boats couldn't keep up. They only had a top speed of fourteen knots on the surface, and five knots submerged. I fondly recalled early in *Bridger's* wartime career our thirty-knot race across the Bay of Biscay, the *Kriegsmarine's* front stoop, to get from Lisbon to Southampton. As Elvis our chief boilerman liked to say, "Speed is life."

After breakfast, I went below to find General Vandegrift's cabin in the tourist-class area of B Deck. His accommodation was a third the size of mine, and I was immediately embarrassed. Here was a man who was about to lead his men into some hard fighting and he was crammed into a tiny box with a single berth and a shaving sink...not even a toilet. His staff had to come and go one by one. Down the passageway, we offered him a small office where he and his regimental commanders could squeeze in. Vandegrift was gruff, humorless and somehow less than shocked when I told him it was possible a member of the First Marine Division may have been murdered.

"Fighting men are subject to all the same passions we encounter on the civilian side, Commander," he told me.

"I have a reservist aboard who is an FBI special agent. Name is Nathan Haggerty. He will be leading this investigation, general," I told him. "But we will need to collect as much information as possible before we release the victim's identity."

"Wise," he said. "Next steps?" He was just like Captain Kelly. He didn't mince words.

"If you can get your regimental commanders together within the next hour and meet me in the theater, I can explain the situation, introduce our investigator and start the process of identifying our victim. We have very little evidence, so we need to start with at least the name of the victim," I told him. "From there, perhaps we can make some connections."

"And we will have to notify next of kin," said the general. "Not sure I like the home front knowing murders can take place while their sons are in our care." I'm a 'just-the-facts' lawyer so I am a little unsettled the general wishes to soft-pedal how his Marine died. I punt.

"I guess we can work it out with the victim's CO when the CO can be located," I told him.

I break clean with the general and head toward Donahue's office in the Master at Arms department, where I know I will likely find Haggerty. Cops are birds of a feather. I find them with coffee cups and Lucky Strikes, leaning back in their chairs.

"We're swapping yarns," said Donahue.

Ship of Tears

"Donahue and I ran across the same mick gangs in Beantown," Haggerty said.

"Those were the days," I told them as I pulled up a chair and sat on it backwards, leaning forward on the seatback. "General Vandegrift's COs are assembling in the theater. The three of us will present what we know. I would like Marchionda to listen—in case we need to put him to work. Nate, the captain wants you to lead the investigation."

"No problem," he responded. "But I will need the Master at Arms Department to be available."

"Always," said our gung-ho Donahue. The chief summoned an underling to go find Marchionda and we broke up to head to our meeting. We were moving forward along the starboard side Promenade Deck, now covered by our big, canvas-and-net survival floats, and ducked back inside. The ship was festooned with those "you-are-here" bullseyes that told us what deck we were on vertically, and what station we were occupying fore and aft. The stations corresponded with the numbered frames employed during *Bridger's* construction, when she was christened *Majestic*.

Our interior spaces were crowded with Marines telling tall tales, curled in a corner asleep, playing craps, or engaged in innocent horseplay. We had pipe cots stacked everywhere and we moved down the passageways single file. We entered the horseshoe-shaped theater, and I saw that Seaman Marchionda had preceded us. He was placing chairs on the stage, and he added one for Donahue when he saw the three of us coming down the aisle. This young man had learned to anticipate. He'd come a long way since he was incarcerated for selling stolen cold cuts. He'd told me his little sister needed the money to get her wheelchair fixed, so I gave him points for creativity and sentenced him to time served. Marchionda was also a "local." He grew up in Penn Yan at the north end of Keuka Lake in New York's Finger Lakes region and I had a small cottage on Keuka's west side—so we'd fished the same waters.

We sat on the stage and I watched our regimental commanders filter into the big space. As the captain informed me, they were a mix from different divisions, owing to the rapid deployment brought on by Australia's urgent need to stop the Japanese. But that's what you get in the military, something of a hash, as war planners prioritized rapid response in the face of an emergency. I got the impression Vandegrift knew working with the hand you're dealt is just a part of being a Marine.

Our COs, colonels all, started coming in. I'd already met some of them: Colonel Clifton Cates of the First Marines, Colonels Leroy Hunt and Merritt Edson, both of the Fifth Marines, Colonel James Webb of the Seventh Marines, Lewis Burwell "Chesty" Puller, a lieutenant colonel in charge of the First Battalion, Seventh Marines. Colonel Webb was Puller's boss, but I was glad to see a battalion commander taking an interest in our plight. All told, they numbered an even dozen, and they were all dressed in their utilities, with pants cuffs inserted carefully into boot tops, which were covered by those natty last-century spats, or "leggings" as the Marines called them. They all had tropical pith helmets on their heads, and they were wearing suspenders that held up web belts lined with pouches for ammo, first-aid kits, and the ubiquitous M1911 Colt .45. To a man, they had Ka-Bar knives in sheaths attached to belts and laced through their legs. It reminded me there was nothing unique about the weapon we were trying to associate with the murder of our unknown Marine.

Ship of Tears

A lot of the colonels knew each other, having come from the same division. But there were newcomers here as well, on their way to the South Pacific because they happened to be in the right place at the wrong time and the War Department could cut their orders rapidly, detaching them from one division to rejoin another. Vandegrift didn't seem fazed. All his men, regardless of their original unit, were still Marines, and they were used to all kinds of adversity...especially when it descended upon them from war planners on-high.

The general entered the theater wearing his summer uniform. We all stood at attention. He was pin sharp and his tie bore the crisp dimple we all strived for. I walked off the stage to greet him.

"General, if you wouldn't mind. Could you introduce me to your men? It will enhance interservice cooperation if we can get a good word from you," I told him. The general was happy to comply. We were a small group, but there was an unmistakable energy in the room. These men were off to kill the enemy. As they sat and kibbitzed and enjoyed a smoke, you could tell they were coiled and ready. They fell silent when General Vandegrift patted his hands downward to signal the all-quiet. You could hear a pin drop.

"This meeting was called by Commander Jonas Pratt, *Bridger's* XO," said Vandegrift. "We've had an incident and it involves all of you. So, pay attention." His colonels were sitting up straight. The general walked off the stage and took a seat with his men in the orchestra section.

I looked out across the theater. I saw close-cropped haircuts, white crows' feet on brown faces from too much squinting at the sun, the hard eyes of men who knew they were about to go into battle with untested troops, and who knew some of them wouldn't make it home. They were appraising me, a lowly member of the rear echelon who couldn't possibly offer anything meaningful as these true warriors were girding for battle. I was just a ship driver, but they couldn't know or understand how important their care was to me.

"We had a man overboard call this morning on B Deck aft at approximately oh-five hundred local," I intoned, trying to match the timbre of my voice with the professionalism the moment called for. "Upon arriving at the scene of the incident, we noticed a great deal of blood on the deck and through a gate in the rail."

I gave them the facts as dispassionately as I could. They wouldn't want to hear plaints or sorrows, just information affixed to a sensible timeline. I watched them squirm in their chairs a bit, but General Vandegrift sat solid as a rock, eyes unblinking.

"We turned the ship around and scanned the ocean on a reciprocal track to try to find the person," I told them. "We failed to do so. We also judged the blood loss on the deck was not survivable. We believe this unknown person has been the victim of a crime, and we are asking all of you to go back to your sections—from regiments right down to individual squads and fire teams—to find out if anyone is AWOL. We would like you to send that information to Chief Donahue, head of the ship's Master at Arms Department, who will forward it to Lieutenant-Commander Nathan Haggerty, chief investigator on this case." Nate raised a hand from his chair on the stage so they could associate the name with the face.

"As XO and the ship's JAG officer, they'll keep me informed of any progress or developments," I told them. "If we can identify the victim, we will be able to draw associations, confirm findings and put ourselves in a position to make a definitive notification to the individual's family. Of course, we want to apprehend the responsible party. I would like to thank General Vandegrift for his swift attention to this matter. General?"

I turned the meeting over to the head of the division and he did me a favor by exhorting his staff to assist. He also added an important point I failed to mention.

Secrecy.

"You heard the man," he told them. "Get the word out. We want a head count. Do not, and I repeat do not, state to anyone the reason for taking attendance. It's just standard operating procedure as we get closer to the theater. We want to keep the investigation under wraps for the time being, and we don't want to cause a panic. We also believe time is of the essence. So, move out." The colonels rose as one and saluted the general, who departed energetically up the aisle.

Haggerty, Marchionda, Donahue and I reconvened near the orchestra pit.

"Nate, this is your investigation," I told him. "What's next?"

"We wait," he responded. But Marchionda had a different idea, and that's why we keep him around.

"How about I get the medical department to expedite that blood typing?" he said. "I know a guy who knows a guy."

Chapter Two
– Ordnance on Target

The United States Navy of 1942 was very similar to the Navy in the day of John Paul Jones. It was all about man and machine working as a unit to bring about an acceptable outcome—whether it was fighting the enemy or fighting the ever-changing weather. Lest one think a ship and her systems are dumb, inert chunks of steel, there is a lot of human spirit that goes into a vessel at sea. The design of the ship, her myriad components, the way she interacts with wind and water: all have evolved from experience.

As with our Revolutionary forebears, we had a trained crew of varying occupations, or ratings, that defined our complement and made our multi-faceted ship run. The modern Navy of 1942 was peopled by radiomen, boilermen, electrician's mates, bosuns, gunnery mates, bakers, and fry cooks. They all came together in a well-coordinated manner that kept our ship fed, fueled, watered, and protected. I had a hand in setting up *Bridger's* medical department when I was in charge of damage control. As per the doctrine, the medical department was actually four medical departments spread throughout the ship. If one area was flooded, crushed, or set ablaze, we had medical assets in other areas, including two surgical suites and a laboratory for testing urine...and blood.

On the day of our suspicious man-overboard incident,

Ship of Tears

Sal Marchionda found me on the bridge about mid-afternoon and informed me he'd pulled in a marker from a poker buddy who worked as a medical corpsman. He bumped our blood sample ahead in the testing line and he'd already obtained the results. Our serologists had concluded definitively that our murder victim had a rare blood type, AB-negative. Sal and I agreed this was a small but fruitful breakthrough. When our regimental commanders reported our missing individual, we could match the blood type with our suspected victim's file and cross check to precisely identify our man overboard.

"Get the test card down to the MA department and tell Mr. Haggerty I've requested he start a file," I instructed Marchionda, and he scampered off.

I devoted the remainder of the day to gunnery practice. Captain Kelly had laid down the law. Every member of *Bridger's* crew must learn how to man every position and fire every weapon. From the XO right down to the mess attendants, we all needed to know how to defend the ship if any of our more experienced gunners failed or faltered. We had four, five-inch, .38-caliber deck guns set in deep armored wells, or "tubs", fore and aft. We also had four, three-inch, .50-caliber deck guns set port and starboard topside. Plus, we had a good collection of Oerlikon machine cannon which were used primarily for anti-aircraft work. At the appointed hour I made my way to A Deck forward of our cargo hatch, removed my necktie and rolled up my sleeves. I climbed up a short ladder and joined our party for a lecture conducted by one of our command master chiefs, Harley Jameson from Wellsville, New York, who would be our gun-mount captain today. A non-commissioned officer, Harley was a member of the elect. He'd served as a gunner in the cruiser *Dallas* back in '18 when I was a mere child aboard *Galveston.* I was on the quartermaster staff back then because I could do the math, but I learned to fire *Galveston's* three-inch guns aimed with a rudimentary rangefinder. Our five-inch batteries aboard *Bridger* were a distinct improvement. They were mounted on single pedestals, so they were out in the open. Modern arrangements aboard dedicated war fighters mounted their guns, singly or in pairs, inside armored boxes set on what's called a "base ring." We'd plopped our guns on top of an ocean liner, so our steel tub mounts for our five-inch batteries were a bit of a lash-up.

I had served in on all positions of the gun mount, but I hadn't functioned as a projectile loader yet, so now it was my turn. We were simulating general quarters, so I was in a kapok life jacket and a helmet. The projectile hoist was at my feet and I had to get the shell out of the hoist opening in the deck and move the shell to join a short line of shells set upright on a track awaiting the fuse setter. Setting the fuse was a mechanical process that twisted the tip of the shell to a prescribed setting to ensure it exploded at the desired range and altitude. After the fuse was set, my job was to pick a shell up off the fuse-setter rack, turn it nose forward, and twist my upper body so I could roll the shell into the loading tray in front of the propellant case. When that was accomplished, I had to activate a rammer that drove the shell and propellant case into the firing chamber before the breech slammed shut.

The mount captain made sure hands and fingers were out of the empty space where the barrel recoiled (we'd already lost several appendages, including an arm) and pressed the trigger with his foot. We got a nice big boom, a terrifying recoil, and we could see the shell burst two thousand yards downrange. Next, we elevated the muzzle of the gun to simulate an aerial attack. It was harder because you had to crouch and kneel while hefting those big shells. After we fired the gun, the chamber was now open for the next round. Multiply these actions by three a minute, and by twenty minutes or so for an average inbound enemy contact, you could see why it didn't take long for loaders to become completely exhausted. It was a young man's game. But I got lucky that day. We shot five rounds, including a high-angle aerial simulation, and I was relieved. My arm and chest muscles were burning and I couldn't unfold my fingers inside my gloves. I was dripping with sweat, and the aroma of male bodies in close proximity inside our little tub gave our gunnery practice a tangible realism—absent the strafing runs we could expect from Jap "Kates" or "Zeroes." All of us needed to have the skills we were acquiring in order to save our ship, and each other. That thought pervaded as I finished my little shootout and let the next man in line take it. I knew him: Bailey, a kid from Syracuse.

"Nice shooting, Mr. Pratt," said Bailey. And I slapped him on the back.

It was dinner time and I took my evening meal with my fellow officers in the first-class lounge so I could listen to complaints and attempt solutions. On this night dinner was turkey à la king, mashed potatoes, peas and carrots, and a blueberry cobbler. There was a young lieutenant junior grade, or j.g., at our table who was grousing he'd rather be conning the deck of a battleship than cruising the ocean blue in the lap of luxury. I'd heard this before from our youngsters, and I advised getting our Marines safely and securely into the theater achieved just as much to win the war as lobbing those big shells. He was mollified, and the older gents at the table like me (I would be forty-one in December of '42) nodded sagely.

The conversation at the table turned inevitably toward hometowns, occupations, strategic observations, and post-war plans. I had a couple of young lawyers at my table. One had graduated from Pomona, east of Los Angeles, and the other from Georgetown. They knew I'd graduated Harvard Law, class of '29, but I always tried to downplay my Ivy League pedigree. I was just a small-town barrister. Later, in more private settings, my fellow officers filled me in on their personal lives. One was trying to get the nerve up to ask his sweetheart to marry him. Another was saddled with a passel of kids and a wife trying to make do on Navy pay. When they asked me about my status, I smiled and said I had a wife, a boy in high school, and a young daughter in junior high. I left out the fact we've relocated to Washington DC, where they can take refuge under the watchful wing of my older brother, the farmer-lawyer-statesman. I avoided mentioning my wife's fondness for alcohol, and our loveless union of convenience. I shied away from the fact I'd found the love of my life, who was not my spouse, and who was betrothed to someone else. There was nothing fancy about the eddies and currents that had swept me downstream. The war was up-ending things.

I also avoided the subject of Lieutenant Commander Nathan Haggerty, our ship's security chief, with whom I enjoyed an unusual, albeit uneasy, day-to-day relationship. I thought I'd be finished with Haggerty once the war had started, and I could do my part aboard *Bridger*. But, like me, he was a reservist, and, small world, he'd been assigned to *Bridger* and tasked with our ship's safety. Earlier in *Bridger's* tour, Haggerty's skills were put to use when we were targeted by saboteurs. Let's just say he liked to shoot first and ask questions later, which ran contrary to my legal grounding. Carelessly shooting two material witnesses dead is a surefire way to stop an investigation. Since then Haggerty and I had achieved an uneasy peace, which had evolved into a close and necessary cooperation. He was a thug—and sometimes that's exactly what we needed.

I saw him working his way across the first-class dining room. He was wearing a leather jacket and I knew he was concealing his ubiquitous .45 in a shoulder holster. He always carried it "cocked and locked": hammer back and ready to fire, slide release in the up and therefore safe position, grip safety always there as a backup. Something must have addled the man. I wiped my mouth with my cloth napkin and begged my party's forgiveness. Ship's business to attend to. I greeted the inscrutable Haggerty in the middle of the room.

"Regimental commanders have found our missing man," he told me.

"Name?" I asked.

"Rizzo," he said, looking around the room. "Seventh Marines." I could tell Haggerty was uneasy.

"Let's go to my cabin," I told him.

"I sent Marchionda up to wait for us outside your door," he said, and off we went to find the central staircase that ascended to the bridge deck and my quarters. We found Marchionda waiting in the companionway and we were quickly settled in the soft leather club chairs of my meeting space. We'd darkened ship, but I glanced behind the curtain covering the porthole to see that sliver of moon rising in the east, which only meant we'd turned a bit more south on our run to New Zealand, first stop before we would move north to the Solomons.

"So...it was Rizzo of the Seventh?" I asked to start the

conversation.

"Yes, according to Colonel Webb," said Haggerty. "Lance Corporal Michael Alan Rizzo, also known as 'Mickey.' Webb reached right down to the squad level and he's got three missing men. Two never made the boat, and this guy Rizzo. He was on the roster and now no one can find him. They think he's the guy."

"What battalion?" I asked.

"First. Puller's battalion," said Haggerty.

"But there's a but," said Sal.

"Continue," I told him.

"Our stiff had blood type AB-negative," he said. "Regimental records show this guy Rizzo's blood is O-positive. He's on a special file of universal donors."

"Screw up in the paperwork?" I asked with an upturned inflection, leaping to the obvious.

"Regimental yeomen claim their records are meticulous, best in the Navy outside the Pentagon," said Haggerty. "Rizzo has vaporized. Over the side? Maybe. Did he take his O-positive blood with him? Not clear. Except we know our man-overboard schmuck on B Deck was abso-fucking-lutely AB-negative."

"It's not Rizzo then," I pressed. "Regimental HQ got this wrong. I'll have to go back to Vandegrift."

"The general has been brought up to speed," Haggerty continued. "Insists Rizzo was our floater. He wants Rizzo's company commander to make the notification."

"But it can't be confirmed," I protested.

"I made that argument," said Haggerty. "But I got some push back from Vandegrift's number two, Rupertus. The First Marine Division wants to move on."

"Glad there aren't any mailboxes out here," said Sal,

dropping into the conversation an oblique but useful insight.

"And our cable facilities are for code traffic only, as of this minute," I told him. "Sal, tell the Seventh Marines' yeoman to give me the official note to next of kin. I'll get it posted when we have a chance. In the meantime, I'll put it in my safe."

"Right, Mr. Pratt," he responded. The three of us can agree it would not reflect well on the Navy to inform the Rizzo family their son is dead when that may not be the case.

"Where is this Rizzo from?" I asked. Haggerty pulls a notebook out of his pocket.

"Michael Alan Rizzo. Born April 15, 1920, Cicero, Illinois. Mom and dad emigrated from Italy in 1909."

"Physical description?" I asked.

"Five-six, hundred fifty-five pounds, muscular, dark... that's about it," said Haggerty.

"Siblings? Schooling? Pre-Marines occupation?" I asked with the lawyerly thoroughness I knew others might find grating.

"Record is limited. O-positive blood type is in the record and presumably on his dog tags," said Haggerty.

"Known associates?" I asked.

"Attached to the Seventh last minute in 'Frisco," said Sal. "I nosed around. Rizzo kept to himself or a small group of friends."

"And your pals in the lab are not capable of a screw up?" I asked Sal.

"Not possible," he responded. "Apparently the test is pretty simple. Something about the antibodies reacting with the antigens. And they've got some quality controls. I think the test is good."

"Okay, gentlemen," I postulated. "Rizzo is our missing

Marine. But, because of mismatched blood typing, he's not our missing marine. One possibility." I let it hang in the air. "Rizzo is our killer."

I could see Sal was surprised, but Haggerty brightened.

"And he switched dog tags with the poor AB-negative ass wipe who got himself knifed," he said. Sal completed the circle.

"And our dead guy isn't missing," he said.

"Rizzo is out there hiding somewhere but he's actually our dead guy," I responded. The three of us fell silent, retreating to our own dark contemplations. Haggerty finally broke the silence with a long, low whistle.

"You've got quite an imagination, my friend," he said, and I struggled once more with the concept of friendship with this man. But I suppose we were friends, after what we'd been through—especially after the Sunda Strait. Haggerty's prowess with a pump shotgun pulled our fat out of the fire. The man got me through that night, when it was only me and my revolver against our infiltrator. Two spies were going after our auxiliary steering gear with fire axes. That's when I crossed the Rubicon. I'd made the grim but necessary choice to take a human life. I was glad I'd never gotten over it.

"We form a hypothesis, then test it with fact," I told them. Sal piped up.

"I like it," he said. "But we don't have a body."

"A challenge," I told him. "*Corpus delicti.* The body of the crime. It's absent in this case, but blood serology helps us narrow down who that might be."

"What's the percentage of people in the general population with AB-negative?" I asked. Somehow, I was not surprised Sal knew the answer.

"I asked my lab guy that question," he said. "Around

one percent.”

“So, we’ve got seven thousand souls, more or less, not including our Navy crew and officers,” I reflected. “That means only seventy men plus or minus amongst our Marine contingent have an AB-negative blood type.” I knew I was oversimplifying. We had to start somewhere.

“Easy enough to comb through seventy records,” said Haggerty.

“But the problem will be getting the regiments to comb through their files to make the initial cut,” said Sal.

“It will have to come from the top,” I told them. “And that means going back to Vandegrift.”

“The general won’t be happy,” said Haggerty. “The people around him are closing in. My contacts tell me he’s just not interested now that they think they’ve found their stiff. He’s got maps of Tulagi and Guadalcanal all over his staff room. He’s got an invasion to plan.”

“You *are* aware that information is classified?” I asked him testily.

“You didn’t hear that, Marchionda,” he said, turning to our collaborator. Marchionda covered his ears, but I knew I could trust him.

“I’m sympathetic to the general’s prime objective,” I told them. “But we can’t allow a murder to go unanswered.” My guests nodded in agreement, and I could tell Haggerty in particular wanted to get his man. I think he was put on Earth to enforce the law. My role as an attorney was to dig and probe and find reasonable doubt. His job was to stop the threat and sort it out later—even if it meant innocent people might get in the way. I edged around something of a plan.

“Sal, you’re making decent contacts among our regiments?” I asked him. It occurred to me Marchionda was the kind of investigator who reveled in sneaking through the back door, while Haggerty was busy breaking down the front. They made a good combination.

"One or two," he said. "Lieutenant Colonel Puller's yeoman, in particular. He owes me money. Maybe my buddy has a buddy, if you follow me."

"Good," I told him. "We have to start somewhere."

"So, we have seventy names, maybe," said Haggerty. "Then what?" I could tell when Haggerty was itching to cut through the nonsense.

"We need complete records, Sal," I told Marchionda. "The key will be finding associations between this Rizzo character and our 'stiff' as you call him. The killer and the victim—maybe Rizzo, maybe not—knew each other, gentlemen. The killer called for a meeting out in that deserted part of B Deck. There's a connection."

"Agree with all that..." said Haggerty, "...and I think it's a logical place to begin. But what's the motive?"

"They had an argument," I told them. "It's usually over something each of them wants. Money. A girl. Revenge."

"Or the killer was trying to hide something," said Marchionda.

"Or maybe find something," I responded. The possibilities seemed infinite, but all the standard human failings helped narrow the motive.

"There's another thing," said Haggerty, his experience with the macabre suddenly aroused. "The killer didn't just stab the guy...He butchered him." I look back on it, and Haggerty's release of that word into the room was the start of our descent into an obscene hell foreshadowing the savagery that was to come.

"Sal, I am going to ask you to find Rizzo's duffel bag.

We need to figure out who he's connected to."

"On it," he said. But we were interrupted. There was a knock on the door and Sal got up to answer it. Donahue came in, eyes wide, his face nearly white.

"There's been a murder," he said. "Forward hold. C Deck." We looked at each other, unspeaking, disbelieving. We were on the edge of cliff, it was a long way down... and we couldn't see bottom.

Chapter Three
– Runaway

We followed Donahue down the main staircase to C Deck, then moved forward. There were pipe cots in all the passageways and Marines were crowding all our spaces. There was laughter, merriment, bravado, the angst and the thrills that attended our complement's incessant crap games. We got to a door marked "Hold. No Admittance" and Donahue used a passkey to get in.

"Is this always locked?" I asked him, surprised. If it is, our perpetrator may have had a key, which limited possible suspects. Also, my damage control parties needed to pass through here freely.

"No," he informed me. "I just locked it on my way up to see you. I don't want Marines traipsing through our crime scene."

Our second crime scene, I reminded myself.

"Wait a second, Commander," said Haggerty behind me. "Let me take point." He pulled out his .45 and took Donahue's flashlight. "Straight ahead?"

"Can't miss it," said Donahue.

I had to admire Haggerty's style. He had his sidearm up, drawn, and sighted—and he was illuminating our path with the flashlight in his weak hand, which he used to steady the barrel. Ever since that incident in the Sunda Strait, I had started to pay attention to these things.

"Who discovered the body?" I asked from near the rear of our single file. Sal was behind me.

"Jarhead snooping around," said Donahue. "Shit in his pants and came down to the MA office. I came back up with a couple of my guys. They are with the victim now."

"Where's our snoop?" I asked Donahue. "I don't want to start rumors."

"I've got a babysitter with him," said Donahue. "One of my security guys. I read your mind, Commander Pratt."

"We'll have to figure out how to prep him before he goes back to his unit," I told him.

We continued forward into the labyrinth of wooden crates. *Bridger's* cargo was slung aboard using our fore and aft hoists. Stevedores on the pier put the cargo in nets. Our men hooked into the nets and lifted them up over the side and down into two big vertical trunks forward and one aft. When one trunk was filled, we lowered a big trap door and filled the deck above, and so on, until all our holds were filled. We had big deck hatches that got battened down on top of it all. There was access to each hold through passage-ways on our lower decks, and we had men coming in and out of here all day to get our goods into the right hands. That was the supply department's job, and I immediately wondered if there was a link.

Up ahead there was light from a flashlight and small talk. Haggerty holstered his weapon and we came up to a scene from another, hideous world. Two of Donahue's men were working their flashlights over a human body hanging by the neck in the passageway. The victim's head was at a freak-ish angle and his eyes were bulging out of their sockets. But that wasn't the worst of it. The body was wearing green Marine utilities. His shirt front was open, and he'd been split open from his sternum to his belt buckle. His stomach and intestines were cascading out of his body, and there was an ungodly stench of blood and excrement. Sal suddenly left us to find a place to throw up. There was a vast pool of blood and stool on the floor and we were careful not to step in it. Haggerty made a few professional observations.

"Nasty," he said. "Wire noose cuts right into his carotid artery."

Donahue queried his men.

"Did you meatheads touch anything?" he asked them. They shook their heads in the negative. It was getting a little crowded and I told them they could take a break.

"Not a word to anyone," I said. "And come back in fifteen minutes with a body bag, a stretcher, and a camera." Sal crept back into the crime scene and he couldn't look at our hanging corpse.

"Go get another blood kit from the forward sick bay on B Deck, Sal," I told him. "And bring Doc McGuire back with you. Tell him it's urgent." Marchionda appeared delighted to flee the scene and he vanished down the passageway, leaving Haggerty, Donahue, and me.

"Two stabbings in one day," I observed, and Haggerty pointed out one element of a possible *modus operandi*.

"Our killer likes to cut," he said. It seemed Haggerty was building a profile. I took Donahue's flashlight and worked it around the periphery of the evening's discovery.

"Looking for footprints, cigarette butts, pieces of paper. Anything at all...," I told them.

I, too, was having a difficult time looking at the bug-eyed corpse. I saw two or three footprints in blood.

"Stay away from that area," I told the group. "Donahue,

get a picture of those treads when the camera gets up here.”

“Aye-aye, Commander,” said Donahue. “Will you look at the guy’s face? Like he’s been worked over.” The victim had black-and-blue welts. There were blue bumps with red peaks and yellow valleys. His jaw was swollen and his lips were slightly parted, showing a gap in his dentition. Had he had some teeth knocked out?

Haggerty took special care with where he was walking, but he was able to get right up to the corpse...and sniff.

“Freshly dead,” he conjectured. “Not a half hour since he bought it. And look at his hands.” Haggerty held up a sleeve and shone a light on the man’s fingers.

“Knuckles are all smashed with a hammer or something,” I observed.

“More important,” said Haggerty. “He’s kind of a big guy. Let’s assume Rizzo’s not our victim on B Deck this morning. Let’s assume Rizzo did this. Marchionda said Rizzo is five-feet, seven-inches tall and weighs one fifty-five soaking wet. Hard to heft this body into position.”

“Still possible,” I told him. “Might have rigged the wire in advance, then threatened him with a knife into standing on that box over there. He kicked away the box and the victim dropped. The slice to the gut came afterward.” I was simply reciting what I saw in front of me. The actual pattern of facts might rest somewhere on either side of this flimsy reasoning.

“Yeah, the gut is the *pièce de résistance*,” said Haggerty. “At least he’s got a dog tag. Have to get a good look at that as soon as we get him down.” Haggerty, Donahue and I spent the time investigating the space while we waited for Marchionda and McGuire. Haggerty brought up the idea our killer may have had a nest in here somewhere. If he did, we couldn't find it. It occurred to me I received a report of a cargo shift on C Deck earlier. Was there a connection? Marchionda finally arrived with two corpsmen and young Doc McGuire, who'd earned his medical degree at the University of Rochester. Somehow, he didn't seem surprised to encounter a crime victim aboard our big ship. We were a huge, moving, floating city...and sometimes bad things happen where human beings congregate.

"This one's a little out of the ordinary, Commander," he said drily. Donahue's men returned with a stretcher and a camera with a flash attachment. Donahue started recording the scene—and those bloody footprints. When he finished Haggerty offered some direction.

"We'll need to get a big step ladder, cut him down, get him in the bag and get him into the nearest medical department. We'll also need to get him overboard after we've cataloged his injuries. Marchionda, go find a pastor, and tell Bowker in housekeeping we need a cleaning crew."

"We'll need to take a picture of his face when we get him cleaned up," I stated absently, and Donahue nodded an acknowledgement.

McGuire and his corpsmen got to work taking blood samples, and they boosted themselves on boxes to cut the wire noose from the overhead pipe. When they got the victim down on deck, Haggerty continued his assessment.

"Beat to a pulp," he commented. "Guy who did this had to restrain him somehow, then bash his knuckles one by one. See the rope burns on his wrists?"

"Trying to bash some information out of him, Nate?" I asked.

"Probably," said Haggerty. "Unless our killer is doing it just for fun. I've seen perps like that."

Ship of Tears

"What's his dog tag say?" Haggerty picked at the chain with his pen to lift it away from the body. The tag was covered in blood but Haggerty could make out a last name.

"Napolitano, James," it said. "Blood type A. Plus his serial number." Haggerty pulled out his notebook and started writing. "MKE6-785412885."

I turned to Marchionda: "Let's run that by Webb and Puller of the Seventh before we go alerting the whole division. Maybe this guy and Rizzo came from the same unit."

"On it," said Sal, and he was gone.

The corpsmen worried the corpse into the body bag and onto the stretcher. McGuire followed them out and I told them I'd meet them in the forward sick bay. Bowker arrived with a couple members of his cleaning team and the night was somewhat restored. Bowker and company were used to unholy messes aboard ship—mostly vomit—and it reminded me why we couldn't Bowker. Haggerty and I made it to the examining room, and McGuire couldn't add much beyond Haggerty's quick take. He and his crew had cut away the victim's clothing, and aside from the bone-crushing injuries to the extremities, the victim had broken ribs, and, as McGuire confirmed, missing teeth. The avulsed and eviscerated abdomen was difficult to look at, but I still wondered if it offered any clues. I asked McGuire to identify and inventory stomach contents. Bridger's doctor had the grace to acknowledge my request with an "aye-aye" and a salute, but his 'Oh for Pete's sake' eyeroll was unmistakable.

"Good idea, Commander," said Haggerty. "Might get us close to a last meal, which could establish our timeline."

"Anything we can learn about the murder weapon from looking at these injuries, doctor?" I asked casually. "Is it bigger than a standard-issue Ka-Bar?"

"Hard to tell," said McGuire.

"Doc, this looks like multiple stab wounds to the chest," said Haggerty. "Do I have this right?" McGuire donned another pair of latex gloves and found a big rag. He doused the man's chest with alcohol and started mopping up blood. At least a dozen deep slits emerged, still oozing.

"You're right," said McGuire. "Whoever did this wanted to make sure he was dead. Killer was in a frenzy."

"Crazy," muttered Haggerty. "These chest wounds happen before or after the gut?"

"I think the gut wound was the last act," said the doctor. "While the victim was hanging. "Kind of a curtain call."

I asked Donahue to take photos of the victim's face. He got busy and then departed to get the photos developed in the small dark room we kept near the brig.

"What about that left ear?" I asked the room, and McGuire stopped what he was doing to have a look.

"Whole outer ear has been cut away," he said. "I got distracted by the abdomen." A yawning silence filled the space, which smelled like antiseptic and the freshly obliterated bowels of the young Marine before us.

"Can you profile our killer?" I asked Haggerty.

"He's either criminally insane, or he's a professional trying to send a message," he said.

"Explain," I asked him, although I think I knew the answer.

"The person who did this has no problem with killing," he said. "It's as natural as breathing. That only means our killer is either deranged or kills for a living. He's well practiced. And he's trying to tell us something."

"Kills for a living? You don't mean the mafia..." I said into the room, disbelieving.

Ship of Tears

"Commander, I've seen mob hits that make this one seem casual. Dismemberment. Beheadings. Genitals removed. Eyes and tongues gouged out. They do it to impress their rivals, to instill fear and respect." Haggerty said it impassively—like this was all in a day's work. Now I knew I had the right man for the job. My problem with Haggerty's overzealous handling of my witnesses now seemed quaint.

The corpse before us yielded its secrets grudgingly. The wounds were so extensive it was difficult to determine just what they were trying to tell us. I went with Haggerty's first impression. This person's agonizing end started with torture—bashed knuckles, the slow infliction of pain—before proceeding to the facial battering and finally the hanging, the stabbing, and the disembowelment. But the ear. Why did the murderer cut the man's ear off, and where was it now?

Haggerty was apparently thinking the same thing. He was down by the corpse's bloody, swollen head, inspecting the ear canal.

"He's a collector," said Haggerty finally. "He needs a trophy, so he's taking ears. If he's been at it awhile, he might have a whole string of them."

"So, *Bridger* has a serial killer," I concluded and both McGuire and Haggerty looked at me as if I had a plan. Nothing could have been further from the truth. That's when Sal Marchionda came back into the examining room after his foray out to Webb's section.

"Remember when the Seventh told us they had three missing? Rizzo, plus two left on the dock back in 'Frisco. One of those missing guys is Lance Corporal James Napolitano," he informed us.

"Mother of God," said Haggerty. Even my hardened chief of security was moved by this information.

I offered a quick analysis: "Either Napolitano made the boat and has been kept prisoner on C Deck, only to be murdered tonight. Or Napolitano was killed back in 'Frisco and the only thing that made it aboard were his dog tags." I was merely ruminating, but the scientific mind of Dr. McGuire had a difficult time dealing with all the missing pieces of our emerging puzzle.

"I'll leave you gentlemen to it," he told us. "I have living patients to see." He departed the room and left us with our disemboweled corpse and our collective disbelief.

"I need to get a cable to CINCPAC at Pearl for forwarding to NIS," I finally concluded, breaking our silence. "I need to find out if James Napolitano is in a brig somewhere, or on another transport making its way out here with another division."

"Or dead," offered Sal. It was an unwelcome thought, but Marchionda was only trying to help.

A corpsman came in and added another layer to the evening's confusion. The bloody dog tags said Napolitano's blood was type A. Testing revealed tonight's victim was O-negative.

"Fucker is playing us," said Haggerty, peering into the deranged mind of *Bridger's* killer.

Chapter Four
– Middleman

We didn't have a good way to store corpses aboard *Bridger*, aside from the big industrial freezers under the swimming pool, and we needed those for perishables. So as soon as Haggerty and I were finished with our examination, I asked the corpsmen to find a body disposal bag and a priest. I was assuming the young Marine was a Catholic, and if he wasn't, a priest could ladle on the necessary appeals to the Almighty to admit this poor creature into His heavenly realm.

The victim was placed in a canvas bag with heavy chain at the bottom to weigh him down, and a hole at the top to allow air to escape. I decided to have the funeral ceremony in the examining room, with the sack of flesh before us draped by a hastily procured American flag. The priest was efficient, the prayers were poignant, and the body had stopped leaking—so even our victim was cooperating. I was not thrilled about walking our departed colleague aft the entire length of the ship to get to B Deck, where we normally attended to such matters. Instead, I ordered the corpsmen to haul him topside forward up two decks to the lee side. With the priest, there were six of us at the rail to heft him up and over. Five of us remained perfectly silent while the priest offered a closing remark, and we committed our brother Marine to the deep.

I was exhausted, and there was nothing I would have liked more than to climb into my rack for a few hours. But I had to check the plot (we were seven-hundred miles southwest of the Hawaiian Islands) and send a cable to Pearl checking on the whereabouts of Marine Rifleman James Napolitano, serial number MKE6-785412885. Plus, there was a note on my door from Captain Kelly, asking me to knock at any hour for a consultation. I splashed some water on my face, straightened my tie and proceeded to the captain's quarters. It was very close to midnight, and I had been charging hard since forty-thirty that morning. But I was there to solve problems, so complaining wouldn't do any good.

I knocked on the door and the captain admitted me. He was wearing his khakis and he appeared fresh and alert. I entered his well-appointed domain and I immediately knew why. General Vandegrift was sitting in a club chair in his summer uniform, and there was a look of displeasure on his weary face, which reflected the pure steel of a Marine about to head into battle.

"Coca-Cola, commander?" the captain asked.

"Glass of water if you wouldn't mind, sir," I responded. Vandegrift looked like he wanted to get directly down to business.

"My regimental commanders tell me someone is murdering my Marines," said Vandegrift. "I need them all. What gives commander?" He's no-nonsense, and I don't blame him. I opened with the current pattern of facts.

"General, sir, as I've stated, we believe this morning's man-overboard episode occurred after a stabbing. And we've just found a mutilated corpse of another Marine in a forward hold. We are having difficulty identifying victims and narrowing down a potential perpetrator because the blood types of the victims don't match their dog tags or their service records. On top of that, our second decedent was wearing a dog tag belonging to a lance corporal named Napolitano, whom your regimental commander told us missed the boat back in 'Frisco. I have a cable into Pearl to get a clarification on Napolitano's status" I stopped to allow the general time to absorb what we knew so far.

"Any idea who's doing this?" he asked.

"Well, a good bet it's another Marine," I told him. "We are interested in a missing individual we've identified as Lance Corporal Michael Rizzo, last known address Cicero, Illinois. This Rizzo may have assumed the identity of this morning's victim."

"And there's a blood mix-up with that victim also?" asked Vandegrift.

"There is," I told him. I wished I could sugar coat it. It was just one more damn thing thrown his way. I imagined it started with the frantic call from the Secretary of War, who received an alert from the Australian ambassador, who had coast watchers in the Solomons all the way up to New Britain. They were reporting on the Japanese build-up. If the Japanese came too far south down the island chain, there was a real risk their aircraft would threaten Australia's supply routes and even her cities. They'd already subjected Darwin in the far north to aerial bombardment. The country would starve and would have to remove itself from the war. Vandegrift and the First Marine Division were being tossed into the fray with very little preparation. The war in the Pacific turned on the talents of the gruff, taciturn general sitting in front of me.

And now this.

Vandergrift turned to the captain. "Aldous, what assets have you got tasked with this problem?" Vandegrift was a major general and outranked *Bridger's* lord and master Captain Kelly, so the captain had no choice but to respond affirmatively.

"We've got the XO's personal attention," he said, looking at me. "Jonas is a Harvard-trained lawyer who has experience in criminal matters. We also have our FBI reservist Haggerty on it, plus additional resources from our Master at Arms Department." This was something of a reversal from the directive I had received at breakfast—to just let Haggerty handle it. But the situation had changed following our discovery on C Deck. I tried to cast some oil on the water.

"We were able to do the blood work quickly, general, thanks to a cooperative medical staff and some solid onboard resources," I told him. "This has pointed us towards some discrepancies that might shed some light."

"It's all talk, gentlemen," said Vandegrift. "I need action. And I need a fighting force that's prepared physically and mentally. I can't have mysterious killings contaminating morale. We have to protect them."

"We are in full agreement," said the captain. "We're in day one of this investigation and Commander Pratt is making headway." So now the captain was inferring I'd made progress when we were far from it. He was putting me in the middle. And that's where I seem to live. All my life I've been the negotiator. It's tiring. But I have to press ahead on one singular issue.

"General, we need some help from your regimental staff," I told him. I can see Vandegrift doesn't want to get his command sidetracked. He just wants the problem to disappear. In his shoes, I would probably react the same way.

"What is it?" he asked, impatience cleaving the air.

"I need to sift through records to find all the Marines on this ship who might have AB-negative blood," I told him. "It's only about sixty or seventy men out of the whole population. But culling the records to tease out our AB-negatives will help speed the process."

"I'm told you already have one of your seamen making these inquiries," the general states. "Seaman Marchionda. He's a pest."

"I asked him to go behind the scenes and make some quiet requests." I am back-pedaling. "If we have your blessing, it will go a lot easier. We need that information."

"Tell me why again?" the general insisted.

"Our victim this morning had type AB-negative blood," I told him. "Your regimental commanders reported our missing Marine is Rizzo, but Rizzo's got O-positive blood. We think Rizzo has taken the identity of this morning's victim. If we can find our ABs, it will get us closer to finding today's man overboard and that will get us closer to Rizzo."

"Alright," said Vandegrift. "I will give you what you need. But you need to give me what I need. And that's a swift resolution." The meeting was over and the general rose to depart. Captain Kelly tried one more time to ingratiate, and he was rebuffed.

"Don't worry, general," said Kelly...immediately regretting his choice of words.

"I am paid to worry, captain. I want a report on progress every night at 2200 local," Vandegrift said, failing to allow Captain Kelly a last, encouraging word.

Captain Kelly and I both saluted and Vandegrift was through the door and on to his next vexation. The captain and I looked at each other and I could feel the tension. He didn't want his XO caught up in a murder investigation and he wanted to satisfy the legitimate needs of our Marine commander.

"Looks like I am throwing another job on top of your load, Jonas," he said. "I want you to delegate some ship-keeping duties to Bryant and Simms." He was referring to two lieutenant commanders from my original posting aboard *Bridger*, when I was in charge of damage control. Bryant slipped into that position, and Simms has a good handle on our deck work. I've watched him con the ship in and out of port and he had a fine sense for wind and current.

"I'll make it so," I told the captain, using the ancient phrase of the mariner to signal fealty and obeisance. But the pressure was building, and I knew I had to get some shuteye so I could hit the ground running in the morning.

I hoped our killer would let me get through the night.

I took a swing through the bridge and our navigation department. All was quiet and we were right on track. Meteorology was reporting a drop, but not a plunge, in barometric pressure. A falling glass meant we were in for a low, and on this side of the equator we wanted to be on the southerly side of that to take advantage of the clockwise flow. I discussed it with Simms and we were eye to eye. I swung by the radio shack on my way back to my cabin and I inquired as to whether or not I'd received a cable from CINCPAC. A young ensign told me it had been sitting in my in-tray for an hour, and I picked it up, consumed by a familiar mix of dread and curiosity. On a day like this, anything might happen.

TO: COMMANDER JONAS PRATT FROM: CINCPAC PEARL

SUBJECT: MKE6-785412885 NAPOLITANO, JAMES MARINE LANCE CORPORAL

NIS REPORTS INDIVIDUAL WAS FOUND DE-
CEASED 062842 VICINITY PRESIDIO, SAN FRANCISCO.
KNIFE WOUNDS. NEXT OF KIN NOTIFIED.

END

Our killer had young Napolitano's dog tags and had slipped them over the head of tonight's victim in the cargo hold. One tag or two? Haggerty will know. They had to have been able to identify Napolitano stateside with a dog tag, unless he had other forms of ID, like a wallet. Still, it's intriguing to think our killer took only one of Napolitano's dog tags so his corpse could show up in two places. Like Haggerty said, he was messing with us. Still, that made three homicides we were investigating. It occurred to me we would have to go back to our regimental commanders and ask one more time if they had reported anyone AWOL. Any missing Marine was tonight's likely victim. I submitted a cable request back to CINCPAC to give us Napolitano's hometown, and my operators told me we might have results in ten or twelve hours.

Associations.

And your first associations were the place where you grew up.

We had to assume for now that our murder victims were being targeted. I refused to believe our killer was selecting his victims at random. That meant they all knew each other, and somewhere in these prior contacts there would be a narrative, a motive, and our killer's name. Right now, the man was slumbering peacefully in one of thousands of pipe cots we'd hastily assembled belowdecks. Was he breaking ranks? Infiltrating other units? Shirking duty assignments to wander the ship looking for prey? Haggerty will know. Haggerty thinks like a killer.

Timothy Cole

I made it to my cabin and stripped off my dirty, sweaty summer khakis. I removed my epaulets, bars and service ribbons and put my uniform in a laundry bag for one of the chiefs, who would have it cleaned, pressed, and re-hung in my closet. All the comforts of home. I took a hot shower to get the grime of the day off my skin. But, as I stood there naked and exposed, I couldn't get that guy in the hold on C deck out of my head. I got out, toweled off, donned some skivvies and turned out the light. I pulled back the blackout curtain on a porthole, and scanned a sea flecked by moonlight. The beauty of the moment was overwhelmed by the enormity of both the war and the crimes right in front of me. I closed my eyes and still saw that man with his neck stretched and his eyes bulging. I also saw the place where his ear was missing. I lay on my bed, closed my eyes, and willed myself to sleep. It never worked. I had to go through my nightly dirge. It began, as always, with pangs for my children.

I felt like an ass for running away from home, leaving my growing kids to deal with their gin-besotted mother. Adding to the night's self-loathing, I allowed thoughts of a certain young lady to enter the mental brig where I incarcerated my most private thoughts. I had met this marvelous person by chance on a trip to New York, where I'd consulted regularly with the marine architects at Gibbs and Cox. The firm was helping us fit out the ocean liner *Majestic* to become the warship *Bridger*. The young woman—name under wraps to protect the innocent—had been waiting for a blind date in the bar at the Algonquin and the nameless bounder never showed. I stepped into the breach and she and I had a perfectly jolly evening. At the end of the night, I accompanied her to the Barbizon in the wee hours, and she gave me a single chaste kiss on the cheek. The next night it was dinner at Sardi's and the Ziegfield Follies, then the Lackawanna ferry dock the night after that, so I could catch my train back to The District.

There were two more weekends in New York—each more soul-satisfying than the last—and I had fallen in love with a woman five years my junior...and nothing like my wife. She was a fisherman, a wing shot, at home in the kitchen or around the campfire. She was fun and sensible and beautiful—and no longer mine. Despite our meteoric rise, our romance was now a smokey cinder. She'd had the good sense to get out of harm's way by becoming engaged to a young beau from Sewickley, a 4F draft deferred executive at Pittsburgh Plate Glass. But I would never forget her...and I understood perfectly why she needed to leave me. The war came between us. I was married less to Tereza than I was to the Navy. But Tereza, enamored of alcohol, had left me, too.

Adding to the evening's dirge was the painful concern for my dear old dad, who was holding down the fort at Pratt and Pratt. He should have been enjoying his well-earned retirement, but his eldest boy and law partner was now serving on the Senate Armed Services Committee, flying off to assess the needs of America's battlefield commanders between sessions on his farm milking cows or drawing in hay. Josiah was president of the local Grange one day, and meeting with Admiral Nimitz the next. Dad's other wayward son—that would be me—was a Naval officer steaming west half-way around the world. Let's just add: this particular wayward son might have been out of his depth.

Add investigating multiple murders to my ship-keeping duties.

The dirge stopped.

I chastised myself for failing to focus on the job. Soon, I was dreaming of finding our latest dead Marine, hanging in the hold by the neck.

I woke up to a knocking at my door.

It was forty-thirty in the morning, and it was time to get up anyway. I opened the door to find a bleary-eyed Marchionda.

"Our AB-negatives," he told me, handing me pieces of lined notepaper with a hand-written table of names, sections, commanding officers, serial numbers and blood type.

"You've been at it all night?" I asked him.

"Yeah," he replied. "Couldn't sleep. General Vandegrift's number two, Rupertus, tracked me down. You must have greased the skids with the big guy. Rupertus dragged in his regimental commanders, and their staffers have been combing through records all night. We found seventy-three AB-negatives."

"Nice work, Sal," I told him, and I could tell he was pleased with himself. He stood a little taller. "Get some rest and a shower and meet me on the bridge at ten hundred hours."

"Aye aye, Commander," he saluted and turned on his heels.

In eight minutes, I was showered, dressed and ready for the day. It's amazing how fast you can get yourself assembled when you're motivated. I made it to my throne on the port side of the bridge, early enough to see a burnt orange horizon gaining definition off our port stern quarter.

Our nightmare had started a bare twenty-four hours earlier.

The mess attendant arrived with my coffee, and a plain kruller, compliments of the bakery staff. I offered thanks and turned my attention to Marchionda's list. He didn't have time to alphabetize it, but that's okay. A random presentation required a closer scrutiny. We had a Kelly, a Farnesworth, five Joneses, at least eleven Smiths, a Cutter or two, a Stevens, a Condon. I am fixated on the idea that there's a subset in this group that might know each other, if my theory holds. I had to remind myself: I was looking for the identity of our man-overboard, an identity now assumed by our killer. But can random AB-negatives be connected? Seemed unlikely. I needed to explore the logic. Our O-positive Rizzo was missing. Rizzo might be our killer. Rizzo knew his victim. His victim was AB-negative. Our missing Marine is AB-negative. Could he be another Italian?

"Lombardi," I said out loud, and I stared forward past the prow of our big ship as it greeted a limitless horizon. Rizzo, whom we knew to be missing. Napolitano, who was murdered in San Francisco before we set sail. I looked for more Italian names.

"Gaudino. Tarrantino. Gallo. Marcello," I said out loud, and the young j.g. overseeing our cadre of watch-keepers asked, "Beg pardon, commander?"

"Talking to myself," I told him, and decided to give Haggerty one more hour of sleep before I tasked him with tracking down our AB-negative Italians. There were a bunch of them. Any missing AB-negative Italian could be considered yesterday morning's man overboard. If the missing Rizzo and our man overboard knew each other, we would have something to work with.

I worked the phone to check in with my stations. Elvis wanted to take a boiler offline to clean some fire tubes. I ran the math in my head and calculated only a fifteen percent loss in efficiency, but I told him to make it so.

"We'll want everything up and perfect the closer we get to our destination," I told him. Speed was our only defense when it came to outrunning the Japanese surface and submarine threats. I worried about their "Kates," aircraft capable of delivering one of those devastating Type 93 "Long Lance" torpedoes. It reminded me we needed more of those Oerlikon machine cannon, and I was determined to look into a couple of those Bofors antiaircraft quads to add to our arsenal. I'd stick them on the shuffleboard courts between our exhaust stacks.

I soon had a handful of yeomen lining up behind me to get their reports signed—housekeeping, nav station, comm, damage control, CIC. Everyone wanted to make sure they got an official sign-off on their bill of health. There were no anomalies at present. I stepped out on the bridge wing to finish my coffee, taking a few minutes to enjoy the air and the softly undulating swells rolling along our waterline. I was heartened to know I didn't have to roust Haggerty out of his bunk after all, because he was sliding open the heavy door leading to my hideaway. He was still wearing his leather jacket, which meant he was still concealing his pistol. He didn't wear it all the time—only when he was getting ready to shoot somebody.

"Did you see Marchionda's chart?" he asked me.

"Certainly did," I told him, as I took a sip of coffee. "Were you there helping him last night?"

"Me and twenty or so sergeants," he said. "We set up in the theater."

"I think I've found a path to explore," I suggested.

"Tell me," he said. "I don't want today to go like yesterday."

"You said something about mob hits," I say. "I don't

like to single out any particular group or tribe, but we've got a bunch of Italians on that list. Add it to what we know. Rizzo. Napolitano."

"And we'll need some hometowns," said Haggerty. "Maybe these guys knew each other from before the war. This is just gumshoe stuff. We can do it. Donahue and his guys can help."

"Use Marchionda," I told him. "I think he might have a career with the Master at Arms shop." Haggerty looked at the sheet. I had placed tick marks next to Italian family names.

"Bunch of these guys are in the same unit," he said. "It'll go quicker. But AB-negative Italians actually knowing each other? It's a reach."

"We just need the name of our AB-negative who bought it on B Deck," I told him. "If that guy is Italian, better yet if he was in the Seventh, we can go on from there and see if there are associations." We strolled back inside the bridge. "We'll interview their COs. I gave Marchionda until 1000 hours to get some shuteye and a shower...so when he materializes, I will send him down to the MA office."

No sooner have I delivered this directive when Marchionda showed up ready to go to work.

"Get enough sleep?" I asked him.

"Some," he told me. "I want to get started." I explained that we will be concentrating on any missing AB-negative individuals with Italian last names, on the theory this loose association might yield a name...and from there, further associations.

"Fellow goombahs," Marchionda said. "Plus, it's all we've got at the moment." Haggerty and Marchionda divvied up the list.

"This is a research job only," I advised. "Don't approach any of the subjects. We just need some information out of their regimental records, hometowns in particular. Rizzo and Napolitano were First Battalion, Seventh Marines. Check there first."

"I wish we could get into the FBI records," said Haggerty. "I'll bet some of these guys have rap sheets."

"Figuring out who and how many will help us form connections. It's the best we can do for now," I told them. I received a Navy-like "aye-aye" and they were off. It was time for some public relations and I made my way down and aft to the third-class mess hall for my breakfast. I liked to stand in line with our guests, with my molded aluminum tray doubling as a plate. This morning it was powdered eggs, link sausage, and a hot biscuit covered by some light brown gravy with mushrooms. There was some canned fruit, hot coffee and a piece of chocolate. Not bad.

There were kids from all over, donned in Marine green. They were wearing their traditional leggings and boots, web belt ammo holders with Ka-Bars in sheaths. They were trim and neat, a testament to their drill instructors, but I could anticipate they'd be a dirty, sweaty, ragged mess after a few days in combat. They had garrison caps or pith helmets on their heads. A few were carrying their unloaded Aught-Three Springfields, punishment for failing to maintain the sheen their overseers demanded. They were all twenty-somethings from Amarillo, Las Cruces, Chattanooga, Tampa, Traverse City. They tossed casual insults back and forth and I could tell a brotherhood was forming. I had a moment's regret I didn't get into foot soldiering, maybe because I was attracted to this kind of spirited camaraderie. But then I reminded myself I likely wouldn't have been very good at it. A muddy foxhole, barbed wire and bayonets. I was a ship driver, with my own role to play.

After breakfast I went out on patrol. I liked to go from stem to stern. I noted our bosuns had spit shined our capstan room on B Deck, where we took in *Bridger's* massive anchor rodes through the big hawse pipes port and starboard. I looked into the windlasses to see if our men had reapplied grease to the gears, fighting off the rampant corrosion that could obliterate machinery at sea if the salt air had its will. I went down a companionway to C Deck and aft. I wanted to make sure Bowker and his crew had cleaned up the previous evening's crime scene.

I got to the very spot—there was still a piece of wire hanging from a hydrant line over head—and I could see a dark stain on the deck plate. I reminded myself to get a paint crew on that. It suddenly dawned on me that we needed to focus on where our killer performed his grisly work. The knuckle bashing would take time, restraints, concealment—a torture chamber. And our faux Napolitano wasn't huge, but it would have taken some doing to control him, then string him up. Did our killer have an accomplice? Were we looking for more than one murderer? I thought I'd detected two tread patterns in the footprints we saw on B Deck.

I knew that Donahue's guys had performed a good search of the C Deck cargo hold the night of the murder—was that only twelve hours ago?—but they had to have missed something. There was a lantern hanging on a bulkhead near an exit leading aft. It was part of my damage control kit. I felt the vibration from *Bridger's* turning props all the way up here, and the ship's roll had added a third dimension—a distinct biangular sway between her rhythmic up and down punch through the swells. A bit of weather, or a change in heading? I'd have to call the OD on the bridge and get an update.

I turned on the lantern and started shining it through the grid of passageways marked by cargo boxes. There were walls of crates, netting, barrels. It was mostly foodstuffs, but here and there I saw footlockers that had contents stenciled in lettering on the outside: Thompson .45-caliber; another submachine gun, the Reising, also in .45; or .30-06 ammo for our Springfield bolt-action rifles and our new M1 Garand semi-automatics. That's when I found a speck of blood on the deck—a few drops, then a good smear. It led to a spot between some boxes and disappeared. I could tell from semi-circular scrapes on the decking these boxes had been pulled, or twisted, out of the way. I removed one of the boxes, and I was amazed the whole pile didn't come crashing down on me. The boxes on top were held up by hastily devised cross members. I shined my light inside the opening and I could see a room at the end of a crawlway. It suddenly occurred to me our assailant had to be physically large enough and strong enough to fashion this hideout. Our original missing Marine, Rizzo, was too small. This kind of setup would have taken several men to put together.

Maybe our killer had assumed Rizzo's identity, too. Maybe Rizzo was another victim.

Then I heard footsteps.

I was not alone.

I felt the heat of this closed-in space, and the sweat that was beading up on my brow under my cap. My shirt was clinging to me, and I could feel the damp on my upper lip and between my eyes. There was a nervous energy searing my temples and choking my throat. The steps were getting louder and it was by God time to move.

I needed a weapon.

Ship of Tears

I looked around for a board or a bat I could use to defend myself, and I was irritated I had placed myself in this situation without Donahue or one of his boys from the Master at Arms Department backing me up. I needed to get deeper into the hold. I picked up a short piece of two-by-two our supply boys had used as a shim, and I had it in my hand as I doused the light and receded into the darkened hold. The steps stopped and I tried to tame my breathing. I told myself that whatever happened, I had to come out swinging. I had a flash on that altercation in the Sunda Strait, when Haggerty and I took on the duo that wanted to hobble our steering gear and slow us down so the submarines could get us.

"It's a fucking war," Haggerty had said into my ear as I followed him into the auxiliary steering locker and I shot the *Nazi* infiltrator with the fire axe in his hands. The lawyer inside me was screaming 'what about due process,' but my animal instincts won the day.

Why didn't I have my revolver?

It was locked in a cabinet in my stateroom where it did absolutely no good to anybody. Haggerty wanted me to upgrade to a .45, and maybe he was right. The steps started again, but this time they seemed to be moving aft. I moved out of the shadows with my club in my hand. I got out to the main passage running down the hold and shined my light toward the door. There was a man running away from me.

"Stop!" I shouted at the top of my lungs. "Stop right there."

The figure kept moving and I had the utterly possessed notion to run after him. I had to see who it was. He was big. He couldn't be Rizzo. And he was wearing the green utilities of a Marine. He was wearing boots but no leggings, and his blouse was untucked. Who was he?

Timothy Cole

He got to the door of the hold. A light from *Bridger's* interior spaces shone into the cargo space, and I could see his silhouette framed in the light coming through the doorway. He had a black brush-cut, something of a neck roll, beefy arms. He looked sideways and I could see the misshapen proboscis belonging to a man with a broken nose. The door slammed in my face, and I opened it to a sea of green Marines going about their daily tasks, desperate battles in a dimly lit tomorrow—chatting, playing solitaire, swapping yarns, jokes, tall tales. They were having fun and avoiding all talk of what might come next.

My big Marine was gone.

Chapter Five
– Stowaway

I was at a half trot trying to get to the port side so I could go aft and down. I needed to get to Donahue's office, and I was hoping Haggerty was available. I was out of breath when I got to the office, where I found my collaborators chatting over coffee and a smoke.

"I need you on C Deck. Now. And I need as many men as you can find," I told them.

They didn't inquire about particulars. They could hear it in my voice and see it on my face. I was on to our killer. Haggerty moved first toward the cabinet where we kept our pump-action shotguns. Donahue had the pistol cabinet open and he was handing out Colt .45s in web holsters with extra magazine pouches. He handed me one, and I was a trifle skittish in the presence of the big bruiser, preferring my gentlemanly .38 in the sartorially correct holster. Hell with that. I took the .45 and mimicked Haggerty as he racked the slide, chambered a round, checked the slide-stop safety and left the hammer cocked and locked as he positioned it at the ready in his holster. I later learned this so-called "administrative handling" was called "Condition One." We headed out into the population and Marines stood aside while our armed contingent struggled through the crowds of green.

"Big guy. At least six-two, six-three. Over two hundred.

Buzz cut. Huge neck. Broken nose," I told them.

"All right you guys," said Donahue. "You heard the commander. Fan out and move forward. We converge on the after door to the forward hold on C Deck."

We moved through *Bridger* with our guns drawn and I filled Haggerty in on my discoveries: "Found the guy's nest, and he came back into the hold. He didn't want to tangle with me and he ran aft. I got a good look at him."

Soon, there were eight of us squeezing into the narrow passage on C Deck between all those stacked crates of Gold Seal flour and Domino sugar and Dole canned pineapple. I got us over to the aisle where I'd found the nest and Haggerty started pulling out the box blocking the entranceway. Donahue told one of his Master at Arms men to go back to the MA office for a camera.

Haggerty gained access and started crawling inside. I heard a less-than-calming "holy shit," coming from inside and I steeled myself to follow. There was a smell of body odor and the slightly metallic smell of dried blood, appearing dark brown under the light from my lantern. The room was ten feet by ten feet. There was a blanket thrown in a corner, a slop bucket with fresh pee and excrement, some food scraps, and a ball-peen hammer resting on a crate covered in blood stains.

"That's where our victim had his knuckles smashed," said Haggerty. "Guy was tortured. He had information our killer wanted." I reflected on that for a moment: knuckle by knuckle, our killer asked a question, and when he didn't get the right answer, the hammer came down. The tumblers clicked. Information. A motive. But what information? Why?

"There's some hemp line over here," I told him. "Restraints."

"Killer is using what falls to hand," said Haggerty. "Still, I don't understand why he left our would-be 'Napolitano' hanging a few feet from here. Had to have known we'd find his hidey-hole."

"And why didn't he come after me when he had the chance?" I asked.

"You're not on his list," said Haggerty. "You'd just slow him down. This is just between our killer and his victims. He knows who they are, Jonas. They have to be connected."

Haggerty was shining a light in every direction. The walled-off room was clear to the overhead above.

"Did he set this up when the cargo was being loaded?" I asked. It's the only explanation that made any sense. It meant our killer had connections on the docks and, possibly, our supply department. Haggerty leapt ahead of my thought process, which was lawyerly and methodical. Haggerty had a criminal mind and went straight to the obvious.

"Dock workers mean the unions, which means the mob," he stated casually. "They're not all bad, but you run into some pretty tough guys."

"He's a stowaway, but he's willing to risk being found. That's the part I don't get," I threw out casually. Haggerty was ahead of me.

"He's not a member of the Corps," said Haggerty. "Explains a few things. He can roam at will. He's not AWOL because he's not on anybody's roster."

"And he won't be on Marchionda's AB-negative list, either," I said.

"The only thing we know is we've got a missing Rizzo from Cicero," said Haggerty.

"And I have a cable out to CINCPAC to learn where our dead Napolitano came from," I responded.

"But we still don't know where last night's victim came from, do we," said Haggerty.

"No we do not," I told him. "But somehow, I think we're getting closer. At least we've got the killer on the run."

"Let's get Donahue's guys to scour through the holds on every deck," Haggerty said. "The guy gave up this hole too easily. It only means he's got a spot, or maybe several spots, somewhere else."

"And let's get Marchionda and go over that list," I told him.

We made our way up to the bridge deck to hail Marchionda on the 1MC when we found him loitering in front of my cabin door. He had a smile on his face, and I was hoping for some good news.

"Fourteen Italians with AB-negative blood type," he told us, and I was now convinced he'd make a fine, permanent addition to Donahue's crew. "One of them was probably yesterday's victim."

"But we need a subset with some commonality," I told him. "I'll take hometowns anywhere in the State of Illinois. Can't be just blood type. I refuse to believe a bunch of guys got together just because they share AB-negative."

"You're right, Mr. Pratt. It's neighborhoods," said Marchionda. "We need to look at Italians who come from the same place regardless of blood type. I mean, fourteen of these guys were from all over hell's half acre. But five of them were within five miles of each other—Cicero, Cabrini Green, Fulton Market, South Loop, Greek Town. They're Chicago boys."

"Maybe the same outfit," said Haggerty. "We need names."

"So far only Rizzo from Cicero. We know his story. Absent without leave. Possibly dead," said Marchionda.

"Hold that thought," I told them. "Let me see if there's a cable on Napolitano's hometown." I stepped out of my cabin and into our radio shack just a few feet away. There was a sealed envelope in my in-tray. I opened it, waiting to be disappointed. But quite the reverse came true.

TO: COMMANDER JONAS PRATT FROM: CINCPAC PEARL

SUBJECT: MKE6-785412885 NAPOLITANO, JAMES MARINE LANCE CORPORAL

NIS REPORTS INDIVIDUAL'S HOMETOWN WAS STREETERVILLE AREA OF DOWNTOWN CHICAGO END

I walked back to my cabin to rejoin Haggerty and Marchionda. I filled them in on Napolitano's origins and Haggerty framed the issue succinctly.

"We've got a paid assassin on board this ship, gentlemen," he stated with his usual self-assurance. "Rizzo. Napolitano. Chicago boys. The fucker doing it is probably from Chicago, too."

"Sal," I turned to Marchionda. "Get down to Vandegrift's office on B Deck. Find Rupertus and tell him we need to locate and sequester anyone with an Italian name on our AB-negative list. MA office is too small. Round them up and stick them in the theater for now. Move." Marchionda was out the door and I turned to Haggerty.

"One of those AB-negative guys will be missing," I told him. "But if that missing guy came from anywhere near Cicero, we're on to something." Haggerty lingered.

"Shift into a higher gear, Jonas," Haggerty said. "We also need to find *any* Italians regardless of blood type from the south side of Chicago. Probably from the Seventh Marines."

"Maybe a big group, Nate," I told him. "We have to think about how we can carve out our victims."

"And our future victims," he added ominously. He continued: "Two tracks. We have to work the personnel side, and we've got to find where this fucker lives. We've got to start going through every inch of this ship."

While I didn't disagree, I knew Vandegrift wouldn't appreciate disruptions—or a panic.

"We'll need extra manpower for that," I told him. "We'll have to deputize a few of the Marines. I'll have a word with Rupertus." Vandegrift's number two was starting to become our go-to, and that was a plus. After the previous night's dressing down in the captain's cabin, I didn't want to bother Vandegrift unless I'd found a solution.

"We also need to up your game, Commander," he said. "You comfortable with that .45?"

"I need to spend more time with it," I told him.

"Needs to be part of your wardrobe. We'll find a quiet place near the fantail and fire off a few magazines," he said. "It will do for weapons handling. I'll break out my Thompson. You can fire that, too." It occurred to me I was probably more familiar with our anti-aircraft batteries than I was with personal defense weapons. Haggerty paused in the doorway.

"Should have had a .45 in the Sunda Strait, when you had to pop that guy," he said. I just stared at him. He knew I didn't like talking about it. He was way too casual when it came to killing. He tried to defend his shoot-first mentality.

"You've seen what our stowaway is capable of Jonas," he said. "When we confront this bastard, we won't be able to ask him nicely to please put the Ka-Bar down while we talk things over."

Haggerty always had to have the last word.

Ship of Tears

He went below to receive our AB-negative Italians and I spent some time on the bridge deck checking in with navigation, meteorology, radio shack, our coding team. I had a conversation with Captain Kelly to apprise him of the status of our investigation and took a few moments in my cabin to type up letters to my kids, which I would be able to post when we reached Wellington. I also wrote a letter to my lady of the heart. I needed to get the words out there on the page. Then I thought better about sending it. She was embarked on her new life, and likely wouldn't appreciate the intrusion.

I made my way down and aft via the port side, stopping by the cabin-class mess to chat with the master chief in charge of our culinary department. Barney Crawford was old school Navy, and his time in service went back before the last war. He knew everyone up and down the chain—and he knew our supply teams. I asked him if he'd seen any funny business in the ship's holds. He'd been around long enough to know theft and thievery of government property was considered just another form of recreation by certain members of our crew.

"I'm interested in any cargo shifts you might have observed since we left 'Frisco,'" I told him.

"We packed the holds from the inside out, just like we always do," Crawford reminded me. "We've got perishables on the outside of the pile. They go into the commissaries first. And then we work inward towards the grains, cereals, and canned goods. Freezers take the meat, eggs and milk."

"Notice anything funny about how the stuff was brought aboard?" I asked him. "Any voids in the loading that could hide a man or two?"

"Stowaways?" he asked. Mr. Crawford is not stupid.

"I can't confirm or deny," I told him. "But Chief Crawford I will be very disappointed if our conversation goes beyond this office."

"Loose lips, Commander," he said, looking me in the eye. "I get it." I needed allies and Crawford was an old pro. I had to inform him of what might be happening in an area of the ship where he had direct oversight. I gave him as complete a picture as I could, including and especially our C Deck homicide the night before. Crawford let out a disbelieving whistle.

"What a mess," he told me, offering a neat summation.

"I've got Donahue and his Master at Arms contingent working their way through the holds, but I want supply parties to enter the holds in force," I told him. "No one goes in without two more to assist. We've got strength in numbers."

"What do I tell my guys?" he asked, not unreasonably.

"Safety oversight order from the XO," I told him. "I don't want them to strain their backs. And I don't want to start a panic." I realized I was in a panic to avoid a panic.

'Remain calm attorney Pratt,' I told myself.

"Understood," he said. "But Commander, you're carrying a .45. Do I need a sidearm before I go into the hold?" I can see he likes that big Marine leg holster Donahue cooked up for me.

"I'm not opposed," I told him. "Talk to Donahue. Tell him I said it's okay. In fact, hell with it. I'll let you use my .38. It's in a holster topside. Walk with me. I've got a meeting in the theater in a few minutes. Let's go." Crawford and I worked our way to the starboard side to move forward, then up. We got to my cabin and I gave him my personal firearm, which I'd used to kill a man. I didn't mention that to Crawford.

"Haven't needed to carry one of these in a long time,"

he said.

"Just tell your guys it's a change in policy as we get closer to the theater," I told him, and we parted as collaborators. He'd entered the inner circle.

I made my way to the stage and took in the scene: There was a clutch of young Marines standing down near the orchestra pit, overseen here and there by squad leaders or even a second lieutenant or two. Haggerty was working the room and he was trying to lighten the mood with some off-color banter. Marchionda was busy with his list, ticking off attendees. He was my first stop.

"Who's missing?" I asked him.

"We've got two more stragglers coming down the aisle," he told me. "Then we should have a clear picture." I saw mere waifs dressed in baggy utilities in that ubiquitous herringbone green. Their M1941 suspenders held up their ammo belts, which also carried canteens, first-aid kits and other paraphernalia in addition to their cartridge clips. I noticed some of our Marines were wearing their ancient leggings; some were without. There seemed to be a struggle over the value of these accessories. Marchionda was finished with his tally and I could tell he was a bit withdrawn. He only had thirteen AB-negatives of Italian extraction in the room with us. His list had fourteen.

"Who's missing?" I asked him, and our victim from yesterday morning's bloodletting, our man overboard, became instantly apparent.

"Gallo. James R. Private First Class. He's twenty," he told me.

"Any information on hometown?" I asked.

"South Loop. Chicago," said Marchionda, and my theory took on a layer of credence. I needed to speak to Gallo's squad leader. His name was on Gallo's row in a column headlined

"CO." I called out his name and I got a few vacant stares, then one of my new AB-negative friends told me Gallo's squad leader was a sergeant named Stan Archibald.

"Just saw him in the tourist class mess," I was told by one of our befuddled Italians, who had no idea why they were being sequestered. Marchionda dragooned the young Marine so he could identify Archibald and they were off at a trot to find the man they called "Sarge." Archibald was soon standing before me. We went through the ritual exchange—hometown, length of service, specialties. Archibald informed me he was on "Lieutenant Colonel Puller's crew," First Battalion, Seventh Marines.

I had been picking up bits of information about Puller. He was a VMI graduate and he'd cut his teeth in the Haitian *gendarmerie* when the U.S. Marine Corps leased out its talent back in the Twenties to the authorities on the western side of the Island of Hispaniola. The objective was to suppress rebellions that might prove contrary to American interests. Puller's next assignment was battling the Sandino rebels in Nicaragua.

"He's a real fighter," I intoned to my new young friend.

"Just what the doctor ordered," Archibald told me.

"Do you know Gallo?" I asked him, and Archibald took a moment to process this simple question. I'm suspicious of the man's delay in responding, but then I tempered this reaction with a dose of reality. We're throwing a lot at these young Marines this morning.

"Gallo is in my squad," said Archibald.

"Do you know where he is?" I asked innocently.

"Fuck if I know," said Archibald.

"Aren't you supposed to count heads every morning?" I asked him.

"Lieutenant said we can relax a bit when we're at sea," said Archibald. "These guys aren't going anywhere."

Ship of Tears

'Except overboard with their throats cut,' I thought to myself.

"When's the last time you saw Gallo?" I asked him, as Haggerty came up to my little interview. We've got Archibald bracketed and I could tell we were making Gallo's immediate supervisor uncomfortable. That's okay with me. Archibald is a position of responsibility. His man is missing. He *should* be uncomfortable.

"Last time?" asked Archibald. "Probably chow line yesterday."

"It wouldn't be chow line yesterday, shit for brains," said Haggerty. "It might be chow line day before yesterday. Evening meal?"

"You're right," said Archibald. "Day before yesterday. Days just kind of blend together. I don't remember seeing Gallo yesterday."

'That's because Jimmy Gallo is on the bottom of the ocean,' I thought, trying to avoid being irritated. I can't relate to this man's 'give-a-crap' attitude.

"Where are you from Archibald?" asked Haggerty.

"Brick, New Jersey," he responded.

'Okay. Not Chicago,' I told myself.

"Know anything about Gallo?" I asked.

"I've had maybe six words with Gallo since we left 'Frisco," said Archibald. "He was an add-on from another regiment. They threw us together last minute."

"When were you going to take the time to get to know your men?" asked Haggerty.

"Big ocean," said Archibald. "I figured we had time. I look to my company commander for all that cohesion bullshit." My dislike for Archibald was blossoming and taking me off task.

"I need to find Gallo's buddies," I told Archibald. "Anybody he might have gotten close to in the past few weeks. Especially anybody from Chicago."

Archibald called across the theater to a crony. "Garner," he said, "get your ass over here." Another impossibly young Marine walked up. "Do you know Gallo?"

"Yeah," said Garner. And then he had a good look at Haggerty and me and added, "Not well." We're the authority figures, naturally unpopular with the lower ranks.

"You're not in any trouble, Marine," I told the boy. "Where are you from?"

"Akron," he told me with a discernible swell of pride.

"We need to find Gallo if we can. It's important."

"I haven't seen him since the day before yesterday," said Garner.

"Where does he bunk?" asked Haggerty.

"D deck, aft," said Garner. "Right over the fucking prop shafts. Impossible to sleep back there." Marchionda walked up and took note.

"Gallo is missing," I told Garner. "We'll need to get into his duffel." I fired a glance at Marchionda and he was reading my mind. He spun on his heels and sprinted up the aisle.

"Ever notice who Gallo liked to talk to? Have a smoke with maybe?"

"Another platoon in the First Battalion of the Seventh," he said. "Chicago guys." A light went on for Haggerty and me. I turned to Haggerty to announce we'll need to get the so-called "Chicago guys" in one room. The AB-Negative track had gotten us this far. Now 'The Chicago Guys' were our focus. That's when Chief Crawford came up to our little group and whispered in my ear.

"Commander, there's a dead Marine in the freezer below the cabin-class mess," he said. The notion of 'surprise' had been knocked right out of me.

'*Of course, there's another dead Marine,*' I told myself.

And they'd keep piling up until I could stop the insanity that suddenly surrounded us.

Chapter Six
– Cold Kill

My beautiful wife Margie was sitting across from me in our comfortable living room. Yes, we'd navigated the shoals and outcroppings of our formative years. She had been married to that bloke from Sewickley, having decided waiting for Attorney Pratt, and for the Allies to break the back of the Axis, was off in some ill-defined tomorrow. She'd knuckled under to mom and dad and married "Joe," who, it turned out, had a wandering eye. I came back from the war. Margie, childless, was figuring things out with her beau. Our timing was off. Tereza and I parted company amicably, but Margie was unavailable. Margie and I reconnected later on. So you see, there were lots of twists and turns in our novella, but now, hoops of steel connected me to the love of my life. She had her reading glasses perched on the end of her nose. She was wearing that lovely white blouse with the upturned collar, and the effect offered a touch of the Katherine Hepburn. She wore a tasteful gold necklace, and her stocking feet were tucked under her woolen slacks as she balanced my manuscript pages and a glass of Dr. Frank's Pinot Noir. She looked just as beautiful wearing camouflage in a duck blind or casting a midge with a flyrod.

"So, you went through all that just to find your missing Gallo?" she asked.

"Only way we could identify our AB-negative victim who got stabbed and tossed overboard on B Deck," I told her. "We had to get all of the AB-negative Italians in one room to find our missing man."

"You had Rizzo and Napolitano. So it made sense your third victim would be Italian, too?" she asked.

"No," I told her. "None of it made sense. And looking for another missing Italian was kind of a Hail Mary. But it was all I had to work with. I was trying to find associations."

"Good idea bringing in Chief Crawford," she told me.

"Had to," I told her. "The holds were the chief's domain. I didn't want any of his people getting hurt. And he could open some doors."

"Who's the victim in the freezer?" she asked.

"That's where the plot thickened, to employ the standard cliché," I responded. "Our fourth victim widened the aperture. But not before we had to sort out his identity, too."

"It's a proper mess Commander Pratt," said Margie.

I looked back on it, bourbon in hand, and I couldn't disagree. Rizzo and Gallo were missing and therefore presumed murdered. The Naval Investigation Service, precursor to NCIS, stated Napolitano was our decedent back in California. So the hanging corpse on C Deck was, as yet, unidentified.

"Did Sal find Rizzo's personal items? His duffel bag?" She had pulled out this obscure piece of information and was holding it up to the light. It reminded me why my wife is so smart.

"Interesting you should mention that. Sal never found Rizzo's personal effects. But his gear did turn up later. There's a piece of that puzzle that became essential." Margie turned back to my manuscript.

"I need to find out what Crawford found in the freezer," she said. "Rizzo will have to wait."

Crawford led us down to the ship's lowest decks. We descended the aft staircase, the ship's furnishings and paint schemes becoming more industrial the lower we went. I could feel the heat from the boilers when we got to D Deck. We went past our waterless swimming pool stuffed with boxes and finally found the big metal door for our cold supply. There were three muscle-bound seamen from Donahue's Master at Arms office standing there, and one of them handed me a pea coat.

"Chilly in there, Commander," he told me. Haggerty took one too and we ventured in.

There was a light switch, and Haggerty flicked it on as he removed his pistol. He had it in his right, strong hand as he pushed aside hanging sides of beef. There were cartons of milk, crates of eggs, and some large tubs of vanilla ice cream.

"Over here, Commander," he told me, and I was astonished at what we found. There was a young Marine in green utilities, his entrails safely inside his belly, thank God. But he had ice tongs jammed in both ears and the tongs were hooked to an overhead pipe. His throat was slit wide open, and with his neck stretched, you could see the structure of his trachea, thyroid and voice box. There was frozen red blood down his shirt front, which had spilled on the floor to form a hardened puddle. His face was a frosty white.

"Knuckles are bashed in," said Haggerty. "And look at that. Left ear is missing."

Why was I not surprised?

"Check his dog tags," I told him, and I braced for his response. My FBI man used a pen to lift the tags off the dead Marine's chest so he could read them.

"Gallo," he said. "AB-negative.

"It can't be Gallo," I insisted. "Gallo was yesterday's murder. We'll check this guy's blood to confirm."

"Guy who is doing this is a real asshole," said Haggerty, frustration open and simmering. Haggerty didn't like to be made the fool. "Switching up dog tags just to slow us down."

"Smart bastard," I told him. "We have to get to Gallo's outfit before the killer does."

"I assume said outfit also includes our dead Rizzo and Napolitano," he said, but then he skipped a beat. "Who do you suppose our stiff on C Deck was?"

"You mean the guy with the tag that read Napolitano who wasn't Napolitano?" I asked him.

"Yeah, that guy," said Haggerty.

"Positive IDs will come when we round up known associates and show them photographs," I told him and he muttered his annoyance.

"If we can find any known associates who are still alive," Haggerty said. Haggerty hated losing control.

"Let's let Donahue and his team cut this guy down. Get him to McGuire for a postmortem, take a blood sample, and get his photo taken," said Haggerty.

"Donahue can also interview the supply team and probe the perimeter for evidence," I told him.

"We have to estimate a time of death and determine who was in here," Haggerty said. "Somebody might have seen something."

The answer to that question became abundantly clear when we found Gallo's bunk on D Deck aft, which was up only two ladderways. We discovered Marchionda pawing through a standard duffel bag. Haggerty assigned himself the task of gathering together Gallo's known Chicago associates, who, at that moment, didn't realize they were being stalked by a killer who preferred using a big knife—and a hammer.

"Any of you guys know Gallo in Chicago," he asked a small knot of green. Five hands went up.

"You guys stand off to one side," he told them. "And do not leave this space."

"What are you finding Sal?" I asked Marchionda.

"Taking an inventory and logging it," he told me. He was fastidious. I liked that.

"Can we confirm this stuff belongs to Gallo, our dead AB-negative Marine?" I asked.

"Person who owns this duffel bag has two or three letters started back home to Mr. and Mrs. Gallo, Chicago, Illinois. Could be parents, or an aunt and an uncle. He's got inbound letters from a girl named Stella, addressed to Lance Corporal James "Jimmy" Gallo. Seems Stella is pressuring young Gallo because she might be in the family way. I've found his military ID, thirty-seven dollars in cash, an IOU from some bozo named Moriarty for a poker debt. Also his life insurance declaration page. A vaccination record. An Illinois driver's license. It's him. Here's his picture."

I looked down at a good-looking kid with wavy black hair, straight teeth, high cheeks, a dimple in his chin, a winning smile. No wonder Stella fell hard for him. He looked like a crooner—and by now he'd made the long, lonely trip to the bottom of the sea.

Haggerty seemed to be having some success corralling Gallo's Chicago buddies. Two were in Gallo's section, and three more were bunking on another deck. They happened to be chit-chatting with Gallo's D-Deck compadres when we showed up. They were all attached to Puller's First Battalion, Seventh Marines, and I got the impression they all went into the service together, performing their patriotic duty. I asked Marchionda to get Gallo's duffel into the MA office and I tasked Haggerty to lead Gallo's outfit up to my cabin. We could use my conference room. There would be eight of us—nine if I could find Donahue—but I thought we could squeeze in.

As Haggerty and I worked our way topsides, our troupe of Italians behind us, Haggerty expressed his concerns quietly but in most emphatic terms.

"Only way to hold these guys is to stash them behind bars in the brig and interview them one at a time," he said. "Best way to catch them in any lies. We don't want them to coordinate any tales out of school." My lawyerly hackles were raised.

"They haven't committed any crimes," I responded.

"That we know of," said Haggerty. "But I think we can suspend JAG rules for at least forty-eight hours. We can arrest them as hostile witnesses, interview them one by one, and note discrepancies. These weenies are being bumped off for a reason, Mr. Pratt." When Haggerty reverted to the formal, I needed to listen...up to a point.

"Suspicion of what?" I shot back, and then I paused for reflection. I couldn't let my occasional distaste for Haggerty's methods interfere with common sense. "Let's put them in the smoking lounge forward of the first-class mess on A Deck," I told him. "There's space, and we can put some of Donahue's guys in there to keep them separated. You can pull them out one by one for interviews up one deck in my cabin."

"My preference is to beat what I need out of them," said Haggerty.

"We'll soften them up with kindness," I told him. "They won't know what hit them." Haggerty was mollified for the moment.

On the way up, we deviated for the smoking room and I was pleased to see it was vacant. We used it for Jewish Temple on Saturdays, and not many of our guests knew it was there. *Bridger's* special ocean liner adornments had been removed, so the paneling, the rugs, the lighting, and the furniture were mid-Century utilitarian—aluminum, non-flammable panels, and ceramic. The ship's designers at Gibbs and Cox had been traumatized by the terrible fires that had consumed the *Morro Castle* before the war, fueled by wood, textiles and other finery. This tragedy was very much on their minds when they drew up *Bridger's* interior plan.

We got our boys in and settled. I called the officer's mess and ordered sandwiches and lemonade for our party. Haggerty was amused by this simple act of gastronomic charity. My host duties completed, I turned to take attendance, with Marchionda serving as recording secretary.

"You guys all knew Gallo from your Chicago days," I told them. "I'll go around the room and you'll give me your full name, your home address, and your unit." I pointed to a sullen young man. "You first."

"You going to tell us what this is about?" he responded, and Haggerty stepped forward and slapped the Marine across the face as hard as he could, leaving a reddened cheek and drawing blood from a lip.

"You heard the commander, asshole," he said. "Name, home address, unit." I knew Haggerty was just trying to set the tone, a bit like first day of seventh grade when the homeroom teacher bashes a yard stick on her desk and shrieks for attention.

"Dominick DiGenova," he said. "Garfield Park, Illinois...First Battalion, Seventh Marines, First Division."

"Now you, smiley," said Haggerty, turning to the next lad to Dominick's left.

"Anthony Petrucio," he said. "Englewood, Illinois... First Battalion, Seventh Marines, First Division." And so on, as we achieved a splendid display of compliance and cooperation. We also had a Mario Ricci from Lawnwood, Illinois; a Tony DeLuca, from South Shore, Illinois; and a Stephen Bianchi, from Chatham, Illinois...all First Battalion, Seventh Marines, First Division.

Puller's boys.

Donahue arrived to oversee his MA regulars, and he was carrying a file folder with crime scene photos. He handed it to me and let me know the pictures from the freezer were in the developer bath. I took a minute to scan the pictures and revisited our hanging torture victim from the previous evening's discovery on C Deck. The stack came with shots of the footprints. The boot treads looked similar to the boot treads on B Deck—our "floater" to use Haggerty's shorthand. But I thought I could also see those smaller, partial footprints on the periphery. How many killers were we tracking? I turned back to my guests in the Smoking Room.

"You gentlemen also knew Rizzo and Napolitano back in the States," I told them as a statement of fact, not a question. They nodded in unison.

"And Rizzo and Napolitano were also from Chicago," I told them frankly, giving them the distinct impression I knew more than I really did. I was just trying to confirm a few things, but what I had in front of me was a little gang of ne'er-do-wells who were heading for the Solomons and the fight of their lives. Still, I couldn't pre-judge. I might have been looking at a future Supreme Court Justice. You never knew.

"Chief Donahue, keep these men in this room," I ordered. "I don't want them speaking to each other. First one who gets out of line goes straight to the brig to think things over."

"Aye-aye, Commander," said the ship's constable.

"Lieutenant Commander Haggerty, please invite Rifleman DiGenova to my cabin for a little conversation," I asked politely. Haggerty grabbed young Dominick by the arm and stood him up. I left the room, the weight of the whole United States Navy on my imperious shoulders, and walked up a flight to the bridge deck. I opened my cabin door, and Sal Marchionda was right there behind me, unbidden, with his notebook ready. I opened Donahue's file and found the least gruesome photo of our C Deck victim so DiGenova could make a positive ID. I had no idea if it was the real Napolitano, or some other hapless hoodlum from the Windy City. Indeed, the victim NIS thinks it ID'd back in 'Frisco might be someone else.

Haggerty brought DiGenova into my domain, and I could tell by the way his eyes roamed around my space he was either impressed or ticked off at one more of life's injustices. How did this guy Pratt merit the fancy digs? Sometimes I wondered the same thing. Haggerty grabbed DiGenova's garrison cap off the boy's head and shoved him down in a chair. I had to remind myself Gallo's pals were being murdered for a reason. It's possible these guys were not exactly exemplary citizens, nor deserving of all the courtesies our ship could bestow.

"So Rifleman DiGenova," I opened. "You and your buddies knew Gallo."

"Sure, we knew Gallo," he responded.

"When's the last time you saw him?"

"I have to think."

"Think hard, asshole," said Haggerty, who continued to stand over the boy. It occurred to me Haggerty had maneuvered me into playing good-cop, bad-cop. I was okay with that.

"He was losing at craps night before yesterday," DiGenova said.

"Who was he playing craps with?" I asked him. "Guys from another unit?"

"Yeah, I guess so…" DiGenova was still wondering if he was in trouble. I could see it on his face. But he was also thinking: *'Which one of my many crimes am I in for?'*

"How many guys were playing craps on this occasion?"

"Four or five."

"Did you know any of them?"

"Most of them," he told me.

"Not all?"

"I may not have known one or two."

"Give me physical descriptions of the ones you didn't know."

"Scrawny kid. From Iowa, I think. And a big guy."

"Big guy have a broken nose?"

"Yeah, that's him."

"Big guy have a name?" Haggerty asked.

"I didn't catch it."

"You see the big guy around a lot?" asked Haggerty.

"Here and there," said DiGenova.

"Any idea what unit he's attached to?" I asked.

"Somebody said a headquarters company or a Raider," said DiGenova. "I wasn't paying attention."

There was a knock on the door and one of Donahue's MA team handed Haggerty a sealed eight-by-ten envelope.

He handed it to me and I slit it open with a pen knife. Tucked within were that morning's forensic shots from the freezer victim. I selected a shot that avoided most of the gore, and I kept it face down on the table alongside the C-Deck victim.

"Did you know Napolitano?" I asked him. "He's the one who missed the boat. Napolitano was from Chicago, too." DiGenova blinked twice and looked down at the table. I repeated...

"Did you know Napolitano Mr. DiGenova?"

"Yeah, I knew him," he said.

"Why did he miss the boat?" I asked.

"He's dead."

"What happened?"

"Knifed in San Francisco," he said. One small mystery was solved. Our hanger on C Deck forward was not Napolitano, despite what his dog tags indicated. I needed to put a little fear into this overly confident young man.

"Know who did it?" I asked.

"Not a clue."

"Maybe it was you," I said, hoping to elicit a reaction. DiGenova's eyes arched skyward. He was registering real surprise.

"No fucking way," he told me, indignant. "I was across the bay in Alameda, at the Naval Air Station, our rally point. Napolitano was near the Presidio. I've got witnesses."

Time to show him the faux-Napolitano from C Deck. I produced the head shot and I watched DiGenova recoil. It was not the reaction of a trained killer, in my experience. The young tough reverted to his boyhood fears.

"Can you identify this individual?" I asked him. DiGenova hesitated, and I pounced.

"This guy in Puller's unit, too?" DiGenova didn't know

what kind of trouble he was in. No one ever told the young man telling the truth was usually the first and best option. Maybe the nuns in grade school, but their admonitions were drowned out by the tough kids on the street.

"That's Mickey Rizzo," he said weakly.

"His bunk aboard ship back near Gallo?" I asked.

"Yeah," said DiGenova. "He was two racks up from Gallo." I looked at Marchionda and he made a note.

"Where is Rizzo's duffel bag?" I asked DiGenova. So now the young tough thought he was being interrogated for theft.

"I didn't take it," he said. He could have said 'I don't know.' His response intrigued me.

"Let's assume you didn't take it," I told him softly. A hard edge won't get you anywhere when you're trying to pull out information. "Does that mean somebody else took it?"

"Maybe."

"Somebody in your unit?"

"I don't know." He'd finally gathered himself, and he was digging in his heels.

"So Rizzo was gone. Disappeared," I told him, relating the clear facts. "And somebody took his duffel too?"

"Not sure," he said, and I knew I was losing him. I'd have to bring him up short.

"You know stealing is an offense that will land you in prison," I told him, and then I speculated. "Guy like you, they'd throw away the key. With all your priors."

"Marine recruiter said he'd get my record cleared," he said. Haggerty piped up.

"They all say that—just to get your ass into a uniform and onto a train to Camp Pendleton," he said, and DiGenova visibly deflated.

"Rizzo's stuff," I repeated. "Where is it?"

"Me and the guys divided it up," he said. And Haggerty once again injected a note of menace.

"Anybody give you permission to steal Rizzo's personal effects? When the commander is finished with all you assholes, we'll go back down and gather up all Rizzo's stuff," he said. "We clear on that?"

"We're clear," he said, and now I had a hoodlum in front of me who was more or less prepared to have a civilized conversation. It was like working with an untrained horse. You had to get their attention.

I was still a little dissatisfied with what I was learning from my interrogation. He and his pals were high-school dropouts. They'd become a feral crew of bums who stole beer and cigarettes for resale, snatched purses, picked pockets, swiped cars, bikes, baby buggies—anything not nailed down. The police chased them all over southside Chicago and they had cubby holes in all the abandoned buildings, where they could play cards, drink whisky, maybe sleep. They remembered their parents vaguely, especially their mothers, but they couldn't recall the last time they'd seen them. I finally got down to that layer of earth where the gems were hidden. Why would anyone want them dead? DiGenova bit his bleeding lip, crossed his arms and fell silent. He was in a pact with his buddies.

I had four more of these galoots below in the smoking room and I released DiGenova to the care and supervision of Donahue's boys. I didn't want them released until all our interviews had been completed. At that point we would go together to find Rizzo's personal items. I had to inject a note of conciliation with DiGenova. Next time, I wanted him to speak freely, and that would begin with an ounce of trust.

"Go get a sandwich, son," I told young Dominick, as I patted him on the shoulder. He looked at me with doe-soft eyes and I wondered when the last time this person had enjoyed any kind of benign human contact.

The rest of our interviews with our little Chicago gang went accordingly, except for Bianchi. I saved Bianchi for last. Petrucio, Ricci, DeLuca: they all tried to out-tough DiGenova. They were belligerent, combative, taciturn—all in a nice stew of anti-authority. Predictably, Haggerty had to use an open slap to get any of them to sit up straight, and with Petrucio, the threat of Haggerty driving his fist "right through your fucking little face" finally overcame the punk slouching in his chair, fending off question after question.

But then there was Bianchi. Bianchi failed miserably at the art of being the truculent gangster. He came in carrying a plate with a massive ham and Swiss sandwich and a tall glass of iced lemonade.

"I let him bring his grub," said Donahue. "Hope that's okay."

"Perfectly fine, chief," I told them and turned, smiling, to my last guest of the day.

"Rifleman Bianchi from Chatham. My name is Commander Jonas Pratt and this is Lieutenant-Commander Nathan Haggerty. I run the ship under Captain Kelly and Mr. Haggerty is in charge of ship's security."

"Take off your cover, asshole," growled Haggerty, and Bianchi shifted his garrison cap into his lap. I began our conversation with a bald-faced lie.

"Your colleagues were extremely helpful," I told him. "They filled me in on what's going on with you Chicago guys. Pretty tough way to make a living, wouldn't you say?" It was the kind of sweeping banality that fit any circumstance, and it was designed to open avenues of inquiry.

"We get by," said Bianchi.

"Let me tell you why we're here," I began. I pulled my freezer victim out of the folder. DiGenova had established our hanger on C Deck is Rizzo. But our killer had placed Gallo's dog tags on the stiff in the freezer. "He's not Gallo, Mr. Bianchi, so who is he?"

Bianchi looked at the photograph and started to weep. There was a human heart beating in that young chest.

"Moretti," he said. "When? How?" Bianchi was showing some compassion for the departed.

"Moretti was part of your squad?" I asked him. "And you knew him from home?"

"...Yes," said Bianchi meekly.

"Moretti ever harm anyone?" I asked him.

"...no," he responded.

"Great guy, then," I told him, and Bianchi nodded.

"Shame what happened to him," I said, and Haggerty threw in his own grisly two cents.

"Picture doesn't do it justice," he said. "Guy who slit his throat hung him up in the freezer with ice tongs poked in his ears. And speaking of ears, one of them is missing. Killer took it. In fact, killer is collecting ears, it seems." Bianchi put down his sandwich.

"I've got four members of your tribe dead, Mr. Bianchi," I told him. Let's start with Napolitano back in 'Frisco. Knifed in the Presidio according to DiGenova. Then Gallo knifed and chucked overboard yesterday morning. Rizzo gutted and hanging in the hold on C Deck. And now Moretti with his throat cut in the freezer. They are all connected to you and your buddies."

"Guy who is doing this is called a serial killer," said

Haggerty. "He's picking you off one by one. But the funny thing is, he's torturing you guys first. Smashing knuckles with a hammer. In my experience, it only means he's trying to get something out of you. Probably some kind of information. Trouble is, he's not getting what he wants. He gets pissed off and moves on to the next poor bastard."

"My colleague Mr. Haggerty is right, son," I told him reassuringly. "It's not pretty. But we can tell the killer is getting frustrated. You guys aren't giving him the information he's looking for."

Bianchi was on the worried side of puking, that stage where you're looking for a place to vomit. Haggerty somehow sensed this and went into my toilet to get a metal waste basket. He gave it to Bianchi and the poor man's sandwich was hurled nearly complete into the receptacle. He was choking now, and there were tears running down his face.

"We told each other we'd take it the grave," said Bianchi.

"Only way to stop the killer is to tell me what he wants," I said softly. "I can help you. But you have to level with me son."

Bianchi rocked back and forth, the truth straining to break free. When it finally spilled forth, I sensed the arrival of a plan.

But we had to catch our killer in the act. For this shark we'd needed bait, and that bait turned out to be me.

Chapter Seven
– Associations

I'd taken to getting up before sunrise on the weekdays and getting into the office early to work on my manuscript. Margie was being patient with me. I told her I couldn't rush this process. I had to delve deep into the events of three decades past, and some of it didn't come easily. I had avoided the topic of the war for so long, and some facts naturally became suppressed. I had pushed all thought of *Bridger's* killer down deep in my subconscious. But I dreamed of those dead men with their ghastly wounds, and I retreated from the very idea there was a human being capable of such atrocities. But then I remembered the fight to hold Henderson Field on Guadalcanal, and my memories of our killer in the cargo hold seemed quaint. Yes, I was there. Haggerty and me. We flew into that embattled island to execute an arrest warrant, landing in a maelstrom of bombs and bullets. It was the events that led up to our brief—and poorly timed—trip that now had my focus. Brother Josiah was looking down on me as I took up my pen.

Stephen Bianchi was a trembling leaf, sitting in that leather club chair in my cabin. There was a killer loose. Bianchi had seen photos of what the killer could do with a standard-issue Ka-Bar. I had chosen to show him everything—Rizzo's eyes bugging out of his head, the wire cutting into the vasculature of his neck, his guts ripped out and spilling on the deck in a stinking pool of blood and shit. I couldn't spare Bianchi. He was the path to finding the person who was responsible for this.

I sensed at the center of Bianchi's terror a tiny flickering flame of conscience. He knew he'd been running with the wrong crowd. But his mates were all he had, and they represented home. Yes, they'd lived in a series of broken and filthy abandoned buildings, but most of us learn home is more than just brick and mortar. It's an intimate congress of souls, a conclave of care. Of course, young men will slap backs and hurl insults and roughhouse. Puppies in a litter will nip each other and bare teeth in loving play. It's the process of maturation. It was hard for Bianchi to go against his litter. But he had to do what was right, he had to do it alone, and he had to follow his heart.

First, Bianchi needed to go through all his belligerent motions and join his brethren in thwarting our investigation. He'd remained silent, stonewalled, rocked back and forth, sipped his lemonade. He wasn't ready to talk, and while I sensed he might be the key that unlocked the door, I decided I needed to somehow get him alone. Better yet, he needed to come to me. I'd get more out of him if it was his idea. I let him return to his buddies. Haggerty and I followed. We got to the smoking room and Haggerty made a general announcement.

"We're going back to your accommodation and you're going to produce every item you stole out of Rizzo's duffel bag," he said. Our lads looked at one another and I could tell they were trying to avoid jail time. With competent counsel, a lenient judge would drop any of these trumped-up charges. They were operating on fear, which played into my hands.

We got to their pipe cots and they scattered to their respective personal spaces to organize their mementoes of Rizzo. DiGenova had Rizzo's card deck and his craps dice. Ricci had two pairs of Rizzo's socks and some Pomade hair gel. DeLuca had Rizzo's dairy, with just a few innocuous entries. Petrucio had Rizzo's little portable checkers set. Bianchi had Rizzo's safety razor.

"That's it?" I asked them.

"Uniform, boots, caps, leggings all went into a pile to re-use if anyone came up short," DiGenova told me. Haggerty and I looked at each other. We'd achieved what we wanted. We'd rattled these poor boys mercilessly in an effort to break loose any bits of information.

"You guys can keep Rizzo's personal items," I told them. "We'll get back to you. I want you guys to stick together at all times. I don't want anything bad to happen to any one of you."

Haggerty and I turned to make our way to the starboard side, up, then forward. I stepped into the passageway and there was a hand tugging at my sleeve. I turned and looked into the pained eyes of young Bianchi.

"There's one more thing," he said, looking over his shoulder. "Can we meet somewhere quiet?"

"Come up to my cabin on the bridge deck," I told him. "The door will be cracked open. Just walk in." Haggerty and I walked away, and I noted the tedious questioning that afternoon would be worth our time if we could get just one concrete fact into position that would lead us to our killer. Understanding what the killer wanted was our priority.

Haggerty, Marchionda and I arrived topside along the starboard Promenade Deck and walked forward. I sensed the heat and the humidity of the tropics in the evening breeze.

Ship of Tears

We were getting closer to our objective, and I wanted to clear up our murder mystery, which had assumed a ghastly scale. Five minutes passed and Bianchi walked in with a small package wrapped in an April edition of *The Chicago Tribune*. Marchionda closed and locked the door behind him, and I started unwrapping Bianchi's parcel. It was a book, *The Prisoner of Zenda*, by Anthony Hope.

"It was Napolitano's idea," said Bianchi.

Questions: I asked, he answered, and the tale left me breathless.

"Issue comes down to the information our killer is seeking," I opened. "What do you suppose he wants bad enough to travel halfway around the world to track you poor bastards down and use his Ka-Bar to cut you to pieces?"

"He wants money," said Bianchi.

"What money?"

"The money we stole."

"How much?"

"A quarter of a million dollars." Massive sums in 1942.

"Who did you steal the money from?"

"Accardo's gang."

Haggarty piped up. This was his bailiwick. "Filled the void in Chicago after Al Capone," he informed us. "Not a nice guy, Bianchi. And he's got a new enforcer. 'Mooney' Giancana. Given name Samuel. Up and comer. You picked the wrong fucking dude to steal from." Bianchi looked ill.

"You didn't just find a quarter of a million dollars on the street, Stephen." I wanted to call him by his given name, the name he'd heard when he was a baby. He was not the young tough tonight.

"Well, actually we did. We followed their couriers. Three guys picking up money from the betting parlors and the extortion rings and the whore houses. We hit them over the head and took bags of cash. Accardo's boys chased us all over Chicago. Napolitano said the only way out was to enlist and get out of town. Let the Marines protect us. He took us into a recruiting station and we were on a train out of there the same afternoon."

"Where's the money?" asked Haggerty.

"Napolitano took it before we left town," said Bianchi. "We trusted him. We were brothers, and he was our leader."

"Now he's dead and all you've got is this book," said Haggerty.

"Napolitano told Rizzo to use the book to find the money," said Bianchi

"So Accardo sent Giancana after you. Then Giancana recruited one of his guys to come aboard ship and beat the information out of you." I stated the pattern of facts and I got Bianchi to nod in agreement.

"Do you know the name of the guy who's after you?" asked Haggerty.

"Jungle drums before we left Chicago hinted it's a mick. Guy named Walsh. Gerry Walsh. Mean. They say he never gives up," said Bianchi.

"Did he have help getting aboard? Somebody on the docks?" I asked him.

"Probably," said Bianchi. "Napolitano said Accardo has connections everywhere, *especially* the docks."

"So, Napolitano took the money. And you idiots don't know where it is?" said Haggerty.

"Napolitano said it's in a code in this book," said Bianchi. "Rizzo took the book from Napolitano's stuff when Walsh got him. I took it from Rizzo. I don't want it anymore."

He handed it to me.

"So Walsh is trying to beat it out of you guys and none of you know where it is because you can't read the code," stated Haggerty. "Fucking brilliant."

I took the book in my hands and started leafing through the pages. I don't have a lot of time for recreational reading, but it sounded like I needed to dig into this. If it was Napolitano's idea, he didn't sound like your standard knucklehead. I looked at Bianchi and he was white as a sheet. His lower lip was trembling and the puffy bloodshot eyes told me he wasn't getting any sleep.

"I'm moving you Marines," I told him. "You'll go with Mr. Haggerty to collect your stuff."

"I don't want the other guys to know we've talked," he told me.

"No problem," I told him. "You're a confidential informant. Mr. Haggerty and I know how to keep secrets. The book stays with me."

"You don't suppose this Walsh guy knows about the book, do you?" Haggerty asked Bianchi.

"I don't know what Rizzo told him," said Bianchi. "He took it to the grave...like we said we would."

"Walsh bashed ten knuckles on both hands with a hammer and he still didn't get what he wanted," said Haggerty.

"If Walsh knows about the book, he certainly doesn't know what the book means, or what's inside it." It was as good a hypothesis as I could muster. I stood up and signaled Haggerty to join me in the passageway.

"Nate, stick these guys under armed guard in the dressing rooms backstage in the theater," I told him. "We'll get them their chow. I want them isolated."

"Not the brig?" he asked. "We've got iron bars on the

cell doors."

"Brig is a little too visible, by my way of thinking," I told him. "People pass in and out of the MA office all day long. I want these guys to just disappear for a while. Make it so." I could tell Haggerty didn't like it.

It was not my first mistake.

We dismissed Bianchi and Haggerty left to set up our quarantine, leaving me to my own sinister contemplations. I had victims, a suspect, a motive, a timeline. We were further along than we were forty-eight hours before, when all we had were some bloody drag marks on B Deck. I needed to bring Captain Kelly up to speed, and I had a ship to run.

After Haggerty and Bianchi exited my cabin, I straightened my tie and walked forward a few steps to the captain's cabin. I knocked on the door and he opened it with a flourish, pipe aglow between his teeth. He had a thick typescript in his hands and I knew it was probably Top Secret—an order of battle, a deployment schedule, one of Chester Nimitz's grand designs. Maybe all of the above. He invited me in, and we took our seats in his club chairs.

"What have you got, Jonas?" he asked me. I brought him up to the very minute, and he was impressed with the speed with which we'd arrived at certain unassailable facts.

"Blood typing was the trick, then" he told me, delighted. "Good idea. I put the right man on the case, Commander," he said, slapping me on the knee. I was happy with this small accolade, but I knew we had a long way to go before we could apprehend *Bridger's* roving killer.

"Yes, serology worked. But only in so far as it helped identify this Gallo fellow," I told Captain Kelly. "Identifying Gallo allowed us to ascertain associations, and that led us to Gallo's den of thieves."

Ship of Tears

"Sequester this group?" asked the captain.

"I've decided to stash them in the dressing rooms behind the stage. Quiet back there. Brig area is too public," I told him.

"Agreed," said the captain. "But make sure Donahue has those spaces covered day and night."

"On it," I told him, giving him the feeling he was in charge, and I felt we could move to the ship's business. "Any changes contemplated regarding our objective, captain? If you're permitted to discuss it."

"I can give you the broad outlines," he said. "We've got intelligence to suggest we can run unmolested to Wellington. We'll rest, refuel, revictual, repack, then move closer to the theater, probably Fiji. We'll offload our guests onto smaller transports and they'll do a rehearsal landing. When the First Marine Division is ready, Vandegrift will try to bag Tulagi and Florida first, then move on to Guadalcanal."

"First shot in our Pacific campaign, captain," I said. "It will feel good after Pearl and Corregidor. After that?"

"Tentatively, we'll run back down to New Zealand to pick up more Marine divisions. Chester wants to feed them into the lower Solomons. It'll be our kickoff for retaking the Pacific." I could tell the captain wanted to get back to *Bridger's* murder investigation. He wanted something positive to tell Vandegrift.

"It's imperative we arrest the guy who is doing this, Jonas."

"Working the problem," I told him. "And yes, speed is of the essence." We parted company and I checked in with the combat information center, radio shack, and the plotting team. Everything was quiet and normal, and we were about seven-hundred-fifty miles from our destination. Five-and-a-half days running if everything went right. I entered the bridge and, as usual, I enjoyed the determined intensity of our quartermaster team in charge of navigation, signaling and maneuvering. Our more experienced cadres were bringing up the young ensigns and it was the constant state of training, readiness and renewal that made the Navy a formidable fighting force. I noticed I had a light on my damage control switchboard. It was coming from the engine room and it appeared the estimable Mr. Foster needed to have a word.

I walked to my elevated chair on the port side, picked up my sound-powered phone and dialed his extension. Elvis picked it up on the second ring. I could hear the steady, comforting roar of Bridger's boilers and turbines striving mightily in the background.

"Mr. Pratt, begging your presence, portside Promenade Deck forward. I can be there in about eight minutes," Elvis told me. He was making me nervous. I only heard from Elvis when there was a problem.

"On my way, Mr. Foster," I told him. I found Elvis leaning on the rail. Our survival floats were attached to the outside of the ship, obscuring a deep blue sea. I could tell he was worried. He wore his blue coveralls with cherished gold anchors on the lapels and he also wore the grease and grime of his exalted profession. Working in a ship's engine room was hot, dirty, and dangerous. But Elvis and I both knew how important he was to *Bridger*, and he carried himself with the erect bearing one finds among the elect. I knew he was instilling this professionalism among the young people lucky enough to be under his command deep in the beating heart of the ship.

"Mr. Pratt, we've had some strange doings around the

boiler rooms," he told me. I loved listening to his West Indian patois.

"When did it start?"

"Two nights ago," he told me. "Missing tools. Two-inch box wrenches gone from a work bench. We've also got a hammer or two gone, and some knives we use to cut our asbestos cladding. We're also finding some leftover food down in our spaces. Chicken bones, bread crust, empty milk bottles."

"See anybody?" I asked him.

"No. Just some signs of things out of place." Ever since the Sunda Strait, the ever-meticulous Elvis didn't appreciate anything awry. Trouble is, I was running out of Donahue's MA personnel and Elvis's warning meant I needed to post a guard in our engine spaces. We couldn't let anything happen to our machinery, or worse, our boiler men. The course of the war was literally at stake. I had no choice but to enlist some of our heavily armed Marine guests to serve watch. It was time to bring in Puller, who had given me the impression he'd go where he was needed.

I thanked Elvis for his contribution, and I made sure he knew he was welcome any time in any part of the ship, including the officer's mess. I got myself to A Deck and started to make inquiries as to where I might find Lieutenant Colonel Lewis Puller. His men called him "Chesty" a reference to his medium-height and barrel chest. I was told Puller liked to lead the ranks on twenty-mile hikes, officers too. To Puller, conditioning and discipline were the essential attributes of the war fighter. I was in what they call "officer country," where Vandegrift and his regimental leaders congregated. They all told me Puller was belowdecks with his troops. I later learned Puller revered his enlisted men and his non-commissioned officers. To him, they were the sole reason for any success the Marine Corps might achieve on the battlefield. Officers could plan and point, but the enlisted men would pull the triggers.

I worked my way through a jungle of pipe cots until I could find a section devoted to First Battalion, Seventh Marines. And there he was, puffing on his pipe, wearing a pith helmet, surrounded by eager young faces who wanted to hear Puller's tales of fighting the Sandino rebels, or projecting American power in Peking. As I write this, he's retired with five Navy Crosses to his credit, his last campaign the successful invasion of Inchon, Republic of Korea. During that conflict, Puller and his regiment captured Seoul, and made the desperate "retrograde movement" away from the Chosin Reservoir, an act that saved countless American lives. But all these exploits were in Chesty's future. As I encountered our consummate warrior on this day in August of 1942, he was discussing the art of the proper machine-gun emplacement.

"Preparation, gentlemen," he said. "You need to understand your topography, clear firing lanes leading down to the enemy's logical point of ingress and fortify your positions with whatever you've got. And that includes from both direct fire from Jap machineguns and indirect fire from his mortars. In these islands we'll have plenty of timber. Your platoon leaders will have you working up a sweat but it'll pay off. You'll see." He was offering encouragement, something he amply demonstrated when I observed him later "leading from the front."

The crowd thinned and I addressed Colonel Puller.

"Sir, I am Commander Jonas Pratt, *Bridger's* XO. Can I have a word?"

"Howdy do," said Puller, in the folksy, engaging manner of northern Virginia, where he was raised. "I was in the theater when you described our issue on B Deck. Damn sorry business."

I asked him to join me on the starboard side Promenade Deck. He was wearing battle dress akin to what his men were wearing, the only adornment a silver oakleaf on a collar signifying his rank. We're equivalent, so I asked him if I could call him Lewis.

"Of course, Commander," he said.

"You can call me Jonas," and we shook hands.

"Any progress to report on our B Deck situation?" he asked.

"Considerable. But we have a problem and I want to bring you in," I told him. "It pertains to members of the First."

"All ears," he said, not realizing the impropriety of the reference. I swore him to secrecy ("Can't cause a panic.") and brought him right up to the present. Four dead, including Napolitano. Organized crime now stalked *Bridger's* holds and passageways.

"Hell of a way to lose good men," said Puller. "How can I help?"

"I need a squad in the theater to protect these people," I told him.

"Can do," said Puller. "I presume we will deliver food and drink."

"Correct," I told him. "And the theater will be closed until we get these men off the ship and into their fighting units ashore."

"I will assign a squad and an eight-hour watch system," said Puller. "Three, four-man teams and a floater." I was convinced the matter was well in hand.

Now I have to turn my attention to Napolitano's obscure reference to *The Prisoner of Zenda*. I returned to my cabin with a cup of coffee. I retrieved the book from my safe and, first things first, inspected every page for margin notes, slips of foolscap, misglued end papers, anything odd about the cover or the binding. I could tell the frontispiece facing the title page had been ripped out. And there was a little pocket on the inside back cover for a library card. Like everything associated with Napolitano's gang, the book had been stolen.

A first edition, it was printed in 1896, and it was about a fictional land called Ruritania wedged between Ukraine and the Carpathian Mountains in eastern Europe. A stranger arrived and local citizens remarked how closely he resembled the soon-to-be crowned king. The new king was poisoned, however, and became incapacitated. The stranger was persuaded to step in for the king and accept the crown until the king recovered. Enter Flavia, the king's designated queen. She fell for the stand-in, and we were off to the races. It was an engaging little romp—and I wracked my brain trying to see how it fit in with the Accardo gang and *Bridger's* murderous monster, Walsh.

What the actual hell was going on?

I put the book aside and concentrated on the myriad needs of our ship: fitness reports, maintenance schedules, disciplinary actions, supply needs. I had a safe stuffed with thirty-five thousand American dollars, which I would use to buy food and fuel when we got to New Zealand. I opened the safe and counted it again. Having that much cash made me nervous.

Think, Pratt!

I wandered down to our well-stocked little library on A

Deck. I found some studious Marines tucked into their novels, or fanning through months-old magazines, trying to pass the time in quiet solitude. I was certain the prospect of combat weighed heavily. I headed for a dictionary and learned the world "Zenda" pertains to the Greek God Zeus—his environment, dictates, and homilies. But in this context, I had to believe Zenda referred to a place, a physical location. It was a hideaway for bags of illicit cash. There was a nice fat atlas of the world, with a huge index. I learned there are Zendas in Idaho, Virginia, Missouri, Kansas...and Wisconsin.

Close enough to Chicago, and right over the Illinois border. I fixated on Napolitano's problem. He's got bags of mob money, and he has to hide it someplace, a physical location with a latitude and a longitude. He is trying to get away from Accardo's enforcer Giancana and make it back to Chicago and a train full of Marines. He's a little frantic. He starts driving north, taking back roads, shying away from any large urban centers, constantly looking over his shoulder. Our boy Napolitano has a lot of responsibilities, including mouths to feed in his little rag-tag outfit of mobster wannabes. He's taken on a lot and he's got to offload his bundle. He runs into a little place called Zenda, Wisconsin.

And then what?

In the book, we've got a Rudolph, a Michael, a Rupert, a Fritz, a Flavia, the poisoned king's betrothed. It's a twisted tale, slightly bawdy and overly convenient when you consider drugging the king prompts most of the action. And let's not forget torn lovers who, in the end, must part and perform their solemn duties. Cue the violins. Is Napolitano trying to take all this action and romance and use it as a means of establishing clues to the little gang's hidden fortune?

If I were back in the States, I would have Haggerty persuade his Chicago field office to send an agent or two up to Zenda to nose around. All this would be hard to convey by Morse, and cable traffic was restricted. We had to wait until we could find a telex so he could touch base with his former FBI colleagues.

In the meantime, I was suddenly seized by the idea of luring Walsh into the open. If he knew I had the book that held the secret to his trove of cash, he'd turn in my direction. I took a swing through the bridge and stepped out onto the port side bridge wing. The Southern Cross had replaced faithful Polaris as our guide star. We'd gone through our ritual darken ship, and I was seeing the Milky Way streak directly overhead and stretch down to the far horizon. I needed to check in with my officer cadre in the first-class mess. We discussed the ship, her systems, our guests, and our role in this mighty endeavor. After dinner I walked through the theater and checked on our protectees. Puller's Marines were cleaning rifles and perusing field manuals. No craps, checkers or Parcheesi for this crew. They were in readiness. Our little tribe was already sacked out. I went back up to my cabin to read a bit, finish some letters and get ready for tomorrow's small-arms gunnery lesson.

I was out of practice.

Chapter Eight
– Condition One

I'd taken my breakfast in the officer's mess, having passed a comfortable night with nary a murder. Hiding our little gang seemed to have worked, at least for the moment. Haggerty had invited me back to the mooring tackle on B Deck, and when I arrived, the sun was hot as blazes and climbing high. B Deck was open but offered some shade with A Deck directly above. We could stand at the extreme aftermost point aboard *Bridger* and shoot across a limitless sea. Haggerty had a table set up and he'd volunteered to run me through the standard issue Marine Corps personal armament of 1942.

He'd loaded some magazines for the M1911 Colt .45; a Thompson sub-machine gun, also in .45 caliber; a Reising sub-machine gun, again in .45; an M1 Garand in .30 caliber M1; and a M1903 Springfield bolt-action rifle, the Marine mainstay, in armor-piercing .30 caliber M2. He'd also promised a Browning Automatic Rifle, the massive BAR, and he reported Puller would be scaring one up for us shortly.

"Your .38 Smith & Wesson is kind of cute," he said dismissively. "But you need stopping power in a personal firearm and the Colt .45 can stop a freight train." He was over-stating the case but there was no question I didn't want to get out-gunned if things got out of hand.

"The 1911 carries seven cartridges in the magazine, and

if you have one in the chamber, you have eight at your disposal, plus two more magazines in pouches on a web belt," he said. "What kind of shooting experience have you had, Jonas?"

"Upland birds and waterfowl with an L.C. Smith .12-gauge double-gun, and waterfowl with a .12-gauge Browning Auto 5," I told him.

"Good choices," said Haggerty. "I am sure you learned in Boy Scouts finger off the trigger until you're ready to fire, and keep the muzzle controlled at all times. Weapon pointed up or down until you are ready. Don't sweep the muzzle over your buddy. Accidents happen." Haggerty had to say these things, and I had to acknowledge. It was like a pilot performing a checklist. He continued.

"Two ways to carry the .45," he said. "Under circumstances where speed is essential, you need a round in the chamber and the hammer cocked, with the weapon stowed at the ready in your holster. This is called Condition One. You have two safeties: The slide stop thumb safety, and the grip safety. Carrying cocked and locked with a live round in the chamber is acceptable behind these two safeties with your finger off the trigger. You can quickly engage a target by removing the firearm from the holster with your thumb on the hammer so it won't move. You train the muzzle on the target, press the grip safety with our palm, move the thumb safety down, and fire. No need to rack the slide to chamber a round, which takes time. And you don't have to worry about using two hands to charge or fire the weapon this way. Bullet's already in the chamber. In less stressful circumstances—a normal day at sea, for instance—you can uncock the hammer and keep it down on an empty chamber. If things change for the worse, rack the slide to chamber a round and you're good to go. Thumb the slide stop safety down, squeeze the grip safety, aim and fire."

He had me holster, fire and re-holster my .45 a few dozen times, and even walk forward into my 'target.' He was working on what he called my 'muscle memory', helping me establish my 'sight picture.' We also practiced making the firearm safe. Drop the magazine and clear the chamber by racking the slide. Recover the unfired round and put it back in the magazine.

"Use a two-handed grip if you can," he said. "The way we do in the FBI. This one-handed stuff is only good for cowboy movies."

We went over the basic function of the latest variant of the Thompson sub-machine gun. It was designed to clear out trenches in the last war, and it was made famous by the Twenties underworld. The 1928 version had a hundred-round drum magazine. ("Hard to load in a hurry, and rattles on patrol," said Haggerty.) It also had a vertical grip for a fore-end, and a muzzle compensator to release excess gasses to reduce recoil. The latest Marine Corps version used a straight fore-end with a sling, and a stick, or box, magazine, which carried twenty rounds. The magazine slid into a track (I needed to practice getting that aligned, especially in the dark). You chambered a round with the charging handle, selected semi-or full-auto and let her rip. Haggerty let me shoot into the endless sea and I could see my rounds spit into the water in a neat line.

I picked up the Reising submachine gun. It weighed only six-and a half pounds, to the Thompson's nearly eleven, and Haggerty assured me that a weight variance that significant would make a big difference if we ever had to engage in a running gunfight. He also explained the Browning Automatic Rifle, capable of cutting down aircraft, was even heavier at twenty-one pounds.

"Squad gives the BAR to the big guys to carry," he said. "But everyone in the unit needs to know how to pick it up and use it."

Right on cue, Lieutenant Colonel Puller arrived at our weapons indoctrination carrying the BAR in .30-caliber armor-piercing M2. The weapon also accommodated tracer or incendiary rounds. He hefted the BAR with its stabilizing bipod onto the table. He dropped the magazine, cleared the chamber and stated, "You can see, gentlemen, this firearm is safe." Puller reminded me it was good firing range etiquette to inform your mates of weapons status. Puller eyed the Tommy gun.

"This is a '28. Prefer the '21 version, personally, but the '28'll do," said Puller. "Ass-kicking rate of fire and that Cutts compensator is great for suppressing recoil. Let me try that thing." He picked it up and leaned into the target. He fired off a neat burst into the water.

"You have to bear down on it to keep the barrel from rising," Puller said. "And you have to have some shot discipline. Aim it well, stock tight into your shoulder, and only fire three-round bursts. Don't spray it. It will stop the threat and you won't waste ammo."

Our weapons orientation was winding down and our discussion turned to business.

"How are our protectees behind the stage, colonel?" I asked him.

"They had a quiet night," he said. "But they are bored and restless. My guys worry a little about keeping them contained." Haggerty gave me what he likes to call "the hairy eyeball."

"Do we need to consider the brig for these idiots, Mr. Pratt?" he asked. Puller was trying to remain neutral.

"I have heard of something called a 'witness protection program' gentleman," Puller stated plainly. "Do our circumstances warrant this?" Puller's voice was like gravel, but he was focused and well spoken.

"It needs to be considered," I told them, throwing Haggerty a bone. But my lawyerly brain still had difficulty incarcerating someone absent their commission of a crime, and I thought we'd get more cooperation with some degree of leniency. Yes, we did have an assault and a theft if you take into consideration how Napolitano and his little gang came by Accardo's ill-gotten cash. Stealing from a mob that had extracted hard-earned cash from ordinary citizens? It was still stealing. Competent counsel for the defense would poke holes in our legal standing to bring charges. The offense was apparently committed in the city of Chicago and would need to be prosecuted in a court of competent jurisdiction, which did not include a U.S. Navy ship in international waters, in my opinion. I was ruminating on the idea members of our little gang were hostile witnesses. We could throw them in jail and sort it out later, but for how long? Even a rookie assigned counsel would have a field day. And this kind of treatment might have the effect of taking our Southside boys out of the upcoming fight. I could tell Haggerty thought I was being overly compliant with the legal niceties, where we have always parted company.

We were skirting around these issues when Marchionda arrived with ominous news.

"One of our gang members is missing," he told us in the flat tone of someone who had seen a bit too much criminal violence of late.

"Which one?" I asked him.

"Bianchi," he told us, and the boy's simpering expressions came immediately to mind. Why would he leave the group?

"Down to the theater, gentlemen," I told them and we gathered up our arsenal to lock back up in the MA office. I was keeping the .45, however, and I tucked it, cocked and locked, into the holster on my hip.

Puller had a guard at the theater door and we nodded at the young man as we entered.

The space could never rival Broadway, but it had seating for two-hundred-twenty people, an orchestra pit, and a stage accessed with steps at either side leading down to the orchestra seats. The curtain was made of an inflammable material, which I'd insisted on when I ran damage control early in our tour. We went backstage and found the assortment of little rooms where the ship's entertainers prepared. I found DiGenova first, who was sitting placidly on his can out of harm's way. He didn't have to open his mouth and I could feel the belligerence.

Haggerty kicked him.

"Stand at attention when officers enter the room, asshole." DiGenova got himself upright, and Petrucio, Deluca, and Ricci arrived at our little scene and stood at attention. Puller's men took up the periphery.

"Where is Bianchi?" I asked him.

"No idea, sir," said DiGenova.

"Anybody else know where Bianchi is?" asked Haggerty. I had visions of the trembling Bianchi about to be hung, sliced, and garroted, with knuckles bashed. It's what had befallen his comrades and that's what seemed to be in store for these fools unless I could stop it.

"He left his gear in the room and vanished, sir," said Petrucio.

"Show me where he was staying," I asked him, and he led me over to a small room offstage, past the cage where the electricians worked the lighting, and where the belaying pins that secured the risers were mounted. We got to a small room equipped with a vanity mirror, and two chairs.

"He slept under there," said Petrucio, pointing under the vanity, and I could see a hastily assembled pile of green Marine twill—dungarees, a blouse—along with his steel helmet and web gear. His boots were lying there, too, and I found it difficult to believe he'd wander the ship in his skivvies.

"Looks like he got up to pee and never came back," I stated to my crime-fighting colleagues. It was Puller's turn and he pivoted toward his squad leader.

"Your orders were to guard these men," he stated, and he's not pleased.

"Might have slipped to the john during a shift change, sir," imparted his sergeant.

"Let me inform all of you," he said. "When you are on watch, you will accompany these men to the latrine regardless of the hour. Is that clear? And you protectees are ordered to have your guards accompany you at all times. Commander Pratt has shown you the photos. You know the reason why. Now I have to pull another squad together to start the search for Bianchi."

Puller had neatly summarized next steps. He looked at me and said, "If you handle the ship, Commander, I will handle the Marines." I extended a hand.

"Partners," I told him, and we shook on it.

Just then we heard a door bang and a rustling out in

the theater section. We parted the curtain and walked out onto the stage, and we saw Bianchi being escorted down the aisle by two large Marines in green. He was wearing handcuffs and his face was bruised and bloodied. There was blood on his white undershirt. I turned to Marchionda.

"We'll need a couple of corpsmen down here, Sal," I told him and our lad sprang into action. Puller turned to one of his squad leaders.

"Water. Pronto," he said and the Marine ran backstage.

We got down to Bianchi just as his escorts inserted him physically into a seat in the front row. He was conscious, but he was bleeding from several cuts on his face and his jaw was swollen.

"We had to restrain him," said one of Puller's men. "Found him wandering around the forward hold on D Deck." Bianchi was shivering now, and his mouth was bloodied. I knelt down in front of him.

"Tell me what happened, Stephen," I asked him. I had my hand on his knee. He looked at me and saw that I was surrounded by tough, eager Marines.

"Got up to take a pee, sir," he said, confirming our earlier suspicion. "Stepped backstage and out a side door. He was waiting back there." I looked at Haggerty and we were thinking the same thing. How did Walsh know where we'd hidden our thieves? Did we have a spy?

"Where did he take you?" I asked him.

"Not sure," said Bianchi. "He put a bag over my head and tied my hands behind my back. He had a knife. He kept poking me with it. I got the idea we were moving forward."

"Did you go up or down any stairs or ladderways?" I asked him.

"No stairs," he said. "We stayed on one deck."

"Did he hit you?" I asked.

"Face. Gut. Kidneys," he said. "Some jabs with the knife." I looked around at my colleagues.

"Give Bianchi and me a little privacy please," I asked them. Haggerty, Puller and the group backed off and I got down to Bianchi's face.

"You're alive, son, so you must have given him something he wanted," I told him. Bianchi looked directly at me.

"I told him you've got the book now, and only you know where the money is," he stated.

Partially true. I had the book in my safe. But I was far from knowing where Napolitano had stashed the money. I had gone from being the big Irishman's pursuer, to being his next victim.

Chapter Nine
– A Place Called Zenda

"So Haggerty won this one," said Margie, who was keeping score. She was not fond of the Haggerty of 1942 (they've since kissed and made up). But I have a different opinion. The man grew on me as our collaboration matured. Yes, that fracas Haggerty caused in the Philadelphia Navy Yard before our first cruise was at least criminally negligent homicide. Still, there we were...charging across the Pacific to fight the Japanese, while looking with building anxiety into these multiple murders. We needed to work together.

"There seems to be a lot of fuss over this book," said Margie. "Wasn't it made into a movie?"

"Starring Ronald Coleman and Madeleine Carroll. 1937. I've seen it five times," I told her.

"Are we a little obsessed attorney Pratt?" she asked me. She had me, as always. I couldn't escape being the fastidious lawyer.

"Yes, you could say that. I've thought about the story from time to time. But I think for those little hoodlums, the story was less important than the book itself. The book was a kind of talisman."

Our discussion was taking place over a civilized drink while our pork loin in a wine reduction brazed in the oven. "These punks... well, most of them...thought the book was the key to untold riches. Their rabbits foot. Whoever held the book held the knowledge of where the money was stashed."

"And this guy Walsh must have thought the book had some kind of secret writing that would reveal all," she said.

"Only thing the book gave us was the name of a place," I told her.

"But the money could have been buried anywhere in that little town, right?" she said.

"Right, but the only thing we had going for us is Zenda's size," I told her. "It's a pimple on the ass of an elephant. I thought it would be easy to find those ill-gotten gains in this tiny burg."

"Colorful counselor Pratt," she said. "I will have to remember that one. So, what was the plan?"

I settled back to reflect on that simple question, and I returned to it in the wee hours of the next morning when, unable to sleep, I took up my pen.

We ordered our protectees to gather up their personal effects. To Haggerty's delight, we were going to troop them into the brig, and a couple of Puller's platoons—eighty armed men—would cover the entire ship looking for Bianchi's assailant. Puller had them arranged to search *Bridger*, deck by deck, station by station, from the bilge to the masthead.

"Like hunting deer back in Virginia, Commander," Puller told me. "We'll go from stem to stern. We'll have drivers—they call them 'beaters' in England—and we'll have posters. We'll make a lot of noise and our boy will move out in front of us, and soon we'll have him trussed up like a goose at Christmas."

"Colonel Puller, I am glad we are on the same side," I told him.

DiGenova had become the *defacto* leader of the 'little

gang that could' and he let me know he wasn't happy being deprived of his liberties.

"Write your congressman, you little asshole," said Haggerty in his delicate, nurturing way. We had only three cells for five individuals, so I gave the single to DeLuca because he hadn't caused me any trouble... yet. Puller went off on his expedition with his men and I told him to say 'Commander Pratt sent me' if he encountered any resistance. I turned to Haggerty and pressed the niggling question:

"Is Walsh getting help?"

"Why? Because he stumbled onto our backstage hideaway so quickly?" he responded.

"Precisely," I told him. "And don't forget both the torture and the murders look like they could only be accomplished by at least two individuals." I was thinking of those telltale footprints.

"We can't haul in every kid from Chicago on this ship and ask if they have mob connections," he told me, the illogic of this kind of sweep abundantly clear. "But it only stands to reason there might be another Marine aboard *Bridger* who would do anything to help Accardo get his money back. If anything, Walsh needs eyes and ears."

"Now that he thinks I'm the key to finding the money, we might be able to smoke him out," I told him.

Marchionda, Haggerty and I huddled for a few minutes on the Promenade Deck. We decided we would need to determine if anyone was paying a little too much attention to yours truly as I went about my many and varied daily activities. Marchionda would keep a close eye on me and Haggerty would be hovering in the background, functioning at what he called 'countersurveillance.'

"You are trying to detect whether or not Commander

Pratt is being followed," said Haggerty

"Easy enough," said Marchionda, to Haggerty's consternation.

"Don't get slap happy," he said sharply. "Disguises. Get yourself a set of Marine utilities, and some officer's khakis. One minute, you'll be a lowly PFC rifleman, next, a young ensign, then an unrated seaman in bell bottoms. You'll also need hats that came on and off. Carry a clipboard or a box. Always have something in your hands and always look like you're going somewhere. Keep the commander in sight, even if it's your peripheral vision. Don't approach him. Ever. And if you need to speak to him, leave a message under his door."

I could tell Marchionda was rising to the occasion. He'd always been a bit of sneak, which I would later find useful in *Bridger's* multi-theater career.

"How do I explain myself to the rest of the crew?" he asked.

"If they do recognize you, tell them it's hush-hush," said Haggerty. "You're under cover for the MA department and you're trying to get to the bottom of a roving crap game taking real money off our jarheads."

"We need an alert system," he said. "If something happens..."

"Okay," said Haggerty. "If the commander is in danger, immediately break cover and get him out of the way. Come down to the MA office where we have reinforcements." I was not enjoying being referred to in the third person, but I couldn't fault Haggerty's methods. Still, the objective wasn't to keep me out of harm's way. Quite the opposite. It was to bring Walsh and any associates out into the open. I was going to be the tethered goat, the bait to bring out the lion.

We broke up and Marchionda went to find his undercover attire. It was time for me to make myself visible. I made my way up to the officer's mess in the first-class dining hall. I stood in line to get some toast to go with my mid-morning coffee and found a seat with a group of young lieutenants. They wanted to know where we were heading and I answered with my customary canard.

"Pretty sure it's the South Pacific," which got a laugh.

"Think *Bridger* will need escorts the closer we get to the objective, commander?" asked a fresh-faced newbie.

"Most assuredly, lieutenant," I responded, a little mystified by the naivety of the question. "Out in the open ocean escorts can't keep up. Any time we need to slow down we'll always take a helping hand."

I didn't wish to elaborate. *Bridger's* top speed was a secret. The Axis powers were well aware of *Bridger* and what she could do to position Allied war fighters precisely where they were needed. It was not clear the enemy enjoyed the same capability, and I had seen intelligence that suggested the Japanese had to rely on cruisers and destroyers, even towed barges, to get their men onto the islands they held in the western Pacific. The movement of troops, using big ocean liners right down to flat-faced Higgins boats with drop-down bow ramps, was getting the attention of Allied leadership from top to bottom. *Bridger* was the colossus at the top of this funnel, and we would be tested in coming weeks. Our five-inchers and Oerlikons were nice, but it was Elvis Foster and his team in the boiler rooms who would win the fight by keeping our engines—and especially our finicky reduction gears—in peak form.

I left those sweeping strategic thoughts in the back of my mind as I bantered freely about hometowns, favorite ball players, and my favorite, hunting and fishing spots. I had a sudden pang for that sweet girl in Sewickley and I pushed it away. I missed that wonderful person, and I had a stone of worry next to my heart for my kids Bart and Bonnie. Their mother would be the wild card, and I hoped she wasn't causing embarrassment with their new acquaintances in D.C. I needed to write a note to Josiah before we touched at Wellington. I needed to find out what was going on back home. Knowing my brother, he will have consulted with one of his Admiral friends and will have anticipated *Bridger's* New Zealand arrival. He'll have used his franking privileges and his courier services to get a package of letters out to me. To reciprocate, a long note to the senator, delivered by the fastest means possible, might help us deal with our brush with organized crime. Josiah knew how to get to J. Edgar Hoover.

I saw Marchionda in a bus boy's tee-shirt, a white culinary cap, and dungarees. He had started out his tour aboard *Bridger* hauling boxes out of the holds and into the galleys. So this under cover get-up wasn't completely out of the ordinary. He was hauling plates, cups and saucers off tables onto big trays and moving toward the double doors leading to the scullery. I watched him quickly scan the room before he hit the door with his butt and disappeared. He was back in a few seconds with a rag in his hands, and this menial chore afforded an excellent opportunity to scan the room and move purposefully among the assembled officers. I had a sense the threat might come from the lower ranks, or from our Marine guests. Still, the threat from the ten-foot-tall Walsh (somehow thoughts of the man made him take on greater height) might come from anywhere. I needed to spend more time showing my face with the Marines below. But I took a minute to explore an idea.

"Anybody here from Wisconsin?" I asked my small circle of young officers. A pimply faced kid raised a hand and said, "Pewaukee."

"Ever hear of a place called Zenda?" I asked him.

"Sure, a little nothing of a town south of Lake Geneva. Blink and you'll miss it," he said with a smile.

"Buddy of mine might settle there after the war," I lied freely. "Tell me about it."

"Not even a stop light," he said. "There's a post office, a two-room school, a church, and a cemetery right next door. Corn fields come right up to the backyards."

"So it's pretty quiet," I asked. "My friend will like that. What about police and fire?"

"All-volunteer fire department," he said. "And the county sheriff covers the crime beat. If there is any."

"How about a clerk's office where I can send my friend to look up land records?" I asked.

"There's a little municipal building and a village clerk. Elkhorn is the seat for Walworth County. That's where you'll find all the action," he said. And then he disarmed me.

"There's more going on in the Zenda cemetery than on the Zenda streets." His pals laughed at this irony but I was aroused.

A cemetery is where you bury things.

I finished my coffee and I remembered my job was to act natural, to let Walsh or his minions come to me while Puller did the work of pushing Walsh through the ship. I had to say I liked this two-fold strategy—a passive and an active approach. But I had to figure out how to let Marchionda catch up with me. I learned I needn't worry. Sal had scrutinized the normal arc of my coffee consumption, and my quick ingratiating gab with our young officers. He sensed I would want to leave soon, and I saw him back in his Navy blouse standing over by our Coca-Cola machine. He had a screwdriver in his hands and he was fiddling with something behind the unit, a popular feature with our crew. He saw me standing up to leave, and true to Haggerty's dictate, he hung back to see if I was being followed.

I walked up to our Sports Deck. It was outside in the fresh air and encircled our two funnels. The after funnel was all-business. That's where our exhaust gases from our multiple boilers were being forcefully expelled. The forward funnel was fake, a cosmetic add-on to make *Bridger* appear more comely in profile. Our stacks were also raked aft to make *Bridger* look fast, a bit of marketing from the time she was *Majestic.* The little access door on the after side of the forward funnel was padlocked. There was nowhere for anyone to hide in there, which relieved me. I saw Marchionda with a broom and dustpan in his hands and he was making a show of sweeping up around one of our radio direction finder antennae on the starboard side. I walked forward to take the air and saw a line of storm clouds to the north and west. It was time to go down to visit meteorology to see what we could expect. I walked down a short flight of stairs to the bridge deck and Marchionda followed me at a distance, then disappeared. I took my elevated throne on the port side and Marchionda entered and headed straight for the ocean chart on our nav table. He was dressed as a Navy ensign, but he wasn't part of the quartermaster team, so people didn't pay much attention to him. Our ship's position was restricted, and I reminded myself to speak to the OD about allowing an outsider to inspect our wayfinding. It occurred to me using Marchionda to stick his nose in all the wrong places might be a good way to entrap our people into doing the right thing when it came to ship's security.

I was busy with reports and sign offs, and I noticed Marchionda had a pair of binoculars. He was looking for specks out there on the horizon when he wasn't looking around the small team on the bridge. That gray line of thunderstorms would cross our path and I called the chief in charge of meteorology to come forward to offer an opinion. Rittenhouse was soon standing at the side of my elevated chair and he showed me a hand-drawn synoptic chart.

"I'll need updates on wind speed, direction and sea state," I told him and he snapped back with a salute and an "aye-aye." I then executed a solid hour of seeing and being seen. I had to issue permissions to release the theater for use, allow our barbers to set up on a top deck to leeward to buzz-cut hair, allowing the clippings to blow over the side, and I had to give supply permission to work down our loads in the holds so as not to upset ship's stability. Having spent time as the ship's damage control officer before assuming the exec position helped me understand the need for positioning our center of gravity as low as possible so as not to upset our righting moment.

I made my way into the after cabin-class mess for a bite of lunch and to kibbitz with the enlisted men and the non-coms. Marchionda was back in his scullery attire and he was busy clearing off tables. At one point he relieved someone in the chow line and he was busy dishing up beans and rice. He could scan the room and look into the eyes of guests and crew alike.

Haggerty came in and slid into a chair beside me. "You guys have had a busy morning," he told me.

"You've been keeping an eye on us?" I asked.

"Absolutely," he said, reminding me once again the

man who was once my nemesis was now saving my life. It was complicated.

"Bear with me on something, Nate," I told him. "Napolitano might have made a trip to Zenda, Wisconsin, just before his little troupe got on a train and headed off to boot camp."

"And you know this how?" he asked.

"Bianchi," I told him.

I described Napolitano's efforts to stash Accardo's money. Napolitano gave Rizzo *The Prisoner of Zenda* as a code to conceal the money, but he got knifed before he could explain what the book meant—and how to decipher the code. These goofballs had no idea what they had in their hands. Walsh was trying to beat the location of the money out of them, and they couldn't answer because they couldn't put it together.

"Zenda, Wisconsin," I told Haggerty. "Easy day trip from Chicago. If Napolitano had stashed the money in this little burg, my bet it's in the cemetery... where you find fresh dirt."

"But where?" asked Haggerty.

"It'll be obvious as soon as we see it," I told him, which only made him grow more frustrated. He was a creature of fact, like me, but he was also head basher, and he was far from subtle. Patient he was not.

"Ten smashed fingers each," he said. "And they still didn't talk."

"They didn't talk because they didn't know what to say," I told him. "And there are limits to what people will say under coercion. It's why confession doesn't infer guilt in most civil societies." Haggerty grew pensive. Maybe he was questioning his career choice. I continued.

"Napolitano managed to impart to whomever killed him—maybe it was the guy we have on board—the significance of *The Prisoner of Zenda*," I told Haggerty, but our lawman offered a keen-eyed counter argument.

"No, Mr. Pratt. Walsh, our killer, discovered the importance of the book from a third party, maybe one of these idiot hoodlums we've got locked in the brig," he said. "My vote is DiGenova. Hate that little asshole. I'm sure he'd turn on his own mother."

I reflected on this, and I had to conclude Haggerty might be right. Why would Napolitano tell Walsh about the book? The book offered a clue Napolitano wanted to conceal. Napolitano remained silent and he died for it. Still, Walsh knew about the book. He's looking for it. One of Napolitano's buddies aboard our ship told him. One of the guys in the brig, a turncoat, is working for Accardo.

"We're waiting for Marchionda to turn up Walsh's confederate, but Walsh's helper is already in the group," he said. I have to admit, his theory is more elegant than mine.

"No argument," I finally told him, turning over my chess piece. "It's one more reason to keep them bottled up. You were right about that, Nate. But there's another thing. I was fooling around with the idea the name of a character from the book is written on a Zenda tombstone. But all we have to do is find a freshly deceased person named Flavia or something and we've got it. But it's a lot simpler than that. We need to find the dates these guys left Chicago. That date will correspond with Napolitano's trip to Zenda. We look at the cemetery records to determine who was buried during that time, dig down two feet and we run into Accardo's loot."

"I like that," said Haggerty, seeming to concede this Navy commander might have something on the ball. "I'll get a date out of one of them when I visit the brig."

"Has to be in late '41," I speculated. "But before the weather turned. They've got to get through basic training, get assigned, muster, and get up to 'Frisco for Napolitano to get stabbed. I am pretty sure they didn't count on voyaging to the Solomons...which brings us up to the present. Can you cable somebody for a run up to Zenda? We need to check that out."

"We'll have to see what kind of telephone or cable service might be available when we get to Wellington," he told me. Just then, Marchionda came over to take away our coffee cups. As he wiped down our table, he muttered under his breath, breaking Haggerty's rules. It was critical.

"Guy near the doorway, Commander," Marchionda said. "I've seen him watching you three times today. Go forward on A Deck all the way to the fo'c'sle. I want to see if he follows you."

Haggerty and I were happy to comply. We got to the Promenade Deck on the starboard side and Haggerty peeled off to head up to the bridge wing, where he could observe the whole foredeck—from the cargo hatch to the gun tubs and into the watertight door that led to our hawse pipes and anchor windlasses. I stopped to chat with a few of our unrated seamen, just kids who'd joined the Navy to see the world. They would save our bacon if we ever got hit. I knew a couple of them from our gunnery practice, and I was glad I stood shoulder to shoulder with these young gentlemen when it came time to put those heavy shells into the breach, even if it was just a drill.

I kept moving forward on a casual inspection, as the clouds obscured a tropical sunshine. It smelled like rain. I could sense Haggerty and Marchionda watching me, and I wondered if I should move into the fo'c'sle enclosure, when a passing squall made the decision for me. Suddenly it was pelting down rain and the dark, open door offered a quick shelter. I stepped inside and moved out of the light from the opening. I stood behind a vertical I-beam support and looked aft. I could see Haggerty up on the bridge wing. He'd moved into the enclosure at the outboard starboard end. I knew Marchionda would be moving in my direction, trailing our person of interest.

And then I saw a single, green-clad Marine enter the foredeck space in the rain and walk my way. He was wearing a utility, like thousands of his mates, and he had a tropical sun hat pulled low over his forehead. He was of medium build, and the first thing I noticed was the absence of Marine-issued leggings. Puller demanded leggings in his regiment. He insisted leggings kept the chiggers and ticks out of your boot tops, which kept your feet healthy and on the march. The Marines moved on healthy feet, which won the wars. Puller was a stickler, and the Marine walking toward me could not be part of Puller's battalion. I looked up to see that Haggerty had moved off the bridge wing, and I was hoping he'd be hot footing it down to my position. He'd have his .45 cocked and locked in his shoulder holster and it occurred to me I should have mine out and ready as the stray Marine continued walking my way.

As I pulled out my sidearm, confronting all the cautions that assailed my inner lawyer, I felt like someone else was sharing this darkened machinery space with me. I could hear the rain and feel the motion of the ship as the soft rhythms of the bow wave parted the Pacific blue. I could also hear a heavy breathing, and smell a sweaty, unwashed presence. My eyes shifted outward to the oncoming Marine and shifted back into the darkened spaces where I was waiting. It took a second for my eyes to adjust, when I heard footsteps to accompany the breathing.

I put my right strong hand on my .45. I shifted into that mindful mode that became necessary when using this deadly tool. My normal means of operation were the deftly crafted affidavit, the swift objection, or the artful plea—all useful in a court of law. Now I had to make sure the hammer of my pistol was cocked, and I had to make sure the thumb safety was in the down position, ready to fire, before bringing the gun up to sweep the muzzle in front of me. In my mind, I could hear Haggerty remind me these moves needed to be quick and automatic, so I could pay attention to any advancing threat.

I heard a shuffling over near the ladderway leading down to our big triangle-shaped windlass space in the very prow of the ship. I walked in that direction, with the gun thrust in front of me gripped in two hands.

"Stop!" I yelled.

And then I heard more yelling outside. Haggerty was trying to get to the Marine who'd been following me. I stepped over to see outside, and through the rain I could see both Marchionda and Haggerty chasing someone aft. They re-entered the ship's superstructure, which led to the Promenade Deck on the port side. Now, alone, I could hear footsteps on the metal treads leading down. I took the steps down two at a time and stood at the bottom looking at a gray, rolling sea move past the hawse pipes port and starboard. Our massive anchor rodes were stretched across this room and turned around our big capstans before disappearing into the chain lockers belowdecks.

Just then, the squall hit us and the bow was plunging

into a building sea. The deck was moving in three dimensions, up and down, right and left, and, once in a while, at a severe diagonal when a cross current took hold of *Bridger's* prow and seemed to shake it. I instinctively moved my knees and hips to find my rhythm. I saw our suspect on the far side of the capstan room, about to go down another deck to C level and into the forward hold.

"Walsh," I called to him. And he turned in my direction. Yes, it was him… big and mean, with the broken nose merely one of his distinguishing features. He had a scar running down the right side of his face from above his buzz-cut hairline to the upper lip. He had huge, broad shoulders and I could just imagine the man hanging Rizzo and Moretti up as his last act after killing them all too slowly.

"Walsh, I've got the book," I told him. "I know all about Zenda." I moved toward him with the .45 brandished in front of me. He smiled at me and I could see bad, yellowed teeth. I didn't have probable cause to shoot. I hadn't confirmed the suspect's identity, and so far, he was retreating. In my personal rules of engagement, I didn't have the right to shoot someone in the act of withdrawing. I held my fire and the lawyer within was satisfied. But the Navy commander wanted to remove this blight so we could sail on to the next battle, and the one after that. Walsh was drawing me in. I knew it.

He was in control.

There were sounds above me, which Walsh could also hear. Haggerty and Marchionda were coming in my direction, and that gave me a reason to move toward Walsh. If he came at me, I decided I'd have to shoot him. He turned to face the ladderway and down, moving quickly for a big man, and I could hear his footfalls on the metal diamond plate of the circular stairs as he descended into the hold. I charged after him, incensed. He wanted me to run after him. I could feel Haggerty behind me, and he whispered in my ear.

"I'll tell Marchionda to go find Puller and his boys and get them into the hold," he said. "Stay down."

"Have them come forward up through C Deck so we can get this guy into a pincer," I told him, and I was pleased my beating heart and the sweat between my eyes, the raw fear, allowed me to even think. Haggerty left me, and instead of staying down, I leaned over a railing to look below into the cargo space. A shot roared out, and a bullet pinged next to my ear, but now I'd seen a muzzle flash. I knew he was below me, armed, and a little aft, somewhere between Crawford's food crates. I had a fleeting thought: Where did he get the gun? But there were guns all over *Bridger* and one could have easily fallen into Walsh's pocket.

I could move back up the circular stairs and wait, or I could move down and get closer to the threat. He'd fired at me and I was now obligated to return fire, as best I could. I couldn't let someone else get in front of this guy, only to get hurt.

I made the decision to move down into the dark.

It would be harder for him to hit a moving target. I pushed the slide-stop safety up and on and kept my finger off the trigger until I was ready to fire. I couldn't lose that discipline. I had my pistol in my right hand and the railing in my left as I headed down in a feeble light coming from our windlass room above. I was trying to move quickly but carefully, when a bullet winged over my head and hit the stairs above me. The sound the gun made was massive, and it echoed around the hold and came back to me. I ducked and raced down to the bottom and, finally, reached the deck. I was crouched, and I had my pistol out in front in both hands, thumb safety off. I thought he was in an alleyway of crates to my right, off the main thoroughfare used by the supply teams. I heard Haggerty on the steel landing above me, and a shot rang out in his direction. It was coming from my right and I headed over that way. I needed to stay low, and I peeked around the corner of the narrow alley. Haggerty made a move on the stairs and Walsh shot at him again. I could see the muzzle flash, and I fired two quick shots. Haggerty used my return fire as cover to get down to the deck.

That's when the shock came.

I was convinced Walsh was in front of me, down the alleyway, shooting back in my direction. But a massive punch to the side of my head came out of nowhere, and I was flat on the deck, dazed. Worse, I no longer had my pistol in my hands. The next thing I knew I was being dragged by the back of my shirt deeper into the warren of crates. All I could see were stars on black. Inside my ears, I could hear my own breathing and my pulsing heart. I tried to move my arms and legs but they weren't ready yet, and I felt a massive being dragging me down the deck—while, in the distance, shouts and lantern light were flying at random through the darkened hold. The dragging stopped, and there was a scarred face with a broken nose right in my eyes.

"The book," the monster said. "I want it."

"You can have it," I told him. And then I added, "Good story." For some reason I needed to be a wiseass.

"Leave it on the tool bench in boiler room four," he told me. "Tonight. No later than eight o'clock. Or I'll rip your guts out, the same way I did Rizzo."

"So...you remember his name." I taunted him. I'm not sure why.

"Just the dog tags," he told me. "If you want the killing

to stop, I need the book."

And he was gone, taking his bad breath and his bodily stench with him. I lay there for a second to take an inventory of what hurt. The side of my face for one, and I was pretty sure I had one eye swollen shut. But I had my teeth, and I could move my extremities. I heard steps coming toward me. It was Haggerty, panting and cursing the heavens—like he actually cared.

"What the fuck, Jonas," he said, exasperated. "What happened?"

"Walsh happened," I told him, smarting, but glad to be among the living.

"Who was shooting at us?" he asked, mirroring my own puzzlement.

"Somebody covering for Walsh," I told him. "Walsh hit me from the side. He was nowhere near that muzzle flash. He's got a confederate, Nate, a shooter."

"Sounded like a .38," he said. "We lost the guy who was following you. He ducked into the Promenade Deck and was gone."

"He might have gotten himself down here to take pot shots at me," I told him. "Help me find my gun."

With thoughts Walsh might now have some extra fire-power, Haggerty and I retraced my semi-conscious journey through the hold. We got to the base of the stairway where I was pretty certain I was attacked, and my pistol was on the deck—cocked, locked and ready. Note to self: A big part of being armed is retaining your firearm.

"Puller's guys are fanning out," said Haggerty. We heard them moving our way, and Haggerty made enough of the right kind of noise we couldn't be confused for the ene-my.

Puller's crew had lanterns, and soon we were scouring the C Deck hold, looking for a vanished Walsh. Haggerty and I got to the spot where I thought Walsh was standing when I shot at him, or at least the guy I thought was Walsh. I was beginning to better understand the fog of war.

There was a nickel's worth of blood spatter on the deck, so at least I scratched him, or a piece of wood crate chipped off and hit him.

Puller came up to report: "We've been all through here. What happened to your face commander?"

"I had an encounter with our target," I told him. "He hit my blind side."

"Lucky that's all he hit," said Puller. I told Haggerty and Puller about Walsh's demand for the book.

"Boiler room four," said Puller. "We can get a few men in position to cover that."

Haggerty was scratching his chin and he was puzzled. "Nothing unusual about that book is there?"

"Not that I can tell," I responded. "If Walsh wants to come and get it, we can be ready for him. But now I think I know how he's moving around the ship, gentlemen."

"Does it have anything to do with the trap door we found on the port side?" asked Puller.

"Yep. It's an escape trunk that leads from the bilge to the Promenade Deck," I told him. "If the ship gets hit, people in the holds and engine spaces need to get out, so we had that made in Norfolk. Navy regs."

"You have that feature in the after holds also?" he asked.

"We do," I told him, and the thought of it unsettled Puller. It disturbed me, too.

"Walsh has complete run of the ship off the major passageways fore and aft," said Puller. "He can go down aft and come up forward and never encounter a living soul."

"He can't have found that by accident," I told him, and now my sense of conspiracy was aroused. Does Walsh have help from the ship's crew? The people who know this ship inside and out?

Just then Marchionda walked up carrying a lantern, and he had more bad news.

"Bianchi is in the sick bay," he told us. "A cutting. Doctor McGuire thinks it might have been self-inflicted."

"Jesus H. Christ," said Haggerty. And Puller looked at me in a way that suggested I better not lose any more of his Marines.

Chapter Ten
– A Man Named Mooney

It was early on a Tuesday, and I was sitting on a bench in Pulteney Park opposite the majesty of the Presbyterian Church. My little town was just coming awake. I saw gentlemen nip into the tobacco shop, stocking up on their deadly habit. The ladies who operate the Clerk's office with such diligence and care were prancing up the front steps with their lunch hampers. The bailiff was unlocking the front door of the courthouse, and if my memory of the current docket was correct, we had quite a slate of legal actions being contested in our county this week. Life in the thriving little town of Bath, New York, was proceeding at a pace and rhythm unquenched since I landed at the offices of Pratt and Pratt, a mere stripling fresh out of Harvard. The bloodstream of our little town ran right through the beating heart of this square, where our town was staked out in 1793.

And here I was trying to set down a tale that took place a half a world away. But make no mistake, a lot of men and women from this little place ventured forth to faraway lands when their country called. We were farmers, store clerks, haberdashers, doctors, lathe operators, nurses...and there was one thing that united us—we all wanted to get back here in one piece and pick up our lives where we'd left off. But first we had to win the war.

Ship of Tears

I walked across the park and entered our little brick edifice. Of course, Bart had beat me to the office, as he always does, and I looked in on him, beavering away. There were manilla folders stacked in front of him, each representing a pressing case. I knew he would be crossing the street this morning to seat a jury for a personal injury matter. My boy had his sleeves rolled, his coffee half consumed. He was working a calculator and chewing on the end of a pencil. We muttered our daily greetings and our understated acknowledgement masked the immense, overwhelming pride I have for this wonderful man, my partner. I am delighted to report I don't try cases anymore, content to advise clients and prepare their documents with a steady pull on the oar. I trudge up the stairs and take my seat at my rickety old desk. I tipped my hat to Josiah and Ike, and take up my pen. As I recall, I've just been assaulted by the dreaded Walsh, and let's not forget that miserable little Bianchi, whose suicide attempt was nothing but a distraction. I know I should have been more caring when I beheld him in his cot in the infirmary. But I had murders to solve, and Bianchi wasn't dead yet. A callous thing to say. But I had priorities. I ventured back to those dangerous days.

I sat at Bianchi's bedside and he was dozing. Doctor McGuire had sutured and dressed his wounds, two slash marks over the inner wrists, hitting all the vasculature in the region, and nicking a tendon on his right arm. I judged these wounds may not take him out of the war, but it was possible Bianchi's lacerations might take him out of the coming fight. McGuire, I was told, was able to perform the intricate surgery that restored blood flow to Bianchi's hands and fingers. So he could still pull a trigger.

I was told he'd been taken to the head to relieve himself, and in an unguarded moment, he smashed a mirror over a sink with a butt from his head. He picked up the glass and slashed at his wrists, causing what Doctor McGuire termed "quite a bit of havoc." Direct pressure from one of Puller's lance corporals and a quick-thinking corpsman stanched Bianchi's blood loss, which, for the most part, remained mostly tucked inside him where it belonged.

He was awake and looking miserable.

"Why Stephen?" I asked him.

"I didn't see any other way out," he said.

"Out of what?" I asked. "We're going to get Walsh." It was a speculative statement and my swollen eye and black-and-blue face suggested otherwise. Bianchi looked at me quizzically but didn't comment.

"I went against my buddies," he said. "He was going to kill me. I told him about the book. And now we'll probably never get the money. I was hoping to help my mother. That won't happen now."

"Well, son," I said soothingly. "You'll fight the war and come home a hero and get a job and help your mom then. You don't need Accardo's loot."

"Easy for you to say," he told me. "I'm a nothing."

I had a ship to run and I was not a psychiatrist. But I did have some reserve left for a fatherly pat on Bianchi's beleaguered shoulder.

"I need some information, Stephen," I opened. "I talked to Walsh. That's how I got beaned, if you were wondering. He said he needs the book. The only thing the book gives me is a place called Zenda. Is there something more I should be looking for?"

"It's in Rizzo's diary," he divulged. "DeLuca's got it. "You put the diary together with the book. It opens the door."

"Does Walsh know about the diary?" I asked him.

"I couldn't tell him," said Bianchi. "I had to hold something back. But the book is useless without the diary."

"Why didn't you tell me about this when you gave me the book?"

"I didn't know what to do," said Bianchi, and I half believed him. The dead Napolitano was the schemer behind all this, and he had information compartmentalized. His sniveling children in his little gang would have to work together to find their loot. But now Bianchi was stepping out of bounds and just wanted it to be over. Did he actually plan on killing himself, or did he just want to get off the ship? Either way, he was no longer my focus.

Haggerty and I made our way down to the brig. I got one of Donahue's men to open DeLuca's cell, and the reprobate had the smarts to stand at attention when we entered. I was in no mood for chit-chat.

"Rizzo's diary," I told him. "Give it to me."

"Bianchi told you," he said, and I answered with a noncommittal glance.

"That little asshole," said DeLuca, heretofore the quiet one, but now betraying a calculating mind.

"I am going to recommend to Colonel Puller that he distribute you idiots throughout the First Division, if General Vandegrift agrees," I told him. "You're not healthy when you're together. For now, you'll stay in the brig where you're safe." DeLuca opened his mouth to speak but we are already out the door, which slammed behind us.

Haggerty and I headed for the starboard side and up and finally got to my cabin. The squall had moved to our south and the sun was dipping below the cloud deck, lighting up the sky in a fiery orange that transitioned upward to a brilliant blue. Haggerty and I settled in, and Haggerty performed the same inspection of *The Prisoner of Zenda* that I had. He didn't see anything out of place. I turned my attention to Rizzo's diary. It was really nothing more than a high-school composition book, and it had pockets on the inside covers for loose leaves. There were a couple of entries from boot camp, and a note about boarding *Bridger* for our cruise to the South Pacific. Rizzo was not much of a writer. Haggerty was paying more attention to the loose items in the cover pockets. Rizzo's Illinois driver's license was tucked back here, along with his military ID, his life insurance application (apparently unfiled) and three folded sheets pocked with vertical and horizontal rectangular holes.

"Here it is," he told me. "That fucking Napolitano. He was no dummy. Pretty standard cryptography."

"Those holes correspond with words and letters in the book?" I asked him.

"Looks like it," he said.

Bianchi had us examining the environs of Zenda, Wisconsin. But maybe the location of Tony Accardo's funds was simpler than that.

"Tell me, Nate," I asked my collaborator. "Why do we give a hoot about where this money is, as long as we can roll up Walsh and any cronies and get them off this ship?"

"You are the bait, Commander," he reminded me. "And Walsh is much more interested in you if he knows you're the key to recovering the money. It's probably why you're still alive." Haggerty's point hit home, but he hadn't answered my question and it had to do with the loneliness of command. All I really wanted was to get this pestilence out of our lives so we could prosecute the war as ordered. I couldn't let Puller or Vandegrift get sidetracked by the stain of the

Chicago mob. I wasn't going to break up and arrest members of the underworld and I wasn't going to return Accardo's loot to the citizens who'd spent it so unwisely on gambling parlors or houses of ill repute. All that was somebody else's job.

I just wanted the killing to stop, and I wanted these heathens to get off my ship. Their money in exchange for *Bridger's* peaceful return to our mission.

That's what I wanted.

I wondered how my FBI lawman might deal with this cold practicality.

I watched him hold up the first sheet. It had rectangular holes for full words, smaller holes for single letters. There was a light pencil number in the upper left-hand corner of each sheet.

"Probably page numbers," I told Haggerty and he grunted in agreement. I took the sheet for page thirteen and lay it over the copy. It took a second to get the right word lined up with the correct hole, but soon the letters 'art' appeared in the tiny window in the upper right-hand corner and I thought I might be making progress. If I could get that first word or letter right, the other words or letters might materialize. At least that was my fervent wish.

"Nate, please run down to the library and grab an atlas," I asked him. "We need a detailed map of Chicago." He was up and out the door and I continued, writing the words that appeared on a separate blank sheet in Rizzo's notebook.

The word 'art' was followed by the words 'inst' and 'west' and 'wing.' Haggerty came back with the fat atlas and started flipping pages to the detailed inset map of Chicago.

"We need the loop, I think... around Grant Park."

"The art institute, west wing," said Haggerty. "There has to be more."

"Bear with me," I told him. "I've only got one working eye."

"Jesus Jonas, let me do it." I was happy to relinquish this chore.

"Okay," he said. "Art institute. West wing. Looks like the word 'bsmnt clning clos. pan over sink.'"

"Gibberish," I told him in frustration.

"Not really," said Haggerty. "Basement cleaning closet. Pan might be panel. And if it's 'over' something it might be a ceiling panel."

"I'm taking notes," I told him. "Next sheet. Page thirty-seven." Haggerty worked his way over to the correct page and got the first word. It was actually a series of letters.

"'Chi un stat,'" he said. And we were both a little stumped until we tried to compare these cryptic jottings with the map. Napolitano was taking us right down West Adams Street.

"Chicago Union Station," I announced in triumph, and I thought this exercise might be fun if it didn't involve serial homicide. Haggerty continued.

"'Trk ten' it reads," he told me. "'Stps end pltfrm stl bx buried und.'"

"Okay," I told him. "End of track ten there are steps leading down and there's a steel box buried underneath. Last one. Page fifty-three."

"Looks like he was staying on West Adams," said Haggerty. "'old st pats kitch back pots cab.'"

"Back of the pots cabinet in the kitchen," I told him. "So Napolitano didn't drive all the way to Zenda. He sprinkled Tony Accardo's loot around three different places in downtown Chicago."

"Now what?" he asked and we stared at each other for

a few seconds to let our gears start turning.

"We leave the book on the tool bench in boiler room four," I told him. "I need to get Elvis and his men out of there. We simply cannot risk any hostage taking. And we need to get Donahue and Puller to set up a stakeout so we can get this guy." Like the barking dog who liked to chase cars until the day he finally caught one, I wondered what I would do when we captured only one of them. Haggerty's next thought beat me to it.

"Guys plural, Jonas," said Haggerty. "We need Walsh, and we need the little fucker who took pot shots at you. We need Marchionda with a camera and a long lens. Maybe if Walsh thinks his buddy hasn't been made yet, we can photograph his accomplice while he's trying to watch you."

"I like that," I told him. "But we can also poke the beast and get him to come out in the open." I wrote a note on *Bridger* stationery and put it in an envelope for Walsh's entertainment. It read: "Book is useless without the code that goes with it, which is under lock and key. I don't want the money. I want you off the ship. Time to talk. Come to the aft side of the forward smokestack at midnight."

"Okay," said Haggerty. "So this assumes our stakeout in the boiler room is a dud and he's got the book."

"It's a fallback," I told him.

"Why not?" said Haggerty. "This asshole has messed with us enough. Time for a taste of his own medicine."

It was only five o'clock and we agreed to meet in the officer's mess at six. He would round up Marchionda, try to get some photo gear from the MA office, and get down to the boiler room to tell Elvis and his crew to come to the library at seven-thirty. We would want an armed guard on the library door. Our boilermen were the key to our survival. I needed to take a tour through the bridge and I found Bryant attending to damage control audits and Simms keeping track of our position. There were atolls and coral outcroppings in this area of Oceania and sailing out here sometimes required a slalom course. I worked my way down to the officer's mess. Haggerty joined me for a one-on-one. He told me Marchionda was equipped with a German Leica with a hundred-millimeter lens and fast-ASA black-and-white film. He should be able to take pictures with available light. Elvis and his ten-man boiler team were in the lap of luxury in the library, working on a puzzle and playing gin rummy. Haggerty thought they might have a bottle of whisky in there but I was not going to spoil their evening unless it got out of hand. Puller and Donahue had placed men out of sight in the boiler spaces, and especially near our after-escape trunk, which Walsh had been using to good effect. Haggerty equipped Puller's Marines with pump shotguns, which would stop the threat without destroying equipment, I hope. Last thing we needed was stray shotgun pellets taking out a steam line or a petcock for our hydraulics.

Haggerty and I had a little time so we lingered over our Welsh rarebit and I could feel my belt start to squeeze. I would have liked a tomato or a green vegetable and maybe Crawford could stock up using some of the ship's cash when we got to Wellington. Halfway through dinner we became mildly interested in where Marchionda might be operating but concluded not being able to see the man probably signaled we were in good shape. Marchionda was diligent and he liked a challenge. He'd be okay.

It was quarter to eight. Haggerty and I finished off our meal with a piece of upside-down cake and worked our way aft to the staircase leading below. We passed through the accommodation decks, working around knots of young Marines talking, playing craps or taunting each other in good-natured play. There was a nervous energy. The décor changed the lower we went, from the simple but attractive paneling along the companionways, to a sickly industrialized green. It got hotter the lower we went until we got to the ship's watertight doors, metal catwalks and asbestos-clad piping. Here and there we passed one of Donahue's men in one-piece boilermen coveralls. They had pistols in their hands. I got to the tool bench Walsh specified, and left *The Prisoner of Zenda*, right on top, including my note tucked under the front cover. He wouldn't be able to miss it.

Haggerty and I wondered if we should await the arrival of our serial killer, then argued against it. Puller and Donahue had more than enough manpower secreted throughout the boiler spaces to kill or capture our menace. We didn't want to spoil things. We climbed back up to E Deck when Marchionda came running by, out of breath.

"Did you see him?" he asked, convincing me he was referring to Walsh.

"You mean Walsh?" I asked him.

"No, the little guy," he said. "Same guy I was following this afternoon. He came down here."

"Haven't see him," said Haggerty. Then we wondered if leaving the boiler room was such a good idea. We followed Marchionda back down to our machinery spaces, and forward to the tool bench where I'd left the book. The book was gone, and Puller and Donahue were looking at each other trying to figure out how someone might have gotten past them. They were looking for the hulking Walsh, not a shorter, skinnier Marine. There were eight of us standing there in various stages of disbelief and armed readiness: pump guns muzzle down, hands on .45s still nestled in holsters. There was frustration and anxiety etched on Donahue's face, and Puller suggested we take lanterns and fan out fore and aft to figure out how our nemesis got away.

"Did you get any photos of the guy?" asked Haggerty.

"Half a dozen," said Marchionda. "He was across the mess hall from you guys, picking at his food and watching you like a hawk."

I had been down in these spaces nearly every week for more than two years, first when *Bridger* was being readied at the shipyard in Newport News, then loading in Norfolk. I knew *Bridger* as well as anyone, and aside from the escape trunks our killers seemed to have found, I was not aware of any other means of getting in or out of this area other than up the aft stack, and that was humanly impossible. Exhaust gases left the boilers at more than four-hundred degrees before dissipating out the after funnel.

And then it hit me. There was an air casing that allowed outside atmosphere into the spaces housing our turbine intakes. Our interloper could climb topside through this vent line. I called for a team to follow me and we headed aft through the engine space to find the access hatch for the air casing. It was ajar. That hatch was supposed to be dogged down tight at all times, and having it loose was a damage control demerit. I put my ear up to the line and I could hear some shuffling inside—boots kicking metal.

"Donahue, this comes out on the Sports Deck aft of the after stack," I shouted to him over the din of the machinery. "Get a party up there and see if you can grab him when he comes out." Our MA team raced off to comply, when a Navy corpsman came up and put sizeable dent in the evening.

"Commander Pratt, Doctor McGuire begs your presence in the after infirmary," he told me.

"What's it about?" I asked him, not wishing to get knocked off kilter. The corpsman looked a little pale and responded.

"Rather not say, sir," he said. "It's important." I looked at Haggerty and Marchionda, and we told Puller's team where they could find us. We followed the corpsman up to C Deck and entered the medical department to see McGuire probing the throat of a young Marine with a tongue depressor.

"Examining room A," he told me, expressionless. Surprise seemed to have been knocked right out of the ship's doctor.

That's where we'd left Bianchi.

We drew the curtain back and the first thing I noticed was a widening pool of deep red blood under his gurney. Someone had thrown a sheet over his top half. When I pulled it back, I could see his bandaged wrists crossed on his chest, then a freshly slit throat. Plus, there was a standard-issue Ka-Bar plunged up to the hilt in the man's left eye. His right ear was missing.

I can't say I'd gotten used to these deplorable scenes. The polite term is that I had become "inured" to the evermore ghastly way Walsh had devised to kill people, the only consistency from one murder to the next being the clean removal of the victims' outer ear. Marchionda was exceptionally unhappy at witnessing yet more gruesome blade work.

"I am going to go get my film developed," he told us, and left the room. Haggerty examined Bianchi's dog tags.

"Reads Bianchi, Stephen," he told me. "Right guy. Right tag. That's new and different."

I am not sure what kind of forensic examination or

post-mortem could yield any more information about Bianchi's killer than what we had already. I asked McGuire to come in and use a gloved hand to get the knife out of Bianchi's eye. He put the knife in a cellophane wrapper and put that in a manilla envelope. I told myself I needed to get it down to Donahue to see if he could lift some fingerprints. Even if we did get prints, we had no FBI database with which to compare them. Haggerty agreed getting prints to The FBI office in San Francisco as soon as *Bridger* returned stateside could be important.

Other than that, we dragooned three corpsmen to lift Bianchi into a disposal bag. One of Bowker's housekeepers got a mop and a bucket and started the not insignificant job of cleaning up Doctor McGuire's examining room. I could tell the doctor was growing tired of this. He couldn't even make eye contact with me. Our task now was to get ready for the confrontation I knew would be coming on the after side of the forward stack at midnight.

I sent for Puller, Donahue and Marchionda and asked them to meet us at my quarters. Marchionda came in last with photos of the small-to middling-built Marine who had figured in tonight's purloining of *The Prisoner of Zenda*. We passed them around and they meant nothing to me, Puller, or Donahue. But Haggerty held the prints loosely in his hands and stared intently at the narrow face, the hawk-like nose, the darting eyes. Finally, when he was sure, he spoke:

"This is Tony Accardo's muscle. This is Sam Giancana."

Chapter Eleven
– Dealing with the Devil

I heard Margie softly singing in the kitchen. My sweet girl from Sewickley liked show tunes, and it reminded me we needed to get ourselves down to New York for a bit of Broadway now that the season had arrived.

I was sitting in my favorite chair in my comfortable old living room. A crisp fall day had transitioned to a soft night. In the waning light, I could see the leaves beginning to turn, and I was gratified knowing there were grouse and pheasant up in the hills that would soon land in our stewpot. In my rocks glass there was a good portion of bourbon over three large cubes as I contemplated a day's end and sent myself back to that monumental night on our final leg to Wellington.

As I write this, it's 1973 and Sam Giancana is considered a principal in the upper echelons of the American mafia. He's positioned The Chicago "Outfit" brilliantly, bringing in a gusher of ill-gotten lucre from loan-sharking, prostitution, extortion, and now that cash cow, illegal drugs. Cocaine has become fashionable, and the mob likes to follow its simple precept, "Give the people what they want."

But I have paid attention to such matters, and Sam Giancana is mentioned in the same breath with the Kennedy assassination. It's said Giancana and our slain president shared the same girlfriend, Judith Exner, and the president's own father had his well-documented dalliance with organized crime as a bootlegger during America's futile embrace with Prohibition. Joe Kennedy may have ticked off the wrong people. Certainly, the president's brother Bobby didn't make any friends with his relentless pursuit of organized crime as special counsel to the Senate Labor Rackets committee, and then as attorney general during his brother's doomed and all-too-brief administration.

Decades earlier, it seemed our rising mobster was making his bones on my ship.

During those dark, terrifying days aboard *Bridger*, Haggerty was making good use of his years as a G-man. He'd spent his professional life looking at mug shots on wanted posters. Back in the trigger-happy times of Elliott Ness, confronting organized crime was one of the chief missions of Hoover's FBI. Haggerty's last assignment, before being called to reserve duty, was the surprisingly active Buffalo field office. But during his career, Haggerty had traveled around to other field offices on temporary duty assignments, once pulling a two-year stint in Chicago. In August of '42, he knew most of the players without having to consult a score card. So, I listened to Haggerty, and what I heard did not make me happy.

As I sat in my creaky old office chair at Pratt and Pratt, writing feverishly on my yellow pad, I was mentally transported back to my sumptuous accommodation aboard *Bridger* in late August of 1942, the battle for Guadalcanal firmly fixed on a near horizon. Haggerty and I were looking at Marchionda's photographic handiwork.

"Yep, it's him," Haggerty said. "Giancana. Made his mark as a head knocker for The '42' Gang."

"The '42' Gang?" I queried.

"Named after Ali Baba and his Forty Thieves," said Haggerty. "Plus, a couple of strays. So, they called themselves 'The 42s'. Small-time hoods. But smart. Aggressive. Didn't step on any toes. Sub-contractors to what was left of the Capone group, where 'Mooney' met Tony Accardo."

"Help me," I implored. "Mooney?"

"Sam Giancana's nickname," he said. "They all have nicknames. Part of being a mobster. Terms of endearment. I have no idea where he picked it up."

"So I've got two mobsters on my ship," I told him.

"Maybe more, Nate," said Haggerty. "Joining the Navy or the Marines doesn't stop you from being part of the mob."

"Let's think about what's in front of us," I told him. "We have to do what's best for *Bridger*."

"What about what's best for law enforcement?" he asked.

"You mean prosecuting members of organized crime? That will come in time," I told him. "Our priority—my priority—is to stop the killing. And, oh yeah, win the war."

"Do you think you can negotiate with these assholes? Get them to be nice?" Haggerty asked. "The only way to stop them is a bullet."

"What if you miss?" I told him. "What if you can't get close enough? What if somebody else gets hurt in the process? Bad enough we took a few rounds in the hold on C Deck."

"So what's your plan, commander?" he asked in that acid tone he knows I hate. This is where the man could be insufferable. He was all blunt force, couldn't imagine a third way that might have involved a little finesse.

"I am thinking at this point we take the midnight meeting. And keep it private. Just me and Giancana," I told him. Haggerty expressed more displeasure.

"If Walsh comes, too, you'll need backup," he said. "I can't let you do this alone, Jonas."

"Okay," I told him. "For the ship. Wouldn't be good for *Bridger* to lose her executive officer, especially with an all-too-public knifing. Tends to upset people." Haggerty laughed.

"Murder can be such a problem that way," he told me. "What's your plan?"

"I will tell him where he can find his money in exchange for no more killings, and to leave the ship immediately."

"Where are they going to go?" asked Haggerty.

"They stowed away to get out here," I insisted. "They can stow away to get home. There might be some eastbound cargo traffic when we get to Wellington. Maybe they can even buy passage."

"There are a lot of ships heading for Panama," said Haggerty. "And then cruise or air service north from there."

"That's it, then," I told him. "We're giving them what they want. And they'll be giving us what we want," I stated firmly. Then, of course, I wobbled a bit: "Do you think we can trust him?"

"Not a chance," said Haggerty. "In my experience, criminals come up with all sorts of reasons to justify their behavior. You looked at him wrong. You had a tone in your voice. You raised an eye. Gangsters take offense pretty easily."

"I'll bring Rizzo's diary with our code sheets," I told him.

"Might make him happy," said Haggerty. "Of course,

he won't know for sure until he gets back to Chicago. He'll want a guarantee, Jonas, and how are you going to do that? When you're dealing with a guy like Giancana, a bullet is much simpler."

"No guarantees, then," I told him. "It's the book, and the code—only—in exchange for a stand down."

"Can't we just arrest these guys?" Haggerty pleads.

"We haven't demonstrated we can get close enough to them, Nate," I told him. "And the killing has to stop."

So once again, I became the negotiator, a role I have played all of my life. It's wearying.

"Let's at least see how this goes," I said.

"Okay," said Haggerty, "We will go up together though. He'll see me, but I'll hang back. He might want us to remove our guns and place them on the deck. I keep a snub-nose .38 on my ankle. He doesn't need to know about that. If for whatever reason you start feeling uncomfortable, keep facing him, but back off. Do not turn your back."

"Not simple dealing with trained killers," I told him.

"And don't forget Walsh might be waiting in the wings," he said.

"Not a lot of places to hide up there," I told him. "Except maybe the forward funnel, which is empty. Donahue keeps the key."

"Shall we go?" he asked, looking vaguely miserable.

I extracted Rizzo's diary from the safe. I doublechecked to make sure the code sheets were in the inside cover pockets. Haggerty and I both checked the status of our sidearms. I dropped the magazine, pulled the slide back and allowed a live round to eject from the chamber. I picked it up off the top of my coffee table, put it back in the magazine and inserted the magazine in the grip well. I released the slide and watched the live round re-enter the chamber, then made sure the slide stop thumb safety was up. I was in Condition One, and the firearm went back into my holster. Haggerty had gone through the same exercise and his handgun was now in his shoulder rig. As Haggerty preached, we went through this little ritual so we could remind ourselves of weapons status. We could never take anything for granted.

I took a quick turn through the bridge. Everything was in order. I then made a stop at meteorology. Rittenhouse had updated the synoptic chart using coded data out of Fiji. There was a cold front moving off the eastern coast of Australia. It was August and therefore early spring in the Antipodes. Winds were expected to be on the beam out of the west at twelve to fifteen knots, and that would kick up a bit of a sea. I picked up the phone to culinary and housekeeping so they could secure any loose gear.

Haggerty and I went up to the Sports Deck. There was a half-moon high overhead, sending light in and out of the scattered cloud deck, delivering a shimmering light in moonlit columns that hit the wavetops. There was a stout, not strong, breeze...but it was building. The stars were magnificent, horizon to horizon, when you could see them through the scattered clouds. The Southern Cross was shining unfailingly. I remembered Acrux, Mimosa, and Ginan and I reminded myself to brush up on the other stars we depended on for navigation in this hemisphere.

We walked up to the after side of the forward stack. Haggerty turned and went back to stand by the port rail. My hands were loose at my sides, and I unsnapped the flap of my holster. I turned slowly around to see if anyone was coming my way, and a medium-built man wearing Marine utilities came out from behind the stack on the starboard side. He was wearing a pith helmet, with the brim pulled down so it nearly covered his eyes.

"Where's Walsh?" I asked him.

"Where I come from, it's standard to exchange greetings," he said. Like Haggerty mentioned, mobsters take offense easily. "How do you do commander?"

"I do just fine," I told him. "I don't exchange pleasantries with people who've taken shots at me."

"I wasn't trying to hit you," he said. "Just give my associate a little cover. If I wanted to hit you, you'd be dead."

"I don't take it personally."

"Hope not," he said. "This is just business."

"Who am I speaking to?" I asked.

"Mooney is all you need to know," he said.

"So you are Giancana, then," I told him, hoping to disarm the man. "Accardo's so-called muscle."

"You're well informed," he said. "But it's not 'so-called.' Who's that guy standing by the rail?"

"My chief of security," I told him. "Nate Haggerty, FBI, serving in the reserves."

"Haggerty?" he said. "Out here? I know the guy. Wish we could sit down and break bread. We're acquainted with some of the same people."

"Where's Walsh," I asked him again.

"He's around," he said.

"We're not going to get anywhere if I don't feel safe," I told him. "Where is he?"

"I told him to stay below," said Giancana.

"I will take that as a gesture of trust," I told him. "Seems like a good place to begin. I want you and Walsh off my ship."

"We want off your ship more than you want us off your

ship," he said. "But I need the book. And your note said it came with a code. I need that, too."

"No more killings. And you leave," I told him. "And incidentally, I broke the code. I know where the money is. That Napolitano was something." I threw this in just to tease the man. He looked out to sea—pensive and calculating.

"I can agree to your request, Commander, in exchange for the code," he said. "But I have a little problem. I can ask my associate to refrain from his activities in defense of my business while he's on the ship. But make no mistake. The people who stole from my organization will pay with their lives. We won't get them on the ship, maybe. But we will get them."

"And if Haggerty and I grab you right now and toss you in the brig?" I asked him, knowing the answer.

"You've seen how inventive my man Walsh can be," he said coolly. "If I don't come back tonight with the code, he's under instructions to widen his net. He's been concentrating on Napolitano's little punks. But if anything happens to me, he's going to grab the first little shit Marine he comes across, and he's going to slit his throat, and rip his guts out. The same thing he did to Rizzo. I was there. I used the hammer to try to get the little fucker to talk. But Walsh did the heavy lifting. He's good. And when he's done, he's going to kill again and again. Navy, Marines, those Blacks in the boiler room. And it will all be on you, Commander. That's why I like your solution. We get the code, we get the money, and you get your ship back. Seems fair."

"How are you going to get yourselves off *Bridger*?" I asked. "You need to be on your way."

"Can't wait. Food sucks. But it will be a mystery, Commander," said Giancana. "A murder mystery. But, like I said, there will be no more killings on *Bridger*. Give me the code."

"I need a guarantee," I told him.

"You're in no position to ask for a guarantee, Commander," he said. Now he was agitated. I'd thrown him a curve. But I had to be the lawyer.

"I'll give you the code. But there's no way to assure you the money is where the code says you'll find it. I make no warranty you'll find anything at all," I told him. Giancana laughs. "Did you crack the code yet?" he asked me.

"Of course," I told him. "You'll figure it out in five minutes. But the money may not be where Napolitano said he put it. I've known what the code reveals for about an hour. But I am not going to attest to the fact the money will be there when you go looking for it."

"I've got ways to find out," he said. "But why don't you tell me what you know right now." He's going to find out anyway, so I let him know what I knew.

"Napolitano divided it in thirds. Chicago Art Institute. West Wing. Cleaning Closet. Ceiling panel over the slop sink. Go west down West Adams. Chicago Union Station. Track Ten. Walk to the end of the platform and take the stairs down to the tracks. Buried under the stairs there is a steel box. After that, keep walking down West Adams to St. Pat's church. Go to the kitchen in the basement. Back of the cabinet where they keep the pots."

"Detailed," said Giancana.

"And plausible," I agreed. "Napolitano could hide the money in one energetic afternoon."

"You've just added what we like to call 'veracity,'" said Giancana. "Good work."

"I'm a lawyer," I told him. "I believe in facts and truth. And I have to see around corners. The code says where the money is hidden. I have no idea it's actually there."

"We could use a guy like you," laughed Giancana. "Our shysters make good money."

"Not a chance," I told him.

"We've got a deal," he said. "Let's shake on it." I was repulsed. But I realized in Giancana's circles, great weight was placed on a man's word, sealed with a handshake. I extended my hand. We shook. And I handed him the notebook. I'd just made a pact with the devil. The killings aboard *Bridger* would stop...I hoped. But the killings of those young toughs in our brig would not, unless Haggarty and I could apprehend the mad man named Walsh. There was nothing in the handshake deal I'd just executed that suggested a covenant not to arrest Walsh and Giancana when they were off the ship. Plus, there was a third way. I could press Puller to keep what's left of our little gang out of sight, or to separate them. I was not sure how to ask that, with every Marine expected to pull his weight. We'd already lost five to Walsh's Ka-Bar. The thought of it disgusted me.

Giancana disappeared around the funnel, and I walked back to Haggerty—wondering whether or not I'd just sentenced to death the remaining members of Napolitano's band of thieves.

Chapter Twelve
– Dress Rehearsal

As we sailed south, getting closer to the Southern Ocean, building headwinds and robust seas gyrated *Bridger* into a disagreeable roll. We were compelled to curtail dining service so we wouldn't injure the culinary staff, and we rigged lines throughout the passageways so our guests could have something to hang onto. Most of the Marines stayed in their pipe cots. Bowker's crew was constantly involved in cleaning up vomit. We were a reeking, reeling mess when we finally made visual contact with the sea buoy standing off Wellington's well-protected harbor. Our plan was to give our Marines a brief liberty, take on supplies, which meant repacking all of our holds, then girding for an extended cruise north to get closer to the coming fight.

Vandegrift and his number two, Rupertus, were planning a rehearsal on Fiji for the second week in August, so we didn't have a lot of time to waste. Plus, there were Marine units scattered on ships across the wide ocean, all converging on Wellington, and later Fiji, where the divisions would be reshaped into a final assault force.

Several problems started to confront the hard-working souls who made up our complement. First, one of our jobs was to sort out and load food stuffs, uniforms, weapons and other materiel that had been pre-positioned. A lot of this cargo had been spoiled through sloppy handling by port staff. Plus, there was a labor action that prevented local stevedores from loading our ship. We attempted interventions at every level of New Zealand authority, right up to the prime minister, but no one was happy about going against the dock workers, who seemed to have a stranglehold on the New Zealand economy. During this period, it occurred to me that Giancana, when he finally did slip away on his surreptitious journey back across the Pacific, would likely be aided and abetted by these labor thugs with their hands out. I finally resorted to getting Puller's men to operate the cranes to get our cargo aboard. It included a couple of squads loaded to the teeth with shotguns and Thompsons, just so there wasn't any trouble.

On top of this, I had Donahue's well-armed MA boys accompany our supply teams into the holds. He reported finding at least three more nests where stowaways might have been hidden. But we didn't encounter Walsh. And I hoped with all my might he had given up his quest and was accompanying Mooney back to Chicago. I pictured them sunning themselves on the deck of a Panamanian-flagged tramp, wending its way toward the Canal.

We were in Wellington a good eleven days, and every minute was spent attending to *Bridger's* hygiene, mechanical systems, tankage, resupply and paint touch-ups. We restocked our magazines of three-inch and five-inch shells and our twenty-millimeter canisters for our Oerlikons. The sick bays were going through inventory, which included a provision for additional body bags, a thought that pains me still. Young, vibrant, fantastically skilled men were about to die, to be buried in some hot jungle or to be sent to the bottom of the sea. They would be shot, stabbed, or blown to bits. And now they were happily camped outside Wellington waiting for the word to mount up and re-board. They were toning up their bodies with twenty-mile hikes after those sedentary days on the ocean. They were listening to their commanders opine about what to carry in their haversacks, how to perfect their riflery, how to work in small fire teams to overcome enemy machine gun nests, snipers and Banzai charges. Only a year ago they had been focusing on algebra, the iambic pentameter, or fixing up some old jalopy. Their biggest stressor was screwing up the courage to ask that pretty girl in English class out on a date. In my quiet moments, behind my cabin door, I wept for the waste and heartbreak we were about to experience. These fantastic kids wanted nothing more than to succeed, to thrive, and to get home. But there was a fatalism that stalked our splendid troops. Every Marine knew the phrase first uttered in the last war by Marine Sergeant Dan Daly at Belleau Wood: "Come on you sons of bitches. Do you want to live forever?"

I was spending more time with Captain Kelly in these hours before we re-embarked. We were going over the map and matching it up with the latest intelligence. We were especially interested in the disposition of the Imperial Japanese Navy, particularly her battleships, heavy cruisers and submarines. Their cruisers—swift, lightly armored ships with guns up to fourteen inches—were damn near as fast as *Bridger*. Moreover, the enemy's battle ships could lob those big, two-ton shells. As we readied to sail north, our lookouts in our twin crows' nests fore and aft would be working nonstop. The sub-surface I-boats were every bit the menace of Hitler's U-boat fleet, but they were dog slow, and we had destroyers with depth charges to assist. The captain reminded me for the hundredth time the protocol when we spotted a periscope was to run right at it or run away from it. We never wanted to present our broadside, regardless of our speed advantage.

Still, there were places in the southwest Pacific where we believed we could avoid enemy contact. We were a troopship, and our survival was our sole aim. We were not designed to take or deliver damage in the thick of a fleet action. We were a tool to convey the rifleman, the machine gunner, the artilleryman, the sapper, the grenadier straight into armed combat. We would therefore approach the theater with nimbleness and care.

"Samoa, Fiji, New Hebrides, New Caledonia," the captain intoned. "They're ours and are expected to remain so as long as we stop Tojo in the Solomons. If we fail there, even Australia will be threatened. The Japanese own New Guinea, New Britain and points north, with big installations on Truk and Rabaul."

"But they are making incursions south," I responded.

"They want to extend their air and sea reach and the southern Solomons is critical to that end," he said. "But we have to nip at his heels before we can start bashing him in the head. That's why our first objective will be here." He pointed to the small island of Tulagi. "And here," he said, with a finger on Florida. "And there are a couple of more islets out here on our to-do list."

"And if that all goes well, Guadalcanal?" I asked. At ninety-miles wide east to west and thirty-miles north to south, it's one of the biggest islands in the chain.

"Yes, but Vandegrift is right not to overcommit," said the captain. "Let's see how it goes out here on the periphery. Aerial reconnaissance shows the Japanese are building an airfield on Guadalcanal, which makes it a more attractive target."

"Where will we be?" This was the crux of my concern. I had to prepare our navigation teams.

"First, Fiji for our rehearsal," he said. "Then either New Hebrides or New Caledonia, depending on the tactical picture. We are faster than the landing ships, and if we can get the fighting man closer to the front, then it's good to try as long as we can keep *Bridger* safe. Plus, we've got more troops to bring out here, so I am guessing we will be ordered back to the States at some point to re-load."

We were soon in a state of readiness, and our passengers were back aboard. I warned Crawford about keeping our holds free of interlopers. He told me he'd inspected every hold before, during and after the insertion of cargo, and he was confident we had no stowaways. I also asked Puller to separate DiGenova, Petrucio, Ricci, and DeLuca to make it harder to find them either on board or when they hit the beach. I really hoped I wouldn't see them again, dead or alive, but I silently wished them happy lives, beautiful wives, clever children, and lucrative careers in something safe like insurance or used-car sales. I released Haggerty to have a private word with DeLuca, whom Nate called "a sneaky little fuck." In a civilian scenario he could have been charged as an accessory and was therefore liable for a felony murder conviction. But Puller needed people and Haggerty had no choice but to let him off with a terrifying warning.

"If Walsh doesn't find you and cut your balls off maybe I will," Haggerty told him.

The weather was a bit better as we steamed north, and I was enjoying the rhythms of the ship. My teams were functioning as planned and on schedule, but I knew Vandegrift and his commanders were a knot of anxiety. Getting our fighting men off the ship, into the landing craft and onto the beach with all their equipment could be a trying experience under the best of circumstances. Attempting it with untested troops under enemy fire and the problems could overwhelm the most competent commander. Mis-judged tides. Mis-forecast weather. Mis-drawn charts, some dating to the eighteenth century. Add mis-aligned landing craft, and those hellish Landing Craft, Personnel or LCPs. It was a miracle it ever went right. And towards the end of the war, it went right time after time, as the Marines clawed their way toward the Japanese home islands. The southern Solomons were the first test, however, and there were mistakes aplenty.

I needed to make sure my little piece of it—getting our big ship secured in the anchorage at Suva, capital of Fiji, went according to plan.

We had been at sea three days, and I checked in with navigation. We were twenty-four hours out of Suva. The quartermaster team was examining an Admiralty chart for the local bathymetry and any sea buoys or channel markers. We wanted to make an accurate approach. The Navy was planning on working with local contractors to move barges into position that would serve as an interim platform before we reloaded them onto the landing craft for the rehearsals.

The bridge deck crew was functioning quite well without me, and I had to say I was feeling a bit redundant. I consoled myself with the belief I'd brought the staff up to a high level and I could now delegate.

We agreed we would need to avoid all the rocky islets and coral outcroppings around Fiji. Approaching Suva from the southwest would skirt most of it. We'd come across the Pacific without having to worry too much about running aground, and now that we'd reached our destination, the water under our keel was of pressing concern. The King's Wharf looked shallow at low tide, so we decided to anchor on the north end of Levu Passage. We would avoid the reefs, and have enough depth, but we would want a clear forecast from meteorology. I worried about swinging at anchor if the wind piped up.

We brought her up the passage between two coral reefs, and soon we had a single anchor down on a piece of bottom that was right for both scope and clearance. Just a bit farther south and we'd be too deep, offering little scope and poor holding. A bit farther in, we'd have decent holding but we'd run the risk of scuffing the bottom. That didn't give me the willies as much as making contact with our props, struts and rudder, what we like to call our "running gear." It was precious, difficult to repair or replace, and needed to be protected. I had a team of divers onboard and I sent them down, led by an old master chief wearing one of those brass Mark Five diving helmets attached to a surface-supply air hose. Chief Guthrie inspected our holding and reported we were nicely settled in a soft sand and earthen bottom. Not coral. Not ledge. And our multi-ton anchor had buried its flukes admirably. So I thought we'd be just fine—at least until the wind whipped out of the west, in which case we'd have to haul up the anchor and get some sea room. Guthrie thanked me for the chance to see all those fantastic fish, and we agreed to come back here with rod and reel.

I had ordered two big barges, which would raft up on our starboard side where we have entry/egress doors on C Deck. On the morning of General Vandegrift's rehearsal we had four of the older style landing craft, absent those nifty bow doors, lashed up to the barges, and our Marines were flowing down the brows and re-embarking onto the LSTs.

There were smaller LCPs swarming around us, and Vandegrift and his staff had taken to a destroyer to observe the action closer inshore. Down on our loading barges, I talked to the all-knowing Puller and he predicted an unholy mess.

"We've got amphibious Amtracks for yellow beach starting in the wrong spot, crossing the line used by the LCPs to get into red beach," he told me. "And the troops for orange beach are getting a late start. It's just beautiful."

"Beautiful?" I asked him.

"Nothing like a good failure to focus the mind," he said. "At least no one is shooting at us."

As Puller foretold, the units hitting the beach in our Fiji rehearsal were a cock-up, and we had unacceptable mechanical and signaling failures up and down the line. Vandegrift and his staff would have plenty to discuss with the regimental staff and their battalion commanders. But it was no surprise Puller's First Battalion of the Seventh Marines arrived on the beach with men and equipment without incident, and marched in full packs, armed to the hilt, to the rally point twelve miles inland.

"Great fun," he later reported as my guest in the officer's mess. But some of his colleagues were ordered to gather afterward in our theater for a top secret dressing down. There was insufficient attention being paid to wind, tide and current-—to the unwary, every bit a killer as bombs and bullets.

The decision was made to move *Bridger* up to the New Hebrides group, which got us six-hundred miles closer to the fight. We had two old four-stacker destroyers escorting us, using their ancient ASDIC sonar, and I chafed at our sacrifice in speed. But Captain Kelly had decided having depth charges at the ready would keep us safe if any Japanese submarines, their I-boats, showed up. He also requested some PBY amphibious flying boats to scout the route for us to determine if we might have any surface threats. Off to our west was New Caledonia and the Coral Sea, sight of a major fleet action in May of '42. The Japanese sank a good number of Allied ships, including the carrier *Yorktown*, during this early test. But the Allies were able to check any further southward advance by the Japanese. The New Hebrides were farther east and north, and we were betting the group would give us a safer jumping-off point for the Marine incursion into the southern Solomons.

When the day arrived for our guests to offload for real, we were settled into an anchorage on Mele Bay to the west of Port Vila on Efate Island, southern most of the New Hebrides chain. We had barges set up to allow our men to get off *Bridger* and onto their smaller Navy transports. I was observing the departure of our guests from the starboard bridge wing. Marines were filing down the brows and milling on the barges before fitting themselves onto the LSTs. Vandegrift and his regimental commanders were taking to heart the lessons learned at the Fiji rehearsal to load units according to when and where they would hit the beach. I was sipping my coffee and enjoying the scenery when Marchionda found me. He was out of breath.

"It's Walsh," he told me. "He's loading with Puller's battalion." I was both amazed and worried. I pressed Marchionda to give me a better picture.

"How do you know it's Walsh," I asked him, hoping he was wide of the mark. "I'm the only one who's seen Walsh for sure."

"Broken nose. Scar on his face. Big, tall guy," said Marchionda, finally collecting himself. "He's all decked out like a jarhead."

"Let's go," I told him. "First stop, Donahue's office." With our depleting passenger ranks, we could move a little faster down *Bridger's* interior passageways. I found Donahue and Haggerty conferring in their usual ribald manner. I allowed Marchionda to relate what he'd observed, and soon I had ten of us working our way toward the big double doors on C Deck. We had to fight through the crowds to get down the gangway and onto the barge.

Marchionda pointed to an LST named the *U.S.S. Joshua Farley*. I was standing on the barge looking at young Marines lining the rail when *Farley's* deck crew hauled in her mooring warps and the little transport drifted aft. I was contemplating chasing her down in the captain's gig, but getting the launch off her davits and into the water would be impossible with these damn barges attached to us.

"Right there," said Marchionda, pointing to a large man standing at the rail. I moved across the barge and got a good look at the tall man in green. He was wearing a pith helmet, but it was Walsh, of that I was certain. Marchionda was right about the scar and the broken nose. But I could confirm it was him when he smiled at me across the distance building between the transport and the barge. His teeth were gapped and yellowed. He was looking right into my eyes.

I needed to get a message to Puller. I had to do everything I could to stop *Bridger's* secret killer.

Chapter Thirteen
Rap Sheet

My sweet Margie was pacing back and forth in the kitchen. She had a big spoon in one hand for our venison stew, and my manuscript in the other. She was rightly worried.

"Where was he all this time?" she asked.

"He must have burrowed into the ship's innards someplace," I speculated. "I have to say I think we let our guard down after I cut my deal with that little son of a bitch Giancana. We weren't experiencing any murders, and I had presumed both Giancana and Walsh had departed. But true to his word, Giancana was after our little band of thieves come what may. Yes, he had the grace to discontinue his rampage aboard ship after I handed over the code, but he got Walsh aimed and ready as soon as he could."

"It begs the question," said my sharp-eyed wife. "Why didn't he get those guys when *Bridger* was in New Zealand?"

"Haggerty and I tossed that around a bit," I replied. "His quarry had dispersed with the liberty we extended? It's possible. I just don't know."

"And he had time and opportunity on your way up to the New Hebrides," said Margie.

"Yes, but that would have gone against my compact with Giancana," I told her. "I suppose there is some kind of code amongst the gangster set. We agreed on no more killings aboard *Bridger* and he and Walsh stuck to it."

"Could you recall the *Farley* and take him into custody?" she asked.

"Tried to," I told her. "But we were under orders. Strict radio silence until the invasion force was secure on the beach."

"Where do you suppose he lay hidden after what, two weeks?" she asked.

"There were a thousand places to hide aboard that ship," I told her. "But no one knew belowdecks like Elvis, who lived twenty feet from the boiler rooms. He's the first one I consulted while Haggerty ran off to signaling to figure out how we could contact Puller. Puller had been involved in the manhunt, so I wouldn't have to explain or offer context. He knew the threat Walsh posed. That's when we ran into Vandegrift's edict on radio silence. After that, my first stop was the boiler room."

Our senior powerplant expert was using our port call to clean the grit out of the fire tubes inside the number three boiler. I found him surrounded by his men, offering a lecture on the parts and pieces that made up our precious superheat machine that created the steam that turned the turbines that powered our reduction gears and spun our propellers. His team sat cross legged in a circle on the diamond-plate deck, watching Elvis go at the interior of the tube with a long, wire brush—the same way you'd clean a shotgun barrel. They were careful to capture any grit in a tarp for later disposal. We couldn't have that stuff clogging any pumps or seacocks. Elvis was wrapping up and turning over the next tube to one of his eager acolytes. I got his attention and drew him aside.

"Elvis, could anyone live down here for the past three

weeks without you knowing about it?" I asked him. He was naturally defensive.

"We've got enough to handle in the boiler rooms and engine spaces," he told me. "We don't go wandering around too much."

"You're not in trouble," I told him. "But remember when you found some food scraps and chicken bones down here? You see anything like that lately?"

"Do you mean do we have another stowaway?" he asked me. He's well versed in what we've been up against but thank God he didn't attend any of the crime scenes. Elvis is a brilliant engineer and master mariner, but he's a bit fragile. I wanted to make sure he could sleep at night. It was my job as exec to deal with the mess. I was there to serve as Mr. Foster's guardian angel.

"Maybe the same stowaway," I told him. "We think we just saw him pull away with one of the Marine units."

"We, if he was down here, he'd probably be forward under the number two hold or aft under the refrigeration system or the swimming pool," he told me. I was armed with my .45, but I was smart enough at this point to get security to help with another manhunt. I called Donahue's office and found Haggerty, who soon joined me below. He'd taken his jacket off and he'd donned his shoulder holster. Our shirts were soaked with sweat and it was hard to breathe, but we ventured forward to the lowest possible part of the ship. There were narrow catwalks that took us over the bilges, which had small pools of seawater that could never be fully evacuated. Our lanterns probed nooks and crannies where a man might possibly live, however uncomfortably. We made our way aft and found ourselves underneath the swimming pool, and we arrived at a piece of the ship I was barely aware of. There was a round access panel for the pool's pump system large enough for a man to fit through. It had a provision for three screws to hold it in place, but two of the screws were missing. Haggerty gave the panel a light bump and it swung out of the way on the single screw remaining. He shined a light inside and we saw what might have been Walsh's hideaway. There was a blanket tossed in a corner, a bucket for waste, breadcrumbs, and bottles of water.

"He's a stoic son of a bitch," I told Haggerty. "He put himself in solitary confinement for the past three weeks."

"Did you get the word to Puller?" I asked him.

"Signal is still working on it," he told me. "The invasion's got priority."

I stopped to reflect. The Marines had their hands full. If their landing was contested, Puller would have better things to do than to perform a dragnet for my murder suspect. But if there was a lull in the action, we would want to let him know what's taking place inside his own command.

"I will get Bowker to send a team down here to clean this up," I told Haggerty.

I ventured topside to the bridge wing and observed the last of our Marine complement boarding our transports. The next act would see these barges hauled off by some of the local harbor tugs. That's when Captain Kelly found me and asked for a quick word in his cabin. I followed him aft, removed my hat and entered his domain.

"Chester wants us to hightail it back to the States and pick up more troops for this fight," he told me.

"It'll mean a deadhead run," I reminded him. It's not very efficient to move a troopship without troops, but the expense of running back to the States was nothing compared to what it was costing the country—day by day, hour by hour—

to prosecute this war. Our job was to get the fighting man into the lines, and that's what we would do.

"Chester doesn't give a damn," said the captain. "He just wants Vandegrift reinforced. The Solomons are where we are drawing our line in the sand. Is the ship ready?"

"In all respects," I told him. "But if we can top off bunker fuel at Pearl, I will be happier."

"I will set it up," said the captain and he allowed me to depart to get my teams in place. I tasked Elvis with getting up a head of steam. We raised the anchor and made turns to the northeast and Pearl. My sections didn't have a lot to do now that our guests had departed. But I reminded them we were still a fat target, even way out here. We couldn't forget there was a war on. I thought of Puller and his men hitting those beaches, and I wanted to pour on the speed to fetch our reinforcements and get back here to help.

Time was now the enemy.

Chapter Fourteen
Flight of the Avenger

"How long did it take you to get back to the Golden Gate?" asked Margie.

"Five days to Pearl, two days in port, and another four to 'Frisco. All ahead full," I told her. "We used the time to get the ship cleaned top to bottom, and to keep our gunnery talents pin sharp. I finally graduated to gun-mount captain of Battery Two on the foredeck after the old chief grilled me, so I was pleased about that. And I also had a chance to update my old damage control manual. Plus, we fit switches on the bridge deck that ran servos to the hydraulics, so I could close all the ship's watertight doors and fire screens myself if we were ever hit. I also staged lectures with our deck officers on sluice doors, manhole plates, air ports and windows, submersible pumps and how to seal the ship in event of a gas attack. We talked over the arcana of our sanitary and deck drainage systems, our fire suppression, our after-damage measures. We spent a lot of time on the ideas of counter flooding and shoring."

"How, attorney Pratt, did you ever get the background to discuss all that?" asked Margie. "I mean, I am not surprised. My husband is a brilliant man. But holy cow."

"I had an old professor at Harvard who terrorized us

regularly," I told her. "He used to say, 'You are not a lawyer until you can be a better expert than the experts you've got on the witness stand.' Miserable old son of a bitch. Grimes was his name. But he made us dig into anatomical texts, engineering tomes, technical specs, reams of financial data... you name it. And in any subject area. We had to be right on our game."

"Impressed," she told me, beaming, while she freshened my bourbon.

"Plus, I had some help," I told her. "A young recruit who worked as a mechanical draftsman before the war. He could take schematics and give them a twist and turn them into a three-dimensional drawing I could take to our print shop. Gifted young man. Plus, before Pearl Harbor I sat at the knee of the great William Francis Gibbs, *Bridger's* naval architect. Mr. Gibbs gave me the philosophy behind the ship's systems, which made understanding her fixtures that much easier. That basic grounding helped burnish our technical proficiency."

"Okay. So you had to get to 'Frisco for the quick turn and get back to the Solomons," she said. "Were you dashing up there to get another Marine division?"

"Turns out we were taking the U.S. Army 164th Infantry Regiment, part of the North Dakota national guard. It later became the famous Americal unit. They were available and Nimitz welcomed them right into the all-Marines show on Guadalcanal, which was not going well as we loaded our Army friends and their gear."

"What was happening back there while you're blasting across the Pacific?" Margie asked. I gave her the rundown and it wasn't pretty.

The Japanese had hurled their Navy at us and sank a

half dozen U.S. Navy ships in the battle of Savo Island, which was a bit north and west of Guadalcanal. After that clash, the Navy hierarchy on the scene did not engender any good will when it stood off to the east a hundred miles or so, leaving our Marines abandoned and exposed. Vandegrift and his regimental commanders rationed stores, and our troops were consigned to eating captured Japanese rice balls. The Japanese tried to retake the flight strip—now known as Henderson Field—in late September during the Battle of Bloody Ridge. The Japanese, under the command of Major General Kyotake Kawaguchi, came through the Guadalcanal jungle up from the south and crossed to the east side of the Lunga River. The ridge was the high ground, and the place where Colonel Merritt Edson ordered a defensive emplacement. The ridge held, barely, but it also schooled the Japanese for their next bold attack on the airfield. To achieve that, they needed to move more troops down the Solomons—through a group of islands dubbed 'The Slot'—and they intended to retake Guadalcanal to the last man.

Bridger had made it back across the Pacific carrying our Army infantry. The trip was blessedly uneventful. But the quick dash to San Francisco had given Nate Haggerty a chance to consult with his former, and future, FBI colleagues. He was well versed in the cruel machinations of Giancana and Accardo, but he wanted to know more about Gerry Walsh, our Irish assassin. He managed to pull prints from the Ka-Bar that had been plunged into Bianchi's left eye. They matched prints belonging to a person named Gerry Flynn, who was known to use Walsh as an alias. Flynn was wanted for at least a dozen murders-for-hire from Boston to LA.

"And that's only the ones we know about," Nate told

me during a meeting that included Sal Marchionda, the Golden Gate now in our wake.

"What's his MO?" asked Marchionda, who had picked up a bit of the lawman lingo from his friends in Donahue's office.

"He likes to get close," said Haggerty. "Knife is his preferred instrument. But other than that, a snub-nose right in the gut or the head. He is patient, and he's been known to stalk his targets for weeks."

"Is he a 'collector' as you like to call it?" I asked him.

"The ears? Something he learned in the fight against the Sandino rebels," Haggerty responded. I am instantly intrigued. Puller fought against the Sandinos.

"Which side was he on?" I asked, tongue firmly in cheek.

"He was one of our boys. Second Brigade," said Haggerty. "Can you believe that? He got turfed out for insubordination."

Now I was worried.

"Who had him removed?" I asked, fearing the answer.

"Looks like it was a review board of some kind," he said. I was only slightly relieved.

Could this fellow Flynn be after Puller, too? I filled Haggerty and Marchionda in on Puller's stellar resume. If this Flynn/Walsh character had any personal animosity against the organization that ended his career as a Marine, Puller was most certainly in harm's way. I was chafing at the fact we couldn't seem to get a message to Puller, and it would have been nice to know about Flynn's Sandino history weeks ago. Maybe our NIS could get involved, only now they were a hundred and fifty miles behind us.

As our voyage back to the South Pacific continued, we

had some stiff gales come at us preceding a handful of thousand-mile-long cold fronts, but the ship and her guests seemed to shake them off. We had the usual assortment of fist fights and petty thievery and intestinal upset—but nothing like the wanton serial murder of the last trip. We got ourselves back into the anchorage at Mele Bay in the New Hebrides group. The smaller transports that would take the 164th north had arrived, and we had been ordered to remain on standby should the command wish to take the First Marine Division—now doing its best to blunt the Japanese juggernaut on Guadalcanal—to Australia for vitally needed rest. It was late spring in the Antipodes, and we could feel the heat build as we went about our ship-keeping duties. We hadn't heard from Puller—or the 164th for that matter—until word came in mid-October that the dastardly Walsh *nee'* Flynn, had been caught near Henderson Field. He first came to the attention of one of our petty gangsters from Chicago—DeLuca, I believe—who pointed him out to a Shore Patrol detachment. They'd surrounded him while he slept and clapped him in irons. Flynn was now occupying a makeshift brig on the field, and Vandegrift's JAG, a Major Finch, wanted to know what they should do with him.

Haggerty and I communicated all these details to Captain Kelly during a brief exchange in the captain's cabin. I made the argument we should go up there and get him, bring him back aboard *Bridger*, and hold him in the brig until we could get him back to the States and into the court system. The captain instantly disliked this plan.

"I am not opposed to transporting Flynn back to the States," he said. "But why can't Vandegrift's people get the son of a bitch back to us here?"

"They don't have the air assets we'll need," I stated

with only a vague comprehension of the challenge—hostile aircraft being high on the list. By contrast, the New Hebrides airfield was a critical waystation for all manner of Marine and Navy aircraft—from Dauntless dive bombers, to the much-heralded Hellcats, to the useful but lumbering PBY flying boats used for anti-sub warfare, recon, and rescue.

"Getting in and out should be fairly routine," I told him. "It will be much harder for Vandegrift's Marines to whistle up an airplane with the spotty comms we're experiencing."

The captain scratched his chin and looked at the chicken salad on his gold-rimmed China.

"*Bridger* needs you, Commander Pratt," he said gravely. "You too, Mr. Haggerty. I don't want you two to get up there and get socked in." What he really meant was, '*I* need you.' Having two of his officers absent meant more work for him, but I guarded against this kind of cynicism. He was the captain, and therefore God Almighty.

"Believe me," I told him. "I don't want to ride up there either. But I am the chief JAG officer on *Bridger*, and as such I feel a duty to charge and extradite our fugitive. The Marines have already done the hard part. And they can't spare anybody to bring our suspect back. Besides, except for the wannabe mobsters formerly supping at our table, I'm the only person who can properly identify the bastard." The captain looked at me and I knew this last remark found its intended target.

"Anything for the Marines," he sighed, adding a reflective comment. "I am giving you forty-eight hours. I want you to bring Bryant up to speed. If anything happens to you, he will be our exec." He looked me right in the eyes and I could feel him building some distance between us. The captain and

I had been close, but it felt like he was already getting ready to lose me. Identifying my replacement before I even got up to Guadalcanal put a fine, hard edge on our upcoming field trip.

As always, the ship would come first. If *Bridger* were called away while Haggerty and I were in the Solomons, the captain needed to have his staff in place. And, if that were the case, Haggerty and I would have to catch up with the ship without orders. This could get tricky if our transportation faltered. But the Marines needed to be considered, too, and taking Flynn off the field and getting him properly incarcerated would help meet our obligations to our sister service.

And then there was Puller.

I doubt the colonel even knew he was being stalked. If anything happened to that fine officer, if we didn't at least try to stop it...it would add another worthy soul to the wrongful deaths I'd witnessed. Those pipsqueak Chicago thugs were, after all, still just kids. I couldn't add Puller to that list. This was something Captain Kelly would never be able to understand, and if I tried to explain it to him, he'd have *me* locked up.

The captain dismissed us, and as we left. I could tell we'd upset his sense of order. It gave me pause. But then I thought of finding justice for our murdered souls—and stopping Walsh's unstoppable lust for murder. I was energized. Plus, Haggerty the hunter wanted...no, demanded... his prey.

It was an October evening, and after dinner we went down to Donahue's department to prepare. Haggerty decided on makeshift Marine utilities.

"Good for the rough and tumble," he said.

I decided to wear my summer khakis as a show of rank and service, but I prepared a bag that had a helmet, some web gear for my pistol, a first-aid kit, extra magazines, and a small toilet kit. I decided on my M1 carbine because it was relatively compact, so I also stocked up on fifteen-round box magazines of thirty-millimeter ammo for my rifle of choice. Haggerty selected the latest variant of the Tommy gun, of course, which meant he could sling it over a shoulder. He grabbed four pairs of handcuffs, some chain leg manacles, and some rags... "to gag that fucker if we have to."

I had Marchionda scare up Bryant and Simms, and we had a late evening meeting in my cabin to go over schedules, damage control priorities, the vital boiler room protocols, and Captain Kelly's typical preferences should the ship be called to action without me. I paid particular attention to working with the bosuns on uphauling the anchor and getting things squared away for sea if duty called. We were not overly sentimental during this talk. I was coming back, I told them. But if they needed to depart quickly, do so without hesitation and we'd see them by and by. I spent the rest of the evening putting letters together in case I found an outbound post office at the airfield, and I finally hit the rack at around midnight.

I passed the night fitfully, wondering if leaving the ship was the right thing to do. And then I thought of those as yet un-murdered kids—and Chesty Puller—and I was compelled to get Flynn locked up as soon as I could. I was grateful to Puller and his crew for catching the bastard, so now I needed to do my part and get Flynn into our brig.

Haggerty and I had requested the gig for sunup, and we'd agreed to meet for breakfast early. We didn't know when we might eat again so we stoked up on pancakes, link sausages, and scrambled eggs. Marchionda was at the helm of the gig when we motored into shore with the sun just touching the eastern horizon, etching the willowy clouds in a fiery light. I thought I saw Sal get a little misty as we broke up the team. I have to say I missed our artful dodger as he putted away to reboard *Bridger*.

We commandeered a jeep to take us up to the airfield, and headed for the biggest building we could find that suggested it might be serving as an HQ. We entered, doffed our hats, and asked to speak to the man in charge. We were soon introduced to a lieutenant commander named Richards who referred to himself as "the air boss."

I immediately assumed we were about to enter a power struggle with this gentleman and I was not incorrect.

"I am the chief JAG officer in *Bridger* and we need to get to Henderson Field to execute an arrest warrant and bring a prisoner back to the ship," I told him. It seemed like a straightforward request.

"Do you people know anything about naval aviation in general and Guadalcanal in particular?" Richards stated to his superior officers, trying Haggerty's patience. Richards clearly thought he was dealing with a couple of lesser beings and his tone of condescension went beyond the merely irksome.

"Why don't you explain it for us, Mr. Richards?" Haggerty asked in that 'don't fuck with me tone' that only works with the ordinary seamen. We were not starting out on the right foot.

"Henderson Field is under frequent naval shelling and air bombardment. Only thing I have going up there are single-seat Corsairs, and tandem Dauntless dive bombers. And they're sometimes waved off if we have some action." Haggerty had studied the challenge, it seemed, because he offered a solution I hadn't considered.

Ship of Tears

"We need a TBM Avenger," he said. "Three seats up top, plus one on a fold-out in the crew compartment aft. If it's got a light bomb load, it can carry four, including the pilot."

"Where's the prisoner going to sit?" Richards asked. "He could decide to mess with the control cables or the fuel lines, and I lose an airplane and one of Uncle Sam's pilots."

"The prisoner will be in leg manacles with his hands handcuffed behind his back. He will have his legs bound so he can't kick anything, and he'll be blindfolded. Plus, I will have a bag over his head and a gun aimed at his balls," said Haggerty. "If he fucks with the airplane, I'll just shoot him in the head and chuck him overboard."

I could tell Richards was running out of arguments.

"I have an Avenger going up in an hour, but we're on a tight schedule" he confessed. "The bomb-bay will be carrying mail and Lucky Strikes. But I will need my guy to refuel and get the hell out of there. And if the coast watchers in the Slot report any inbound 'nips', I will have to turn you guys around."

The idea of getting up to Guadalcanal and back was suddenly looking like a major military operation. Richards pointed vaguely toward the airfield, asked us to check in with a crew chief named Olmstead, and returned to his many and varied frustrations.

Haggerty and I found Olmstead and reported Richards's directive to take us to Guadalcanal. He asked us to cool our heels while they loaded the bomb bay with cigarettes, which the more enlightened troops called 'coffin nails'. The Avenger fighter bomber was a very large aircraft—big enough to carry a single torpedo, or one two-thousand-pound gravity bomb. Alternatively, it could load smaller packages of four, five-hundred pounders as needs changed. The war loads were carried in the belly, which closed up with two clam-shell doors. The airplane also had twin .50-caliber machine guns in the wings, an aft-facing ball turret gun on top with a .50-caliber off-center machine gun, and another man-operated thirty-millimeter machine gun in the belly facing aft to cover the Avenger's ventral side.

Soon, we were each kitted out with a parachute, a flotation vest, and a one-man life raft. All we needed was a plane and a pilot, when a frightfully young lieutenant named Rogers showed up. It seemed the air boss had already filled him in on the variation we represented to his morning mission.

"We're bringing back a prisoner?" he asked. "Seems do-able." Rogers couldn't be more than twenty years old. He hadn't lost that youthful deference towards one's elders. He wanted to help us.

"I guess it'll be more interesting than a dog fight...but we won't know what the Japs will throw at us until we get a little closer. You gentlemen ever experience aerial combat?"

Haggerty and I looked at our shoes and answered with a mumbled "no." Already Rogers had bettered us, and he went on to demonstrate a prowess with his flying machine that was impressive for such a young man. Turns out he was a student of the Avenger.

"We can handle the load," he said. "But it's going to be mighty uncomfortable down in the crew compartment below the gun turret. We might get into some heavy maneuvering." Haggerty repeats: our prisoner will be chained and gagged.

"And I'll be sitting on him," he adds.

"Should work," said Rogers. "Commander, you will get up on the wing on the starboard side and take your seat in the middle. There's a way to get aft if you need to by crawling on your belly under the gun turret. If I ask you to go back there, you'll need to take off your parachute because it won't fit through. This should be a milk run, so I won't ask you to do anything except report bogies or friendly traffic. Mr. Haggerty, you ever fired a .50-caliber machinegun out of the rear turret of an Avenger?" I can tell young Rogers had a flare for the rhetorical.

"Not even in my dreams," said Haggerty.

"As soon as the commander gets settled, you and I will go over it," said Rogers. "Not that complicated. But if you're sitting there, you might as well know how to use it."

Olmstead and his men had finished loading the bomb bay and had closed the doors.

Young lieutenant Rogers was in a huddle with Haggerty and I eavesdropped.

"This is a Grumman 150SE ball turret. It's got a single .50 with a reflector sight. I've already pre-flighted the fuses, the circuit breakers, the electrical lines and the cannon plugs. I've loaded a 400-round ammo can, but you'll need to charge it in the air," Rogers said.

Haggerty asked the obvious question. "How do I keep from shooting the tail off?"

"The turret has a fire interrupter that shuts down the gun if the muzzle sweeps anywhere near it," said Rogers. "I've pre-flighted that, too." He went on to describe the intricate minuet required to get into the turret, facing forward, with a twist to an aft-facing position, without knocking into anything vital. The occupant then unstowed and secured an armor plate to sit on, and got acquainted with the gun's charging crank, slewing levers and sight picture. Rogers's final instructions were communicated from a step ladder outside the airplane with the turret's emergency egress lowered. He's got Haggerty belted in with the final comment, "You'll want it tight."

I watched Rogers perform his walk-around, sump the fuel tanks to guard against the intrusion of rainwater and check the oil on the massive Wright Twin Cyclone. He directed a line crewman to walk the prop through a couple of turns to "pre-lube the tappets," then climbed up the plane's flanks using built-in foot-and toe-holds. At last, he wound up a pre-start system that began to turn over the big fourteen-cylinder radial. A belch of oily smoke and the prop was spinning, with the airplane shaking like a wet retriever.

Rogers asked the tower for permission to taxi, and we were soon number one for takeoff. The morning sun was climbing over the island of Espiritu Santu as Rogers jammed the throttle forward and the big Wright engine came alive. The airplane's tail flew up on her *empennage*, a beautiful French term dating from the days of Bleriot, first pilot to cross the English Channel. The big bird screamed down the runway on her two main gear and I could feel her lighten and finally levitate. Rogers cranked in a wind correction and we were climbing at a yaw relative to the runway centerline, owing to the crosswind. The details of our terrestrial life—houses, farms, hamlets—all receded, to be replaced by green jungle mountains with rocky peaks. Up to that time, I had only flown in a Curtiss Robin off the little grass field in Hammondsport, so our speed and angle of climb was a bit surprising. I reflected on how our sense of scale and perspective expanded when we were lucky enough to come up here to see this side of the sky.

Rogers came on the interphone: "Six-hundred miles to Guadalcanal and we're just shy of two-hundred knots. So, it'll be about three and a half hours over the water, then a climb over Guadalcanal's eastern side before we make the run into Henderson. It will be a combat arrival—a tight, descending turn from around eight thousand feet. Ground control reports no bogies, but that could change. Mr. Haggerty, we'll want to charge your weapon and fire a couple of test rounds to make sure the belt feed is correct. I will walk you through that."

"Aye aye," said Haggerty, who may not have liked flying backwards, but certainly enjoyed shooting big guns. Our pilot explained the process of cranking a cable-mounted charging lever to feed the belt's first round into the chamber. The action snapped closed and Rogers describes how to use the foot pedals and the pistol-grip slewing lever to rotate and elevate the turret. He asked Haggerty to make sure there were no friendly aircraft at his ten o'clock position (looking aft) and to fire off a quick burst to make sure everything was okay. Haggerty complied and we got a little 'whoop' of delight through the interphone. I spent the next two hours enjoying the scenery. The sun was turning the sea into a shimmering silver, and I knew those little waves down there were big enough to give *Bridger* a snappy roll. The cumulus clouds scudded past below our wings and the air on top of this cloud deck was glass smooth. Once in a while, we blasted through a white wisp and the airplane offered a solid bounce in response. I spent my time looking at a big chart the aviators called a "sectional." It had outcroppings here and there marked in brown, and I could apply the correct island names based on the shape of the topography—Vanikoru off to my right and Tapui off to my left.

They had coral reefs stretching around parts of their perimeter, with a green opalescent water inside them. I could only imagine the sea life that could be found around these little oases, and I vowed to return to this place when we'd won the war. At this point in the fall of 1942, especially after Pearl Harbor, we were definitely losing...but we dined at the table of hope.

At last, the rocky eastern shore of Guadalcanal came into view, and it was hard to believe the fantastic struggle both sides were waging to control this piece of geography. Most of the fighting was taking place in the northwest corner, where the airfield was located, plus the now-secured islands of Tulagi and Florida. I was contemplating an unmolested arrival, a refuel, a turn around, and a leisurely flight back to all the comforts *Bridger* could bestow. Just then, something white, hot and moving fast streaked by my sliding hatch.

"Fuck," said Rogers. "Tracers. Haggerty you see anything back there?"

"Now I do," he told us. "Three planes. Looks like two behind are chasing the one in front. Coming up fast." There was another burst of fire and Rogers didn't spend time chitchatting. He firewalled the throttle and started a climb.

"Get your oxygen masks on," he said in an urgent tone that suggested we might want to comply. "We have to get on top. I will tell you when to turn on your oxygen regulator." It occurred to me we should have briefed this chore from the safety of the ground, but there was no time for second guessing. I watched the altimeter and we were above twelve-thousand feet when Rogers told us to move our oxygen delivery system to the "on" position. Haggerty chimed in with an aye-aye, and, perennially the middleman, I was feeling useless.

"They're climbing up to us," he reported. "There's a meatball on the side of one of them. He's a Jap, and he's getting chased by two Corsairs."

"Okay," said Rogers. "Chance-Vought Corsair. Blue. Gull wings. Single seat. Do not, and I repeat do not, fire on the Corsairs. Highly embarrassing. You are cleared hot on the Zero. Make damn sure before you pull the trigger."

"Roger," said Haggerty, and then our adolescent pilot threw me a curve.

"Mr. Pratt," he said. "I think we need to use our ventral gun, too. Not as complicated as the turret gun. Ammo magazine is already in place hanging on the wall. Just pull the charging lever and pull the trigger. It's down in the aft crew compartment. It's also got an automatic gun camera, so you'll have pictures to show the grand kids. Just unplug your interphone and your oxygen. You can plug them back in when you get down there."

I was pressed into my seat by the G loads, but I got unbuckled, out of my parachute, and down out of my perch, inching on my belly past the ball turret. I got positioned pretty much unscathed in the crew compartment. I had bumped my head a couple of times, of course, and I could taste blood in the corner of my mouth after I bit a lip. I saw the machine gun and I also saw I'd have to get down on the floor in order to sight it in. The gun had a paltry range of motion, essentially down and aft. The right-left sweep of the muzzle was highly limited. My cooperative Zero would have to fly right into my sight picture so I could shoot him down at my convenience. I knew it wasn't going to be that easy. My heart was racing as I plugged my interphone back into the two jacks I found to my right and found the oxygen port. Rogers was jinking the plane around, and at one point I was lifted off the floor when he performed what I can only describe as some kind of barnstormer wingover. I could hear Haggerty making a contribution to our dog fight, and I was eager to help, but all I saw through my ventral viewing port was blue sky interrupted by puffs of cumulus then green mountain jungle in the near distance. I had to concentrate on my job, and, at last, I saw a plane come into my sight picture. It was one of the Corsairs, and he was firing on the Zero who was firing on us. They were too low for Haggerty to depress his turret. But then I saw the Zero come up into my firing range and he just as quickly disappeared overhead, followed by our two Corsairs. I told myself better to fire late and make a good ID than panic and knock one of these big Marine fighters out of the sky. It would be hard to explain. Still, I could hear Haggerty's gun working the problem, and I could hear Rogers and the Corsair pilots negotiating firing sequence and positioning to avoid a mid-air collision or a friendly-fire incident. Our adversary was stubborn, however, and he was spending time trying to knock down the less nimble Avenger, with us in it. I heard Haggerty over the interphone.

"Jonas, he's coming down into your field of fire." And just as quickly I saw the clearly marked Japanese adversary passing down and right. I led the target a few inches ahead of the cockpit and pulled the trigger. The machine gun bucked in my hands and recoiled into my forehead, causing more blood. I saw my war shots enter the Zero's cockpit, with a spray of blood over the inside of the cockpit hatch. I was pretty sure I'd killed the man when his airplane made a slow turn, down and away, followed by the Corsairs. I watched them follow our adversary down and pump a few more bullets into him. I couldn't see anything more through my limited view port, but I could hear the pilots cheer each other on.

And then... "Splash one," according to one of the Corsair pilots. No one saw my bullets enter the cockpit of the enemy plane. It happened too low for Haggerty to register what was happening, and Rogers had his eyes forward. Not that I care, but there was gun camera footage of our encounter and I decided to let the film speak for itself. It would be tawdry and low to take credit for a kill the Corsair pilots deserved more than I did. I asked Rogers for permission to come back up to my position and he told me to "make it so, Commander." Haggerty wanted to know if I "got in any licks" and I told him I thought so.

"Let's wait to see the film," I told him and Rogers was wondering if I'd gotten myself buckled in. I got that finished when he announced we were right over Henderson and we'd been cleared to land. He lowered the landing gear and put in a few degrees of flaps ("To help slow us down," he told me) and all I could see was the green jungle and brown earth fill our field of view and come straight at us as we descended. We made at least three spiraling left-hand turns right over the center of the field, and Rogers let me know this maneuver reduced the need for a long straight-in approach that might take us over enemy positions. I saw the arrival end of the field and we were still flying fast in a left bank angle. Rogers put in more flaps and then executed what he called a "forward slip" ...when the plane flies forward with a wing down and the nose to the right of the runway centerline. He straightened us out when we were thirty feet up and we were down on the rough gravel field in a few seconds.

"Welcome to Guadalcanal," Rogers stated over the interphone. "And welcome to hell on earth."

Chapter Fifteen
Perfect Timing

"So did you really shoot down that Zero?" asked my Margie. She was in our old sleigh bed and she was reading my manuscript with her knees up and her glasses on her nose. She was wearing that dainty pajama top she knows I find devastating, and I am once again delighted I have my first and best critic perusing my tale with her critical eye.

"Well, we almost didn't have any gun camera footage, because we almost didn't have our Avenger following that ride into Henderson Field. We got ourselves and our duffels out of the airplane, and the bomb bay relieved of its nicotine cargo, when we started to take incoming fire from a Japanese naval bombardment. There were explosions on the field and Rogers accepted a rapid re-fueling and made a hasty departure, alone. He got the plane back to New Hebrides and my gun camera showed my contribution to downing that plane. So, we all took a little credit. But those boys in the Corsairs deserved the kill."

"Oh brother," she said. "So now you and Haggerty are stuck on Guadalcanal with 'incoming,' as they say in the movies."

"I fully expected the prisoner Flynn to be ready and waiting by the side of the runway," I told her. "But not only was he not ready, he was in a hastily arranged log box at Puller's battalion command post a half mile from the field."

"Best laid plans," said Margie.

"I have studied the Battle of Guadalcanal. I can tell you with confidence our timing was perfect."

"You mean perfectly awful," she said.

"Precisely my love," I told her. And then I looked at her gravely and stated: "Your Jonas very nearly remained on Guadalcanal for all eternity." I left her hanging right there. It would take a few days for me to sketch out what Haggerty and I had just stepped into.

We watched Rogers and our Avenger spew dust and gravel as our young pilot firewalled the big Wright radial. He took the active runway and beat it out of there just as more enemy gunfire raked the field. Haggerty and I grabbed our bags and ran toward a ditch near a fuel tank, then thought better of that plan and found shelter near a mess tent. We weren't sure where they were coming from, but the ground shook and clouds of dust and grit were hurled into the air. Our ears were filled with an incessant ringing from the pressure bursts. And the first of many horrors visited my eyes when I saw a human leg wearing green pants, leggings, and a combat boot fly through the air. Bombs were finding the fuel dump where we'd sheltered just a few seconds earlier, and sheets of flame found tents, planes, jeeps, trucks—all the implements of war, including young Marines who lived their last as they were set ablaze. I was not prepared to die and yet I knew I would have to get ready for it. I said goodbye to my kids, thanked God for my many blessings, and gritted my chattering teeth. I was dumbstruck at the destructive force that suddenly surrounded us, when a sergeant plunked down next to us and screamed in my ear:

"Fuck you doing? You're the exec off *Bridger*. You don't need to be here!"

His observation was woefully obvious, but it was not the time to explain my obligation to the military justice system, and our five murdered Marines. Believe me I was debating the wisdom of being at this time and place, and I told myself I needed to one day adopt Captain Kelly's talent for common sense. It was not the first time, nor the last, I would second-guess one of my decisions in this war. But right then, flailing myself for this failure of judgment was an utterly useless exercise. I couldn't know the Japanese Navy would decide to rake Henderson Field with deadly gunfire at nearly the instant of our arrival.

"Where's Puller?" I screamed at him as more bombs streaked into the field from offshore.

"Southwest perimeter," he told me. "Big shit show coming. This shelling might be the first part of it. I'll see if I can get you down there. Anything to get the fuck off this airfield."

I learned his name was Baldridge and his friends call him "Baldy." He was from Salamanca, New York, where he worked as a truck mechanic. Later, when the shelling petered out a bit, and we only had four-or five-thousand Japanese soldiers in front of us from the vaunted Sendai Division, Baldy explained he'd joined the Marines in '38 to provide for his family. But he hadn't seen his wife and two boys in two years and he wouldn't blame Mrs. Baldridge if she'd sought comfort elsewhere.

"Because let me tell you, Commander. This shit is fucking insane."

When we got away from the field, we stopped for a minute to catch our breath and Baldy gave us a sip from his canteen.

"No telling what kind of fucking pestilence you're getting but have at it. I've got malaria but so does everyone else and nobody gives a shit. And did I tell you we're also starving? Oh, and we're low on ammo. Fucking Navy left us here to rot, no disrespect."

We used the interlude to take out our helmets, our web gear, pistols, holsters, and my M1 carbine. Haggerty was similarly equipped as he worked his Tommy gun magazines into his web belt. I had blood on my face from my tangle with the Avenger's belly gun, and I already had holes in the knees of my khakis. It looked like Haggerty's choice to dress like a Marine made better sense, but he had the grace to remain silent on the obvious. I had to congratulate myself on my choice of footwear—heavy lace-up, ankle high shoes—the only sensible choice I'd made that day. Haggerty and Baldy were now a bit unsettled by the blood on my face and Haggerty produced some gauze and alcohol swabs. We were out of the direct line of falling explosives, but we could hear shouts from the fire brigades. There were secondary explosions, and we started running toward a crater when a line of exploding shells started walking in our direction, each concussion short, sharp and pummeling. The last shell stopped fifty feet in front of us, and I could feel my insides shake and vibrate from the blast wave. There was a fear like a caged animal inside me. I knew I was going to die, and then the threat ended and we moved on. How many times can the human body withstand so many near-death experiences? The surge of stress and adrenaline was an hourly occurrence for these Marines.

"We've been under naval bombardment and night aerial bombing raids since we got here," said Baldy. "But this is a bit more intense. I think we're in for it. Let me take you up to Colonel Puller's command post. We call it a CP."

By my reckoning, we were moving southwest through a tall stand of jungle that came out on a meadow of head-high grass. There was a dirt road that tracked deeper inland to the west and finished in a trail.

Baldridge took us from the trail into a trench that appeared to be part of a large fortification. We soon took a right-hand turn into another, perpendicular trench and finally came to a log and sandbag bunker, Puller's command post. It was surrounded by Marine's occupying deep fighting holes looking out on double strands of barbed concertina wire. Baldridge raised a flap and we entered the hot, dirty, choking domain of Lieutenant Colonel Lewis Puller, "Chesty" to his beloved troops. He looked up from a wad of dispatches on an overturned ammo crate serving as a desk. He was wearing plain utilities, with a lieutenant colonel's insignia in a lapel. His helmet was at his feet, and he was drinking a cup of tea with his reading glasses perched on his nose.

"Delightful!" he told the crowded room. "Men, the executive officer of *Bridger* has decided to pay us a visit on this of all days. Commander Jonas Pratt! And his faithful security chief Lieutenant-Commander Nathan Haggerty!" Everyone stood at attention and a young Rifleman asked me if I would like some tea. I was not opposed, and I took a seat on an adjoining ammo box.

"Happened to your face, Jonas?" Puller asked me, and I described my tangle with the machine gun in the belly of our Avenger.

"Rookie mistake," he said, making me feel minuscule, but I was sure he wasn't trying to be insulting. I was a rookie. Make no mistake. Haggerty rose to my defense.

Ship of Tears

"I think the commander got in his licks," he said.

"I suppose you gentleman are here to take Walsh back to *Bridger*," Puller said. That was indeed our objective, I told him.

"We would be very happy to accommodate that," said Puller. "But the tactical picture has changed, which will mean a delay in your departure. First, the naval bombardment you just experienced is only a prelude. Our airplanes, our fuel, our ammo dumps, our food supply, our people...they are all under the immediate threat of total annihilation. I also have at least four-thousand Japanese soldiers coming this way, according to my company-sized patrols skirmishing just west of here. Sons of bitches want to take the field back, but they will have to go through us."

Puller's reputation as a warrior was now on full display, and seeing as there wasn't a damn thing I could do, I listened carefully as we spent the next hour and a half getting a briefing and a tour of his perimeter. He started with a map. Puller told us the battle for the island was concentrated in the northwest around the airfield, and offshore near Savo Island, where naval engagements had cost both sides dearly. There were so many sunk warships north of Guadalcanal that wags had started calling it "Iron-bottom Sound." There had been three attempts by the Japanese to overrun the field. The first, to the northeast of Henderson Field, was now called the Battle of the Tenaru River, which had taken place in September. The Japanese were repulsed, but not without significant Marine casualties.

"To our right is Edson's ridge," said Puller. "Second attempt to take the airfield was through there in September. Colonel Merritt Edson's boys of the First Marine Raider Battalion stopped them. It was The Little Big Horn, let me tell you. If the Japs had taken that piece of dirt, it would have been all over." He stopped to fill a pipe and light it with his Zippo.

"We seem to be at the start of their third attempt," said Puller, drawing on his beloved tobacco. "They've been massing on the west side of the Matinikau River, and we think they'll once again try to sweep south, cross the Lunga, and hit our underbelly. Right where we're standing."

And let me emphasize, it's right where *I* was standing. I was now sharing the full gravity and peril felt by these Marines. I knew I didn't belong here...but I was here. And if I was going to be here, I had to decide. Do I add my own gun to this fight, or do I find a place to cower back up with Vandegrift and Rupertus in their headquarters? And just what kind of protection would that offer? This rough sketch forming in my mind later tracked with the dangers of my new reality.

Puller described the work his Marines had accomplished to harden defenses. His men had been clearing vegetation to create interlocking fire lanes for his machine gunners. The Marines were digging deep fighting holes and stringing double barbed-wire barriers. They'd been placing tin cans filled with pebbles as alarms to catch infiltrators. The machine gun emplacements and the firing pits had been getting reinforced with big coconut logs and sandbags—with heavy log roofs—to deal with indirect mortar fire or naval bombardment.

"This jungle down here is helping us," said Puller. "Absolute hell to cut through. When they get up to us, they'll be tired, hungry—and ready to die for the Emperor. Right now, we've got the Seventh Marines taking on the lion's share of the First Division's responsibilities. Elements of the third battalion are on the ridge, parts of the second are on the left flank and we're right in the center. We've got the eleventh marines providing artillery support, as well as the First Marine Raider battalion. Problem is, we're occupying a soft spot. It's six hundred yards from flank to flank and our ranks are a little thin. So, gentlemen, I see you've brought your personal weapons. I can't order you, but we could certainly use two more guns in this fight."

I was edging around a growing instinct square in my gut called survival. There was a battle brewing. The airplanes needed to haul me and Haggerty out of here with our prisoner were either destroyed on the ground or safely secured where we'd just come from. Everyone around Henderson Field was in the thick of it, and Puller had just called on me, another sworn American service member, to join the fight. I was a relatively young man, and I was facing death...but I was composed. I focused on living, and that meant paying close attention. I was in class, and I needed to sit up straight. And did I mention I was scared shitless?

Puller and his executive officer, a young lieutenant named Seamus from Youngstown, Ohio, pulled back the flap and we scrambled out of the CP into a gentle rain. Baldy was right there, unfailing, and handed us a couple of ponchos. I would need to ask Puller who Baldy had been assigned to. Seemed like he'd been assigned to us. Puller walked quickly and it took some concentration to move at his pace.

"Took us a good two weeks to build these works," he told us. "But we've got the Fifth Marines under Edson and the First Marines under Cates worrying about the perimeter north of the field. We're on our own down here and that's got us scrambling. The Japanese seem fixated on this spot. So, this is where we will prosecute the fight."

He took us out to a high ground that overlooked one of his "firing lanes," having studied the handful of logical routes the enemy would have to take toward Puller's position. His men were still cutting and placing timbers, and he had sandbag brigades filling and moving these critical elements into position on top of the log roofs and in the chinks below the shooting ports. All along the line Puller stopped and talked to his men and offered psychological support—perhaps more than timber and sandbags, the true underpinning in the defense of Henderson Field.

"How you doing, Lou?" he asked a young Rifleman, then, turning to me to offer an aside... "another Virginia boy like me."

"Ready to kick some ass, Colonel," said the boy, whose helmet wobbled on his red-haired teenage head. Puller got down on one knee and looked into Lou's fighting hole.

"They're going to throw some more artillery at us a little later, son," he said. "So, I want you to stay low, cover your ears and get set for a charge against that wire right there. The wire will slow them down, Lou. We've talked about shot placement. That's what will win this fight. Don't fire over their heads. You're lucky you drew that Springfield. Armor-piercing rounds and bolt-action so you can slow yourself down and shoot to kill. Aim for the center mass. Don't just wing 'em."

"Right Colonel," said young Lou.

"Get some chow and take a good crap now, son," he said. "Attend to business while it's clear." All along the line behind the wire, Puller stopped to offer advice and encouragement.

"Stanley, your ammo box is set up for a left-hand feed, but you're feeding from the right. Get that fixed."

"Art, I like the way you've got the top of this hole covered. But make sure you can get out of the fucker if we need to fall back."

"Mike, tell the rest of your fire team to focus their attention on that little gully. That's how the bastards will try to take this position."

Soon there was a small cluster of Marines gathered around Colonel Puller.

"You men remember this: Your adversary will be coming into our fortifications tired, hungry, lost, pissed off at his non-coms and his leadership. To shoot his rifle, he'll have to stop, take a breath and aim. If he's charging with his bayonet, even better. He'll have to come up this little rise and he and his buddies will be plum tuckered. You have the advantage in this fight." He thus steeled his troops for the coming fray, and for this I could say the American taxpayer was getting its money's worth out of the likes of Colonel Lewis B. Puller.

His senior enlisted and his young officers were watching and listening as the old man reached down and touched the youngsters, and he later told me he hoped this personal inspiration would spread forth and help advance the cause. Puller took us back fifty yards to the trench Baldy brought us in on. It ran the entire length of the six-hundred-yard breadth of his responsibility, connecting to his brother battalions to the right and left.

"This way we can get messages up and down the line if our telephone lines get cut," he said. It was deep and it zigged and zagged in spots, an attempt to create a natural split in the enemy formations if they should get this far. Puller had set up a couple of cook tents back here under a thick log and sandbag cover, plus a few latrines where

Marines in his battalion could perform their necessities sitting over a log with their buddies, cheek to cheek.

"Seen worse," he told me by way of encouragement, as he handed me a half roll of toilet paper. "We ration these, so use sparingly."

He took us back up to the line. He wanted to show us a typical machine gun nest. He had eighteen of them along his defensive line and they were staffed by experienced sergeants... "with a few newbies so we can educate the young 'uns."

He had pulled together Browning crew-served .50-caliber machine guns, older water-cooled Browning heavies in thirty-millimeter, lightweight Brownings, also in thirty, and even a few .50s he'd pulled out of wrecked aircraft and re-purposed on mounts his boys had welded up.

"I've got the .50s and the Browning heavies anchoring the ends of the line to drive the enemy toward the center firing lanes. We'll hold our fire until they're right up to us. Discipline, Commander. And physical fitness. That's how we'll win." His optimism was infectious, and I could see how his men would do anything to serve this compact, barrel-chested titan.

"Where do you want to put us?" asked Haggerty with his Tommy gun slung over his shoulder.

"Giving you a choice," said Puller. "You can go back to the airfield and bivouac with Rupertus, General Vandegrift's deputy commander. He knows you're on the property. The shelling will be just as bad back there, I have to warn you. Or you can hunker down in the CP with Seamus and me while we take in information and direct fire. Or you can go with Baldy here and take over a couple of fighting holes he and his buddies dug for you this morning." So now I knew where

Baldridge had come from. He was our babysitter, and I didn't mind one bit.

"If you guys want to stick it out with us, I'll put Nate with Baldy, and Mr. Pratt you can go with my friend Smitty here," said Puller. "You two will be next door neighbors and will offer fire support."

A young Marine stepped up to me to offer a salute and extend a hand.

"How do you do, sir," he said. "Reggie Smith. My friends call me Smitty." Smitty was tall, lean, and had a strength in his grip that I found reassuring. I learned my young friend hailed from Ogallala, Nebraska, way out on the western periphery of the state west of North Platte. He'd played on the defensive line for the Ogallala Indians, and he had a football scholarship to the University of Nebraska waiting for him when he got home. He was wearing a pair of round spectacles with the temples tied together in the back so he wouldn't lose them. The bridge of the nose had been taped over, and the lenses were dirty. But Smitty's smile added a brightness to the fevered preparations all along the battlefront where Puller would make his stand.

"I've got a good spot for us, and Baldy and me...we've been making it hell for stout."

"Hate for Baldy's and Smitty's hard work to go for naught," I told Puller. "What do you think Nate? Couple of fighting holes?"

"Two more guns in the fight," he repeated Puller's line. I offered a nod in agreement and hoped it wasn't coming off as a little anemic. But how could I let kids like Lou and Smitty fight without putting my own shoulder to the wheel?

"Colonel, when we have a few minutes, I want to get back to talk to your machine gunners, in case I need to shoot one," I told him. "And I'd like another crack at that BAR."

"Commander, I admire your spirit. Good to have everyone proficient with all our guns. Smitty will make the introductions," said Puller. "I see you guys are equipped okay. You guys ever get 'buck fever?'"

I'm a Steuben County deer hunter, so I know the syndrome. You either freeze or misfire when your season's big buck comes into your sight picture.

"Know it well," I told him in all candor.

"So, you know what I'm talking about," said Puller. "The noise will be godawful, and close, and your enemy will be charging up the rise, screaming. Your number one job is, stay calm, and number two, stay calm. Number three? Pick your target, shoot, pick another one, shoot. Breathe. Keep breathing. And keep your weapons clean. No jams. Let me see that rifle, Commander." Puller reached for my M1 carbine. In a show of etiquette, I removed the magazine and opened the action. Smitty picked up my ejected round and gave it back to me. Puller peered into the chamber and stated: "Extractor needs oiling. Smitty will get you what you need." He performed the same inspection with Haggerty's Thompson and he was not happy with a hint of corrosion around the magazine release.

"Baldy will help you get set up with ammo," he told us. "And get your hands on one of our Aught-Threes just to familiarize yourself. Love that rifle. None of that semi-auto folderol." It was getting to be dusk when I remembered our primary mission.

"Colonel Puller, do we have time to interview our prisoner?" I asked.

"I've got him tucked away behind the CP," he told me. "Let's go have a chat."

Ship of Tears

Haggerty stopped us and looked at Puller: "When we were in 'Frisco on the last run home to fetch the 164th I checked with some friends at the local office of the FBI. The prints on the knife that skewered Bianchi belonged to a Gerry Flynn. Walsh is an alias. He's got a few arrests on his rap sheet for assault, kidnapping and attempted murder. Back channel: He's an enforcer for the Chicago outfit."

I take over. "Colonel Puller, this guy was in the Marines. Served in Nicaragua against the Sandino rebels, about the same time you were there. He was given a dishonorable discharge. He was collecting ears off dead *federales*. Do you know this character?"

"Seems I do," said Puller. "He came before a review board I put together. We got rid of him."

"Colonel," said Haggerty. "This guy was trying to get our little thieves. But he may have been trying to get you, too. He's not just a serial killer. He's an assassin. And he's carrying a grudge."

"That would explain what we found in his bag," said Puller. "Let me show you." We went back into his command post, lit by candlelight. There were coded Morse signals darting through the air, broken up by voice traffic. "Baker One" was trying to get ahold of "Charlie Actual." Puller explained the messages pertained to his forward patrols trying to make contact with the enemy "to gauge his intentions." He asked his exec "Where did we put Walsh's stuff?" And Seamus found a small duffel thrown in a corner.

"Flynn. I remember him now," said Puller. "A souvenir hunter. We've got no use for people like that. Killing the enemy is a solemn business." He pulled out a piece of wire thick as a coat hanger that had been bent into a circle. Embedded through the wire were dozens of human ears, some black with age and rot, some more recent with flesh and blood.

The exec piped up: "We caught him after the action on Edson Ridge. He was walking among the enemy KIA with his Ka-Bar, cutting off ears. Crazy fucker. We arrested his ass and put him in the stockade. One of the guys off *Bridger*, DeLuca I think...or it might have been DiGenova...ID'd him."

"How is he enjoying his captivity?" I asked.

"He's pretty pissed off," said the exec. "Wants us to let him go so he can kill nips. We've got him in handcuffs, leg irons, and a choke chain. Takes four guys to feed him and take him to the latrine." I immediately wondered how we were going to get him to remain calm in the crew compartment of the Avenger, if we could ever get Rogers to come back and pick us up. Maybe Vandegrift's medical department could get us a tranquilizer.

"Let's see what he has to say for himself," I suggested, and Seamus shook his head. "Not looking forward to this."

Chapter Sixteen
Battle Cry of the Sendai

I've been going into the office early so I can work on my manuscript before my appointments. I am gripped by the sheer momentum of those days. I've got in my hands the Asiatic-Pacific campaign medal Puller gave me to commemorate my presence on Guadalcanal. My biggest contribution—aside from at least twenty-two confirmed enemy killed—was my own survival. But I can tell you flatly that other individuals—Haggerty, Baldridge, Smitty, even Puller—were doing their best to make sure I didn't get hurt. I was demonstrating something that was not quite cowardice, but certainly a distinct absence of bravado. I don't know what possessed me to choose a fighting hole with Smitty over what later turned out to be Rupertus's palatial bunker. I think it was Puller. He made you believe in the mission, the coming fight, and most of all... yourself. His knowledge, his sense of caring, his commitment to keeping his people safe, made you want to stand shoulder with that man and his young Marines. Still, I learned that confidence in combat was an utterly useless commodity, given the random lightning bolt that could come out of nowhere and kill you at any second. I will amend that: some confidence didn't hurt, but the outcome depended fifty-fifty between concerted plan and blind chance.

Besides, Haggerty and I thought we could be of use. Another pair of hands, another set of eyes, two more guns—to be thrown against the hordes we knew were coming. We couldn't walk away from those young men. Delusional hubris? No doubt. I wasn't trained for what was to come. I had to operate on an instinct so raw I almost ceased to function. But when the time came, I somehow did one thing right, and then another, and another after that...and in time, dawn broke and, much to my surprise, I was still alive.

As it had been from the beginning, our immediate problem was Flynn—the former Walsh and the present conundrum. Puller walked us over to the stockade he'd had his men fashion out of logs and barbed wire. The round enclosure was behind Puller's CP, and down a short grade. It was open to the sky and I considered for a moment any aerial bursts from the Japanese Naval bombardment might expose the prisoner to danger. He was being held on suspicion, criminal matters that demanded a presumption of innocence. Putting him in harm's way would cause a mistrial in any other setting. Proper adjudication of this killer's wanton crimes was still uppermost, and I didn't want to give him any room to appeal.

It was still daylight, and I could see the rough-hewn logs, and the concertina lining the top of the enclosure, and also forming around it a chest-high ring. There was a way to move the barbed wire aside and we all filed into the space outside the door to Flynn's temporary accommodation. There was a rattling of a padlock and the clink-on-clink of chain, and I heard from within the growling presence of our demented killer.

"Get the fuck away unless you're letting me out to kill more Japs," he said to our small assembly of unimpressed authorities, who were armed to the teeth. Seamus the exec had his hand on his pistol and he directed a sergeant to get his Reising submachinegun up and ready. There was a wild animal inside the enclosure, and the Marines weren't taking any chances.

"Mr. Walsh—or is it Mr. Flynn?—is one angry man," said Puller. "Don't unlock it Seamus. Mr. Pratt can talk to our guest through the port." The Marines had fashioned a small door for passing items like food and water in and out. I liked Puller's suggestion. My first obligation was to ascertain the suspect's true identity. I opened the port and I beheld a bearded man with long-ish hair sitting on the ground opposite the port with his back against the inside of the stockade. I looked at him long and hard. The build was right. He had a broken nose and there was a scar running down the right side of his face. He smiled at me, and his teeth were yellowed, gapped, and even missing in a few spots.

"Is your name Gerry Walsh?" I asked him.

"It's you!" he told me. "Mr. fancy-fucking pants from *Bridger*. Come to arrest me? And no, it's not Walsh."

"Your rap sheet with the FBI is correct then," I stated flatly, as though I knew much more than the suspect wished to divulge.

"You've seen my rap sheet? Flattered," said Walsh, who, at this point, is most certainly Flynn.

"My associate Mr. Haggerty saw it," I told him. "Your busted nose and your facial scars match your mug shot. You're Flynn."

"Proud of yourself, commander? You broke the code."

"We don't have lineups out here, and we don't have mug shot books," I told him. "But I remember you from the capstan room, and the C-Deck hold aboard *Bridger*. I still have a ringing in my ears, from when you boxed me. I'm adding assault to your list of charges."

"Yes," he said. "You were a little sideshow. Needed to get that book. Mooney said so."

"Then you really fucked up," I needled him. "You let Mooney get away with the book and the code so he could get all the money for himself and Accardo. How much is he paying you? Do you think you'll ever see any of it?"

"You don't know Mooney," he said. "He's always played it straight with me."

Flynn was a talker, and he had a right to counsel. My job was to identify him, transport him, keep him locked up, and get him into the system. But there was a side to me that wanted to get some answers. These were the days before law enforcement had to abide by the Miranda warnings, informing a prisoner of his right to remain silent. Back then I was not thus encumbered. I wanted to know why he tortured those poor, dumb kids before he killed them? Why did he smash their fingers one by one with a hammer? What turned a man like Flynn into a monster? Haggerty was used to yanking nuggets out of his suspects. He didn't expect the strait-laced lawyer, this gentleman Pratt, to dig in quite so hard. First, I had to goad Flynn, crack open the tough-guy shell to find the kernel inside.

"Mooney and Accardo," I told him. "They really fucked you over."

"I'm telling you. You don't know them."

"I don't need to know them to see what kind of pricks they are...and to you, probably the hardest working son of a bitch in the whole outfit. Haul yourself all the way out here to do Tony Accardo's dirty work? And for nothing?"

"I'll get out of this and I'll get mine."

"Flynn, you fucking dope. They played you. Send that dumb lug-head Flynn to bust up the little gang of thieves that stole our money. Yeah, Flynn will do it. He's dumb, and he's cheap."

"I'll get mine!" he yelled.

"Never gonna happen," I responded, winking at Haggerty, who had played this game before, with punk idiots who might have information, but shit for brains. 'Get 'em pissed off and they'll spill,' Haggerty liked to say.

"No. Mooney and Accardo are laughing their asses off right now. And you're stuck out here. If the Japs overrun this place, you're going to get stuck like a pig. You kind of look like a pig. Did you shit yourself Flynn?"

"Fuck you. Fancy-pants ass wipe. I'm going to get those little bastards, and then I'm coming after you."

"We're going to have you hog-tied like the pig you are. I'm not worried. Whole thing started with Gallo, didn't it? Our man overboard? You stuck him in the neck and tossed him over the side. But wait a second. You got Napolitano up in the Presidio. Did you take their ears, too?"

"I always take the ears."

"Why?"

"I need a hobby. Helps me keep count."

"Then I guess it was Rizzo in the hold on C Deck. He wouldn't give up where the money was because he didn't know. Why did you have to rip him open like that?"

"The terror. I need everyone to feel the terror. They need to smell it."

An opening.

I stopped goading him and looked at him...hard. My voice softened. The aggression, the taunting, was replaced by simple questions delivered in a quiet voice. It's funny how the softness finds the evil. You couldn't pound it out of the really bad ones. They were all defiance and resistance. You had to coax it to the surface by taking away the pressure.

"Why Gerry? Do you want everyone to feel the same terror you feel? So, they'll know what it's like?"

"Yes. Goddamn it! I want all of you motherfuckers to know what it's like!"

"And what is it like Gerry? I mean when you're terrified. What does that feel like?"

"It's a beast, and it wants to get me." He'd lowered his tone.

"And where does the beast come from, Gerry?" He's a deviant, but he's part of the human species, which means he's a part of me.

"Fuck you."

I needed to take him elsewhere. Back to the very beginning.

"Did your mom and dad call you Gerry? Or was it Gerald? Sometimes moms and dads have nicknames for their little ones." I needed to take him to the time when the beasts arrived, probably in the cradle.

"I was 'dearie' to my mom," he said, looking away somewhere, trying to remember. "She died. My dad called me Doofus." And that's where it all began. Parents could be a child's worst enemy.

"Not Gerry?"

"Or Goofus. Or Dummy."

"And he wouldn't stop, would he?"

"Nope, and he was right."

"What did dad do? I mean, for a living?" I asked him, softly.

"He was a meat packer. Worked in the stockyards."

"So, he was a butcher," I said flatly. And that was it. That's where Gerry learned to cut. And Gerry wanted to please dad, so he cut very well. I paused. I wanted to know if our boy Gerry might qualify for an insanity defense.

"You do know that stabbing people, taking ears, is the wrong thing to do, don't you?"

"Why. They're dead. They won't miss their ears."

"But you killed them first. That wasn't right, Gerry. Was it?"

"Aren't we supposed to kill the fucking nips?"

"What about the people who aren't the fucking nips, Gerry?"

"Bunch of cheats. They had to go."

"So, killing them. And taking their ears. They got what they deserved, right?"

"Mooney said so."

"And you do everything Mooney tells you to do?"

"He's my friend."

"Why is he your friend?"

"He found me an apartment. Buys me booze. Found me a couple of women. Lets me play poker with him and his buddies." So Mooney was the provider, unlike Flynn's dad.

"And then when Mooney needs you to do a job, you do it, no questions asked."

"That's right."

"And you don't care who knows it."

"No. I don't care." Another point of inflection. He had no conscience, no fear of consequence. It doesn't mean he can't be prosecuted. I think the man might be able to stand trial, although his capacity to distinguish right from wrong offered a degree of reasonable doubt. I paused.

"Are you scared Gerry?" I asked him. A reasonable

man would be scared.

"I don't like the explosions," Walsh said.

He'd lost that monstrous temper, and I seemed to have tapped into that scared boy who lived inside all of us when those bombs fell. I knew right then I'd have to let the wheels of justice turn. Fear is a consequence. It helps an offender distinguish right from wrong. Fear is also a side effect of sanity. Another attorney could argue whether or not Walsh could stand trial, but I was satisfied he could enter the justice system without going directly into an insane asylum. Walsh bore all the hallmarks of competency. We needed to get him out of there, back to the brig on *Bridger*, then the nearest court of military justice to hear an extradition argument. He was a civilian, but he'd committed crimes against members of the military aboard military property. A decision would have to be made as to whether or not he should pass to civilian authority. His crimes were committed in wartime, which would be relevant to any final judgment on jurisdictional standing. It would be a federal matter if I could get him in front of the right judge.

"Okay Gerry," I told him. "I'm going to ask the colonel to get you some food. And we'll make sure you visit the latrine on a regular basis and you're safe from any fighting." I saw him relax that grimace and that knot in his stomach start to loosen. I had to summon the lawyer at my core, the one devoid of emotion. "But I need to have you help me. I need you to cooperate. If you can cooperate, we can take that choke chain off you. You're not a dog, Gerry. You're a man."

Maybe it was the first time in his life anyone had called him that.

Seamus had taken down the gist of the conversation and told me he would see to Flynn's victuals and his toileting. We followed Puller back to his CP and one of his young lieutenants approached.

"We've heard from Papa Zulu and Delta Mike," he told the room. "Enemy contact seven clicks south. Approaching in force." I ran the quick math. That was seven thousand yards or about four miles.

"Perfect!" shouted Puller. "They're coming right into us." He turned to a radio man. "Get our companies back inside our perimeter. Get today's password—'DiMaggio'—up and down the line. No friendly fire. Baldy, you and Smitty run down to the mess tents and stop the chow lines. Colonel said back to your holes lickety-split. We'll have incoming howitzer and naval rounds shortly. He turned to me and Haggerty. Gents, get into your fighting holes. Helmets on. Heads down. Grab your balls and cover your asses."

I look back on it now, and I can't decide what was worse: The incessant shelling that shifted our insides and rattled our teeth, or the prospect of screaming Banzai charges, Sendai warriors with swords drawn coming straight at us.

Haggerty and I got back to our side-by-side fighting holes, and soon Baldy and young Smitty had rejoined us. They made a good pair. They'd brought back satchels of thirty-millimeter ammunition in magazines for my carbine, armor-piercing rounds for Baldy and Smitty's standard Aught-Threes, and plenty of .45 rounds for our sidearms and Haggerty's Thompson. They also had four canteens of water for each hole. ("Laced it with iodine pills," Baldy informed us.) Plus, a godsend, a couple of little pots with rice and beans. There were some C rations amidst this trove and, and I began to understand the small blessings that could lift the spirits of the fighting man. I shared in their rapture, and it made me glad I was with them. I didn't quite comprehend it at the time, but there was a bond forming, and it took on greater weight than the whole of the conflict roiling the world. I was fighting for Smitty, Baldy, Puller...and yes for Haggerty, too.

Our fighting hole was an inverted cone, and it got tight at the bottom. I could see the work that Smitty and Baldy had put into getting the logs, the sandbags, the camouflaging, the vegetation just right. We could lie in the dirt in our own separate half, and there was a double stack of logs and sandbags on top, with a fairly wide shooting port looking south and west. When we sighted through the port, Smitty and I could squeeze in shoulder to shoulder. Smitty and Baldy had taken the time to cover the ports with vegetation, so we were camouflaged. There was a good-sized hole under the logs on the northeast side to come and go. Smitty was pretty proud of their creation. Preparation was all a part of the fight. Aboard *Bridger*, the war was distant, abstract. Here, it was right before my eyes.

A little time passed.

We were in our holes and settled. We'd each dined on the basics, and we'd each taken one more quick visit to the log latrine, joined by dozens of our fellows. It felt good to void, and get that over with, and I didn't care a wit for the lack of privacy. Now I could concentrate. I got back to our hole and tried to get comfortable.

"How long have you been playing football, son?" I asked our future Cornhusker.

"We all start out with the local police athletic league games and then go on to J.V. from there. It's just something you do," Smitty said. "When I'm not helping my dad."

"What's your dad do?"

"Farm implements. Sales and service," said Smitty.

"He's got a little Stinson airplane he uses to get around and visit customers. Flies it out of our back pasture. I soloed when I was fourteen. Wanted to be a Navy pilot but my near vision isn't so hot. Marines seemed like a good fit."

"Marines are lucky to have you," I told him. "What's your advice for this old man?"

"Breathe and shoot," he said. "Just like the colonel said. I'm usually a belt feeder for our machine gun crews. But the colonel's XO tapped me to help Baldy get us set up. If my machine gun buddies get in a tangle I might have to run over there. You okay with that?" I guess I'll have to be.

"No problem, Smitty. Do what you have to do."

"My dad taught me how to weld so I ginned up a few mounts for those big .50s we pulled out of wrecked planes. Sometimes they get a little wonky."

Smitty made a brilliant observation.

"Colonel just saved our fannies with an early word to get ready," he said. And my estimation of Colonel Puller rose even higher. One of those fannies belonged to me. Just as the words left Smitty's lips, we heard a sharp report coming from the northwest, somewhere offshore, then a screeching, tearing sound, and an explosion somewhere behind us, probably up on the airfield.

"That's just a sighting round," said Smitty. "They've probably got forward observers calling in fire. Sneaky fucks. 'Scuse my language." Just then we heard six more big bangs in rapid succession, and a shrieking sound followed by a series of nearby explosions.

"They want to mess up the airfield a little...airplanes, fuel dumps, maintainers, air crews. Then they'll turn it on us when their troops are ready for the assault," said Smitty. The boom and the shriek were coming more rapidly.

"We were under some of that this afternoon," I told Smitty.

But the shelling was getting closer. Those fighting holes wouldn't take direct hits, and I feared we were going to lose some people. Maybe me. It was a lottery, and the odds were terrible. I was going through these musings when a shell exploded right in our emplacement.

It caught me off-guard, and the pressure wave hit me in a full-body tackle. Now I understood what we were in for, when the second, the third, and the fourth came into our fortifications. I could feel my insides move inside my body. I had my index fingers stuffed so far inside my ears I wasn't sure I'd ever get them out. There was dirt, dust and fine grit floating in the hole, and Smitty somehow had the presence of mind to wrap our rifles and my carbine in some oiled cloth. I looked at Smitty and he had his teeth clenched. I couldn't even conceive of how I looked as we took this battering. The worst was psychological. We were utterly trapped. There was nowhere to run. We could hear the shrapnel whizzing overhead, walloping into the trees, and cutting down the growth. There was nothing left to do but curl up in the bottom of the hole, stuff our ears, cover our heads and hope we didn't take a direct hit.

I stopped counting the incoming shells at one hundred and thirteen. I could not imagine anything left of our encampment. I fully expected Puller's CP to be pulverized, our fellow riflemen left in shredded bits, our mess tent, Flynn's stockade, the latrine...nothing but stinking craters.

That's why I was amazed during a brief lull in the bombardment to see Puller at the door of our hole.

"You guys don't worry," he said. "Their barrels got hot so they're giving us a little break. They're letting their troops rest up at the bottom of this rise. So next break in the action, expect a Banzai charge. Lot of whooping and hollering, maybe some incoming mortar rounds. Start firing when you've got a clean target. Aim for Chris' sakes. Don't shoot over their heads. I'll order star shells so we can light up the area. It'll help with your aim point."

The colonel and his faithful Seamus were running to the next fighting hole, offering information, encouragement, and, occasionally, a shout for a corpsman. His men were getting hurt. They were just kids really, but to him they were men. So far, Smitty's fighting hole was holding up, but he rushed outside to get a log repositioned on our roof, and to hurl another sandbag on top. He and Baldy conferred on more camouflage and decided more is always better.

There were more shells falling on the airfield, and, through the trees, I could see expanding blossoms of flame rising into the night, fueled by aviation gasoline. Soon, the whole northern sky was lit up, and there was an acrid, oily smoke drifting to our east. Small blessings. It was not coming our way...yet.

Was I scared? Fool not to be. But there was another emotion...resignation. I fully expected to die on this little rise on this ninety-mile-wide island in the Solomons. The war would go on without me, and so would Bart and Bonnie, my stalwart kids. I thought of them constantly through the barrage—their first smiles, their first ungainly toddling, their homework assignments, the books they read, our walks in the woods and our visits to the local fair. I was desperately sorry I no longer loved their mother, but maybe the falling bombs caused an epiphany: Maybe it was better for the kids to see a functioning adult deciding he could no longer tolerate the loveless sham of the marriage I was in. Maybe they needed to see me picking up the pieces, striking out on my own, perhaps finding Miss Right.

They would have to deal with that, and they would have to deal with their absent father, who might become the dearly departed. The kids would not be alone in having parents separated or removed by the war. Besides, I could only deal with my job, my ship, my responsibilities, this war, and the Japanese soldiers soon to assault this delicate rise of earth on which we lay. Would the luck of the draw reach out and find me? When it was over, if I ever got home, I could try to make up for the time we'd lost. And if I didn't come home, at least I'd tried to stand up and fight. That might make a difference to them, if they one day learned what became of their father. But every man occupying this hellish piece of ground was going through the same ruminations. They were facing the idea they'd done the best they could, and they may never see their families again.

I wasn't special.

The shells were falling, and so were my tears.

Chapter Seventeen
A Hole in the Line

I was looking down on Bath from the overlook on Mossy Bank. We had the good sense to elect Johnny Langendorfer, who runs the Esso station, to be our mayor, and he was the driving force behind the park that offered brilliant views of our valley. If you looked closely, you could see the little brick building that housed Pratt and Pratt. My schedule had been reduced, owing to my semi-retirement, and on a nice day, I liked to come up here, sit on a stump, and watch the Conhocton River flow by below me. Lately, I have brought my yellow pad, and I spend the time looking at the clouds, and scratching away with my pen. It's hard for me to write about Guadalcanal, except for the part about Puller, who was born to wage war and who went on to greater glory. He took his men up the island chain and fought the hard fights. Where does America find such men, who are right there when we need them? One would think the defense of Henderson Field would be the crowning capstone of any military career. But Puller went on to victory at Bougainville, Peleliu, Tarawa, Cape Gloucester—all the tough battles that would take our forces closer to the home islands of Japan. I remember him running from hole to hole, moving logs, shoring up sandbags, talking, talking, talking.

"The ground assault will begin with mortar fire," he yelled over the line.

His men adored him not only for exposing himself to enemy fire, taking the same risks and burdens as the average rifleman, but also for designing defensive works and offensive emplacements that moved the troops toward victory—time after time. It was a rare privilege to be in company with that gifted man.

The last I saw of Puller that night was his backside as he ran back to his CP to pick up his own rifle.

It was right when we heard the thump that occurs when a shell leaves a mortar tube, and you could hear the shell whine through the night, destined to maim or kill. The sketchy part was not knowing where it was going to hit. So, you did your best to duck, cover, and hope. About that time, Puller ordered parachute flares to light up the ground in front of us, and Smitty and I could see masses of Japanese soldiers down the grade, their bayonets glinting in the artificial illumination that swayed and swung under their little parachutes, causing the shadows on the ground to move in awkward spasms. Our enemies looked like maggots crawling over a piece of meat. There were so many of them, I wondered if we'd have enough fire power to slow or stop them. We had sixty-millimeter mortars, and eighty-one-millimeter mortars, and the big ones fired first. I watched the shells drop into the Japanese lines, explode, and hurl bodies through the air. More star shells filled the night, and the first enemy wave came charging up the hill screaming. Baldy yelled over to hold our fire until "the little fuckers" got right up to the wire. There were bullets whizzing like bees over our log roof, and I watched Smitty bring out his big Aught-Three, squint through his busted spectacles and sight it in with care.

I got my carbine up and ready. Next door, I was pretty sure Haggerty had his Tommy gun out with five full twenty-round magazines positioned within easy reach.

"Our fire lane is right in front of us, and twenty feet to either side," Smitty yelled. "Let the other guys handle what's in front of their own hole. Concentrate the fire on what's in front of you."

The Japanese were charging toward the wire, and I could hear our machineguns begin their deadly work. I could see the first wave right in front of us carrying bangalore torpedoes used for breaching concertina, essentially long explosive tubes that could be forced under our coils of wire to blast a hole in it. Smitty fired the first shot of the evening from our fighting hole, and a man pushing the torpedo fell face first. Another man took his place, and I heard Haggerty letting off a three-round burst of machinegun fire, shooting the next two torpedomen. I aimed at the chest of another Japanese soldier rushing the wire with his bayonet thrust in front of him. I saw the small, ragged explosion where my bullet entered his body, and I saw the spreading blood. I couldn't think about the life I'd just taken. There was no time. I moved to the next target and shot to kill. I was calm and deliberate. I don't know why. Maybe it was because Puller let us know what to expect, and maybe that knowledge helped remove the toxic fluster of surprise. I needed to breath, aim, squeeze...and move to the next human being.

Now they were just targets. I fired into the body of another adversary. I took a minute to borrow from Haggerty's page and placed more magazines for my carbine within easy reach. Puller ordered more star shells into the sky to illuminate the battle front. The Japanese were sending in waves of men, who were dying in droves, some hung up on our wire.

Others were wounded and out of commission, and we could hear them crying. We'd been at this an hour, and I was thinking we might be able to roll back the tide of men making futile, fanatical attacks on our line.

I was wrong, of course, as the Japanese began to pepper our defenses with more mortar shells. There were at least a dozen thumps and an orchestra of whines that descended into the wire barrier in front of us. We had to look away from the dirt and dust that entered our hole, when a well-placed round landed directly in front of our hole and blew off Smitty's roof. Logs and sandbags were lifted up and scattered somewhere behind us. The enemy seemed encouraged by what they saw as an exploitable opening and begin charging through it. We shot them dead as fast as we could. And about this time, I later pieced together the fact that Baldy in the next hole had taken a bullet through the clavicle on his left side where it meets the neck. Haggerty was calling over for more gauze padding to stop it. I rummaged around and Smitty, just a bit excited, stopped me...

"Get to your fucking carbine goddamnit, sir!" he said frantically, and I left him with the gauze and slammed another magazine into my rifle. I was covering our immediate front, shooting as fast and as mindfully as I could. I was not getting clean kills, but I was stopping the enemy at least, and there was a pause. Smitty used the scant lull in the action to toss our first aid kit into the next hole so Haggerty could see to Baldy's needs.

"Shoot to the right, Commander," Smitty told me. "Cover their hole."

I was happy to oblige, when I saw Japanese infiltrators streaming past us into the pocket swelling in our lines behind us.

Ship of Tears

"We've got to get Baldy out of here," Haggerty yelled over to us, and it struck me as undoable, as Smitty and I continued to fire into the throng of Japanese soldiers, who had so many bullets coming at them they failed to register this Naval non-Marine was managing to lay down effective fire.

"I think Baldy is going to bleed to death if I can't get him back," Haggerty yelled over. It seemed like a fool's errand, but now my chief of security had left his fighting hole and grabbed Baldy by the back of his shirt collar. He was dragging him up and over the lip of their fighting hole. Haggerty tossed Smitty his Thompson and a half dozen loaded magazines. Smitty gave me the machine gun and I started firing three-round bursts into the attacking force that had just blown a hole in our lines. The Thompson was heavier than my carbine, and it bucked angrily in my hands. I had the stock right in the meat of my shoulder and I pulled the weapon into my cheek. I leaned into the recoil to keep the barrel down and centered on each target. I remembered Haggerty's admonition from our shooting exercise on *Bridger's* fantail. Don't flinch. The Thompson had a devastating effect on the enemy in front of me. I went at it for thirty minutes or more. I was not sure what was happening to my sense of time. It ripped away from me, as if it didn't exist, and just when I thought we might be gaining the upper hand, a Japanese mortar shell burst right in front of me and hurled me on my back into the bottom of our hole. I'd lost the Tommy gun, I couldn't find my carbine, and I pulled out my .45, which I'd kept in Condition One.

And where the hell was Smitty?

A Japanese soldier was standing at the top of our hole, casting a shadow from the light of a descending flare. He had an Arisaka rifle in his hands with a long bayonet, and he lowered the muzzle to shoot down on me. I brought up my .45 and shot the man in the chest. He fell into my hole bleeding, and I rolled out of the way when another Japanese soldier appeared, and I shot him too. He fell in on me, and I was now partially under the first, and entirely under the second. I could hear the battle raging around me and smell the cabbage breath of the men I'd just killed. One moved and I shot him again, this time under the chin so the bullet from my .45 exited out the top of his head. His brains mixed with the dirt, and his blood was warm and red and covered me. I could hear Japanese soldiers run by my hole, see two of their dead comrades, and keep moving. I had these two lifeless beings pinning me to the ground. I smelled their sweat, and one of them had black motor oil on his face, a kind of crude camouflage paint. I sensed more Japanese soldiers surrounding my hole, looking in, moving on—to be shot dead by members of the Seventh Marines. There was a wave of machine gun fire, and amidst all the clatter I could start to distinguish our thirty-millimeter M1s and Aught-Threes from the enemy Arisakas. There was more fire from our side than their side, and I knew I had to get into this fight somehow. I pushed the dead Japanese off me, grabbed Haggerty's Thompson, and got myself to the lip of my hole. I found more of his twenty-round magazines and then started ripping into the enemy as it retreated back through the wire.

Puller later called the enemy breach a "salient," a bulge in the line, and it was nearly our undoing. There were fire teams from different parts of our line coming in to fill the gap. They were working together to lay down a withering fire as the Japanese bodies piled up. Very few retreated through the hole they'd created. They would rather die. And this said volumes about the men we were fighting. They were maniacal. But they also broke and bled. They could be stopped. The Japanese had dominated the war up to this point—Manchuria, Singapore, the Philippines, the devastating attacks on Pearl, Wake, and Manilla. But on this spot of ground—the defense of Lunga Perimeter and Henderson Field—the tide seemed to be turning. This was their high-water mark.

Haggerty came back to his fighting hole as the shooting continued through the night. Baldy was in an aid station and he was getting patched up. Haggerty was part of the team that had pushed the salient back. Smitty arrived. He apologized for leaving me, but he had stopped hearing the comforting sound of the Browning crew-served machine gun to the right of our position. He sensed there was something amiss, so with that Nebraska farm kid 'get 'er done' attitude, he got himself over to the machine gun nest that was occupying a critical firing lane and came up with a quick solution that restored order to the gun's belt feed.

"Sucker has been giving us trouble," he mentioned, still a little shame-faced he'd abandoned his charge, the old man exec off *Bridger*. I told him all was forgiven and I hardly knew he was gone. Haggerty added some texture to the story of our little pocket.

"Like an ass I left my gun back here," he said. "So, I kept picking up those Arisakas and shot into their retreat." I told him about the two dead Japs in our fighting hole, how they protected me, and he slapped me on the back.

"Nice move, Commander. Almost like you planned it." We both laughed, as the sound of gunfire petered out across the line and the first grains of light filtered through the trees to signal another dawn. We were delighted to be alive, but out here in the Solomons, you could celebrate one day and be dead the next. It was a brief reprieve.

"We have to get our prisoner and get back to *Bridger*," I told him, and his response was vintage Haggerty.

"Let me put a bullet in that fucker's head and be done with it," he said. "Save us all a lot of trouble."

The odd thing was, I considered it. There'd been so much bloodletting, what was one more corpse? Especially one as troublesome as Flynn. I pictured him taking a fire axe to our homeward Avenger while we were in flight, bringing us all down in a flaming pyre. But the lawyer within wouldn't allow it. Flynn was a suspect, not a convict. That last interview with the man told me he was *compos mentis*, could understand the charges against him, might even participate in his defense. He had committed serial murder, and he'd defiled corpses all across the Pacific. But rising from the central insanity that seemed to have seized the world, there had to be some kind of civilized order. He needed to be arrested, charged, tried, and convicted—then the state could hang him. I tried explaining all this to Haggerty, but I could tell I was losing him until I stated the obvious: "You're a law man, Nate. Not a wanton killer. You have to bring in your man."

"I don't have to like it," he told me, and I assured him neither did I. I was reminded for the ten-thousandth time the wide gulf that often separates justice and the law. But I saved Haggerty all those comforting frills regarding the majesty of jurisprudence. This was not the time.

Neither of us realized at that moment that the guns falling silent on that morning-after was only a small break in an action that would continue for two more days and two more nights. Puller informed his men that his reconnaissance units were coming back into the line and had reported the enemy massing again west of the Lunga. He expected they would try to find weaknesses in our perimeter and continue sliding to our left. His fellow battalion commanders were working on shoring up defenses, clearing enemy dead out of our firing lanes, and registering artillery and mortar tubes to improve critical shot placement. There was sporadic sniper fire back and forth all along the line.

Haggerty and I spent the morning dragging dead bodies into a heap that would be bulldozed under the earth as soon as possible. The smell I fully expected had begun and we had to wear bandanas around our faces to try to stem the stench. Getting these corpses into the ground as soon as possible was just another necessary job and we didn't have time to be appalled. That would come later.

Our twin side-by-side fighting holes were a little battered and bruised, but we found enough logs and sandbags to restore them to some kind of order. We ducked and covered and got ourselves rearward to an aid station to check on Baldy, our brother in arms, and found him fixed up and very close to smiling. He'd been evacuated to the airfield, where the only danger would be from random falling shells. We couldn't decide what was more terrifying: staring into the eyes of the Japanese soldier who wanted to shoot you dead, or waiting for the bolt from the sky that would end your life in a blast of shrapnel and dirt.

Baldy had some words of wisdom.

"You can live for a few days without food but get some clean water aboard. And I don't care what you have to do, make sure you don't run out of ammo. Hoard it. Don't waste it. And stick with your buddy."

Yes, I had to stick with Haggerty and that tireless youngster Smitty, both of whom were better at this than me. I had racked up countless kills, and I conveyed an outward calm, but I was out of my league and out of my depth. I was not so much scared of dying than scared of causing a blunder that would in turn cause harm to our people and our cause. Failing to stop a charge. Failing to keep my rifle clean. Failing to keep my fighting hole protected so I could put more fire on targets that came in screaming waves. Mostly, I was afraid of failing. Yes, I had failed and fallen short elsewhere in my life. But I didn't want to fail in this fight, because it meant I might inadvertently take one of these fine Marines with me. How could I live with that?

It was noon on the second day. There was shooting and mortar fire all along our front, but I sensed it moving further to our left, and Puller came by to check in.

"You guys can stay put or fall back and move left to help plug a weakness to the south and east," he told us.

"We'll go where we're needed, Colonel," I told him, pushing away that nagging pull from my sense of self-preservation. I resisted my fear of failure with a willingness to put myself forward, however unschooled. I kept telling myself the least I could do was contribute another gun. Puller went on to give us information about the bigger picture. I decided that was part of his talent. When apprised of their tactical situation, his men fought with spirit and confidence. He didn't treat his people like children or cannon fodder.

He also took the time to describe certain successes, like the field day being enjoyed by Gunnery Sergeant John Basilone of Buffalo, New York, later a Medal of Honor recipient for his actions on those three crucial days in October. I didn't know Basilone, but I certainly heard about him. His exploits in keeping his machinegun going all night and into the next day and the next were becoming the stuff of legend up and down the line. A machine gun in the hands of

Ship of Tears

Basilone had accounted for scores of enemy dead, and that meant scores of Marines as yet unharmed. He had risked his life to procure more ammo, fix what was broken, and bring more concentrated fire into pockets of enemy resistance. Basilone had been a one-man Marine Company on that first night. And I was hearing Smitty's welding talents had been helping Basilone keep his guns in the fight.

"Like I said, we will go where needed." Haggerty chimed in.

"Just point us," I told Puller and he smiled. There was sniper fire whizzing over the man's head and he didn't flinch.

"Get your ammo ready," he said. "When there is a break in their artillery you can get some water and maybe a captured Jap rice ball. When Seamus identifies a problem you can solve, he'll come get you."

Puller was gone to the next fighting hole and the next word of advice, encouragement, warning. Haggerty and I were waiting for our next assignment and the next wave while our machine guns under Basilone relentlessly harassed the enemy. Aside from their terrifying burst through our lines to create the previous night's salient, they'd had an increasingly difficult time finding their toehold. They had landed serious punches, however, and I could see dead Marines here and there. But the enemy dead was simply stratospheric, and I had to believe the battle had swung in our favor. In later Pacific battles, especially Peleliu, Tarawa, and Iwo Jima, the Japanese would learn how to engineer better defenses. On Guadalcanal they thought their Banzai charges would yield results and we were showing them the error of this mindset.

Still, it would be another night and another day before we would start to believe we were safe. Finally, in the early morning hours of the twenty-sixth of October, the firing on the ridge protecting Henderson Field stopped. Inexplicably, the last charge came from a single suicidal Japanese officer who lurched toward our line with Samurai sword drawn. I can still see that blade glinting in the dawn, a rising sun reflecting back and striking weary eyes that had seen far too much. The officer stood amid heaping piles of his own dead, shrieking his mother tongue. Then he joined them with a single shot from an unknown Marine in our blood-stained line. Puller and Seamus came up to us and congratulated us on being among the living, and for helping repulse the infiltrators at the salient on that first night.

"Fine piece of shooting, gentlemen," he told us. "Sure, you don't want to join the Marines?"

"I have a ship to run," I told him. And then I looked at Nate, who was now my brother in arms. The Sunda Strait was now well behind us. "And I need my chief of security."

We looked out across the rise and it was simply littered with enemy dead. Some of the wounded sat up or tried to stand and raise their hands in surrender, while Marines or GIs from the 164th went down to take them prisoner.

"We need to annihilate the rest," said Puller. "I have to see about pulling together a few companies to form a posse. Meade let Lee go after Gettysburg. We'll have none of that."

He moved off to perform more wonders, with the faithful Seamus in tow. Haggerty and I picked up our weapons and magazines. We'd need to clean them and reload. He told me how godawful I looked, between the dirt and the blood, and we wondered if we could find some fresh water between here and the airfield. And we needed to go by Flynn's stockade to check on our prisoner. But when we got there, the barbed wire enclosure was pulled away. A hole had been blasted from the outside from what looked like a mortar round.

We looked inside, and Gerry Flynn, the butcher of *Bridger*, was gone.

Chapter Eighteen
Smitty

Waking up put all my bad dreams back in the vault where I stored my most private thoughts and agonies. I reached out for Margie on her side of the sleigh bed. But she was gone, and the door to the loo was open, so I knew she was probably downstairs. The days were getting shorter this time of year, and first light wouldn't come for another thirty minutes or so. I turned on my reading lamp and swung my legs around to attain the vertical. I was mightily pleased I had all my parts, plumbing, and appendages at this stage of my life, and I proceeded to the lavatory to perform my ablutions. I've noticed my elderly clients degrade slowly at first, then seem to go to hell all at once. Soon, we're crowded around the bedside while I take out the documents and get the last signature. It's completely unlike the shocking kind of death I witnessed on that goddamn island. Young, vibrant, smart, funny people were taken from us with a precision bullet or an indiscriminate explosion. And somehow, I survived? I still don't know why, and this thing they call survivor's guilt continued to track me down, tap me on the shoulder, and speak into my cocked ear: "It should have been you, Pratt. It should have been you."

I found Margie at the kitchen table, and it was my turn

to make the coffee and scramble the eggs. She was reading my account of Henderson Field, and she didn't know it just got worse. Later, after chores and a touch more coffee, I went back to that stinking hell where I faced more terrible choices. Later, I stared out the window as the trees bent to near braking by a sudden squall. I returned to Guadalcanal, and I took up my pen.

"This complicates things," I told Haggerty, looking at Flynn's blasted enclosure.

"As if it's not complicated enough," he responded. I knew when he was annoyed. Right now he was kicking himself for not taking the matter into his own hands. But then, more trouble found us. Seamus let us know Flynn's duffel was gone, and he'd used a Ka-Bar to stake a note to a vertical pole inside Puller's CP. He handed it to me, and in a childlike scrawl, it read "Puller You Die!"

"So, we've got a fugitive," I told Seamus and Haggerty. They kicked the dirt and looked up into the trees. We were wondering if Flynn was watching.

"And a dangerous one at that," said Haggerty, exercising his talent for understatement.

"Flynn and the colonel have some history," I told Seamus. "Dates back to their time in Nicaragua. Flynn started his collection back then, and Puller saw to it he'd be booted from the Marines. Dishonorable discharge. Flynn is part of the Chicago mob and he stowed away on *Bridger* to murder some minor hoodlums his outfit had a quarrel with. But I think he took the assignment partly because he figured he could get to Puller. We'll need at least a squad to go looking for him."

"Maybe we'll get lucky and the Japs will get him first," said Haggerty.

"I can order a squad," said Seamus. "But we'll have to give our boys some direction."

"We'll go too," I said. Seamus nodded his consent, but I knew he didn't like it. I'd done okay in my fighting hole and during the Japanese push into the salient, but my resume as a warfighter was still woefully thin.

"And we'll need more men around the colonel," Haggerty said.

"That'll be the hard part," Seamus said. "Colonel likes to keep moving."

"The other problem is Jap rifles and ammo all over this battlefield," said Haggerty. "Flynn could be setting up a sniper's nest."

Seamus was looking beyond us, somewhere into that jungle hell.

"What a mess," he said to the world at large, and I could tell he was missing the flush of victory. His job wasn't over. He continued:

"Here's what I think we should do. Commander, there's a pile of clean utilities down where the mess tent was. Your web gear, your carbine and your .45 look like they're holding up. But you need to burn those khakis. We've got a pool in a tributary of the Lunga River where you can clean up a little. You too, Nate. Then we'll get a squad of volunteers together and go looking for this fucker. But we have to be careful. There are Jap stragglers everywhere, and they like to leave behind snipers up in trees or down in their spider holes. Might be some booby traps."

Haggerty and I embraced Seamus's plan, and soon we were buck naked in the fresh-water pool Seamus had commandeered. We had at least forty Marines in there with us, with more standing guard. Hell to get shot while skinny-dipping. I was standing on a flat rock in the waist-deep pool and I dunked my head under. When I came up for air, I could see the Japanese blood and dirt from our Solomons fighting hole wash downstream. It couldn't wash away the visions from the last two nights, though, and I wondered if I'd ever lose the sight of that soldier aiming his rifle at me, or the cabbage smell of his hot breath and his oily sweat as he lay dying. Then, of course, I have to thank the man for keeping me hidden while his comrades pushed into the salient, only to be repulsed by Puller's First Battalion, Seventh Marines. God love them.

I was out of the water, dripping dry, and I found the utilities Seamus had requisitioned. He included extra underwear, socks, a tee-shirt, and a sun hat which I stuffed into my haversack clipped to my web gear. Some Marines had set up a shaving stand and I even ran a razor over my face. When I got myself together, I was a new man. Haggerty seemed to be back to his old contrary self. I was approached by Seamus and a squad leader named Jerry Barnes from Knoxville, Tennessee. Barnes had been apprised of the objective. We didn't have a mug shot, but we had a description, and we could start by circulating behind our lines and asking Marines if they'd seen a big guy, busted nose, scar face, bearded, long-hair...someone who might be drifting around our blasted-out emplacement.

Puller's neat machinegun nests and fighting holes were now a wreck, and Marines were re-assembling the redoubt that had kept them alive. Everyone thought there might be a counterattack at some point. I looked down the subtle grade the Japanese had had to cross in order to kill us. There were more bodies piled two or three deep in front of the wire. The flies were starting to swarm. Our intelligence teams were down there among the enemy dead pulling anything of value out of pockets, especially maps, dispatches, orders, or anything stamped official. We had native Japanese speakers in Vandegrift's headquarters unit who could begin to make sense of it. I saw Puller had made a priority of disposal. There were more bulldozers off to the right digging out a trench and shoving in bodies. I couldn't decide what was more hellish, the screaming Banzai charges, or this ghoulish aftermath.

"We've got company-sized units moving south to harass the enemy's' retreat," said Seamus. "You can follow, or you can patrol a bit closer." I knew Haggerty would have an opinion.

"Beg pardon," he said. "But I think he will want to stay close. Flynn's objective now is Puller. And he thinks he's safe if he can blend in." I had to offer a counter opinion

"He's the most raggedy-ass Marine out here," I told them. "No way is he just going to blend in."

"Maybe he's getting cleaned up with the rest of our guys?" said Barnes. "We've got haircut and shaving stands set up. A 'high and tight' is easier in the jungle."

"Let's keep the squad together, Mr. Barnes, and go have a look," I told him. We found the communications trench that led right and left behind the lines. Barnes took us to a tent and there were Marines lined up outside. We went in and I approached a young rifleman who was using mechanical hand clippers on the top of another Marine's head.

"We're looking for a big guy," I told him. "Busted nose, scar on his face. He's let his beard and hair go for a while. Did you see anyone matching that description this morning?"

"Nope," he responded. But then he turned to a buddy.

"Hey, Ronnie. You see a big guy come through? Busted nose? Scar on his face? Kinda shaggy?"

"About two hours ago," said Ronnie. "Fucking guy stank."

I walked over to Ronnie. "Did you see which way the guy went after his haircut?"

"Towards the CP," said Ronnie.

And I feared anew for Puller, the man who'd saved our bacon. I had a word with Seamus, the man closest to Puller.

"He needs at least a four-man bodyguard," I emphasized. "Flynn likes to get close. He uses a standard Ka-Bar. Killed five that I know about, four on *Bridger*."

"I knew he was a bad one," said Seamus. "But I didn't know how bad. Jesus. But the colonel won't pay attention to his personal safety. Never has and never will."

"If you can get four good people to stay close to him, he should be okay," I told him.

"I'll make it so," said Seamus. "One of those people can be me. He won't resent the intrusion if it's his exec."

"I like it," I told him. "While you're playing defense around the colonel, Barnes and his squad can work with me and Haggerty on offense. We have to find the son of a bitch."

Seamus pulled out a map, which was divided into squares called 'grid references.'

"We have advance elements of three companies chasing down what's left of the Sendai." Seamus pointed to our current position and moved his fingers across the Lunga River to the north and west.

"Where do you think they might regroup?" I asked him.

"Inland to the west a few miles and then a turn toward the northwest coast, across from Savo Island," he told me.

"We intercepted some messages. Their leadership was convinced it would be able to overrun the field, and guaranteed Tokyo as much. They haven't planned an evacuation, and what's left of the Sendai won't be picked up anytime soon. The Japanese are having the same issue with landing craft we are. They're resorting to putting food in barrels and towing them in long strings behind destroyers. The barrels wash up on shore. It's no way to feed an army."

"Encouraging," I told him. "But Flynn isn't constrained by the same issues. He could live off the land, at least for a while."

"So, he could be anywhere," said Seamus.

"If I had to guess, I'd say he's within a thousand yards from where we're standing." It was mere speculation. "He's biding his time. He's watching. And he wants to get within shouting distance so he can come back to Puller's CP. If the CP moves, he'll want to move with it."

"Guy know how to use a rifle?" asked Seamus.

"For sure," I told him. "And there are Jap rifles with bayonets all over the place. Haggerty and I will tag up with Barnes and get moving. Does Barnes have a radioman?"

"He does," said Seamus. "You are call-sign 'Kingpin.' Barnes will check in every four hours...Good hunting."

I found my squad, and I discovered to my delight my friend Smitty had volunteered to join us.

"Something to keep me busy until we build the next perimeter," he said, and his optimism and enthusiasm gave me a sense of hope.

Haggerty and Barnes already had a rough plan. We would cross the Lunga well south of where we believed the remnants of the Sendai crossed over. We were trying to think like Flynn. He would want to hide, bide his time, gather his strength. At the same time, staying near the river gave us—and him—an easy way to navigate. It was either upstream or downstream. We had a topo map, a compass and a protractor. I wasn't sure how Flynn was equipped, but I was betting he'd want the reassurance of having the river over his shoulder.

It was mid-afternoon when we entered the jungle, a bit cooler under the canopy of trees. But the sun came unleashed as we came out to the wide water of the Lunga. It was shallow enough to wade across, and the tropical heat seemed to choke and burn. Barnes spaced us out to reduce the chance of casualties if we were hit by mortar or sniper fire. He had me and Haggerty positioned in the middle of this procession, and he called us forward when we got to the other side.

"The grass is beaten down in here and there's blood spoor from their wounded on the vegetation," Barnes told us. I could tell he might have been a deer hunter back in the Smokies. "If we get close, I'll want to get word back up to battalion, but I don't think we'll want to engage, unless it's just a few stragglers." He was thinking of his men and I admired that. No sense in getting anyone hurt.

"Seamus said something about snipers and booby traps," I reminded Barnes, who didn't need reminding.

"I know. Complicates matters. Trying to get into the head of this Flynn guy," he said.

"Scary place," said Haggerty.

"Guessing Flynn will want to get himself nestled into the jungle so he can rest and think," I pondered.

"We're lucky there's no high ground in here," said Barnes.

"At some point he'll want to circle back so he can get

what he came for," I said. Was I starting to think like Flynn?

"The colonel," said Haggerty.

"Yep," said Barnes. "The colonel."

He "volunteered" a couple of his men to take point down the river trail we were on. He kept us spaced. The floor of the trail had loose vegetation, but it was well traveled, and I guessed it was how the Japanese had come into our zone three nights earlier. I was watching the trees, listening to the birds, trying to detect any natural flush or footfall that would signal the presence of the enemy. The pressure was fantastic, and I wondered how our Marines withstood this stress day after day without breaking. It was getting dark, and Barnes came back to confer with me and Haggerty.

"Don't feel too much like stooging around out here much longer," he told me. "We can set up camp off the trail, post guards, and hit it again in the morning."

The word went up and down the line and our squad buddied up and moved ten or fifteen feet off the trail east or west into the jungle. Haggerty and I heard the sounds of entrenching tools digging in the earth to make some rudimentary fighting holes, enough to keep us low if we got surprised by any shell or rifle fire. Haggerty and I found a flat dry spot and started digging. In a few minutes we had a rectangular hole about three-or four-feet deep. We packed dirt around the perimeter, forming a dam against the rain, and we snapped together two ponchos. We mounted this weather proofing over the hole on four sticks and added a center pole to induce some run off. We put some vegetation over that.

"Homey," Haggerty wisecracked as a black night fell. We got ourselves settled in the dirt, and I amused myself by exploring what I liked to call Pratt's Theory of Relativity. Our accommodation was relatively poor, compared to the splendid log and sandbag redoubts we shared with Smitty and Baldy. But we also thought, relatively speaking, it was better to be out here in the dark, where the only sounds were chewing insects and mating calls, than curled up in our fighting holes waiting for the Sendai while the shells dropped. And the last two nights, relatively speaking, we were facing hordes of Japanese soldiers who'd wanted to hasten our trip to heaven. So, tonight's fox hole in the jungle was relatively better than the fighting hole we'd occupied for the past three days.

Haggerty and I got our magazines loaded. We spent a few minutes running cleaning rods down barrels and oiling actions, the cautionary exhortations of Colonel Puller animating our labors. We then opened some godawful C rations—some kind of deviled ham concoction. We wolfed it down, and I leaned back in the hole smelling the clean ozone in the atmosphere and waiting for the rain. I was dozing when it started an hour or so later, and Haggerty put his hand over my mouth. He was right up to my face and he put a finger to his lips. I'd been sleeping, but I strained to hear. Even through the big drops hitting our ponchos, I could tell we were not alone. Boots were moving down the wet trail. There was a metallic clink of swords knocking against tin drinking cups. Clothing was pushing past wet vegetation, and here and there, someone was coughing...or moaning. I could hear a few words in Japanese, not quite conversations. And occasionally, a non-com would hiss an order into the night, and the pace would quicken. Haggerty and I were stunned into silence, and we just hoped our own squad members weren't in the mood to take on what might be a superior force. The enemy may have been weakened by the previous days of fighting, but I didn't want to test this theory. There was the sound of coughing, crying, arguments. The Emperor's defeated army was trying to reconstitute itself or find a way off this bloody island. The small unit—a squad, a platoon, something larger, we were not sure—finally passed down the trail and the natural sounds of the jungle returned.

Dawn arrived with the slow, steady gathering of a gray, wet light as rain continued to drop from the vegetation. I ate a Hershey bar for breakfast, and it was the most delightful experience I'd had since before our first cruise. It was my Theory of Relativity fooling me again. When you are wet, tired and hungry, any comfort or sustenance seemed fit for a king. The light continued to build, the rain stopped and there were shafts of sunlight penetrating the jungle, causing little rainbows that danced on the mist.

Soon, Barnes came up to our fighting hole.

"Time to mount up, gentlemen," he told us. We chatted a bit about the Jap stragglers who had come through the night before and we agreed engaging the enemy needed to be undertaken with care.

"'Kingpin' checked in with our CP last night and we gave them the word about that Jap unit," said Barnes. "We'll see if it comes to anything. Cover your holes with dirt and put some palm fronds on it. And Commander, there's something out here you should see."

We got ourselves packed up, our hole filled in and covered and stepped out on the trail.

Sitting with his back to a tree was a dead Japanese soldier. His throat had been cut, and his right ear was missing. Haggerty turned to me with a question.

"What did Flynn say about terror?"

"Part of his plan," I responded. "He wants to keep everyone spooked."

"Do you think he knows we're out here?" asked Barnes.

"We have to assume he's watching," I told him. And that aggregated in my mind a poorly formed idea.

Just then we heard the crack of a rifle shot and the muscular staccato of a submachinegun, probably a Reising, according to Haggerty, who had an ear for gunfire.

"Sounds like Charlie Actual making contact with that bunch that went through here last night," said Barnes. There was more rifle fire, then the random 'wump' of grenades. It was a smart little fire fight taking place less than a mile to our north along the west side of the Lunga. I tried to keep our focus on Flynn.

"He's a scavenger, gentlemen," I told them. "He'll want to pick up the sick, the wounded, the tail enders...like a wolf or a coyote. Let's give him what he wants."

I asked Barnes to configure the squad so Haggerty could take the tail end. Haggerty liked it.

"Countersurveillance," he said, brightening. "Good idea, Commander." It's not often I get a pat on the back from Haggerty.

"Sergeant Barnes, I need one of your big guys to walk with me," I told him.

"And we need to reverse course," said Barnes. "I don't want to tangle with that fire fight. Company can handle that. Let's turn south."

"Even better," I told him. "If we make contact, we know it probably won't be the Japs."

Barnes got us turned around, and ordered Smitty, my good luck charm, to hang back with me.

"Smitty, you and I will be well back from the body of the patrol," I told him. "Mr. Haggerty here will be the squad's tail-end Charlie. Helps, Mr. Haggerty, if you walk with a limp or something. Smitty, you and I will try to see if anyone takes an interest in jumping our colleague."

"I'm expendable," said Haggerty, and I found this dedication perversely noble. I also knew he was armed and ready, and he would love to cut short our stroll in the woods with a bullet through Flynn's brain. Haggerty would bring a pistol to this knife fight, evening up the odds. We broke up, Barnes and Haggerty headed south with the squad, and Smitty and I took a seat behind a tree, well off the trail. We were straining to hear footsteps through the bird calls and the slight ruffling of the treetops. We talked in a whisper.

"You a hunter, Smitty?" I asked him.

"Ducks, pheasant, deer," he told me. "They used to let us out of school on opening day."

"Great traditions," I told him. "Eager to get back out in the field when we get home."

Smitty was familiar with the great midwestern flyways that sent migratory pintails down to Nebraska from Canada.

"We all like the outdoors," he continued. "My dad and I like to fly the Stinson over our favorite spots before the season starts. We've got a few potholes west of North Platte that are always pretty promising. I fly while he scouts with the binoculars. We can land the plane, camp for the night and, before first light, set up a blind. Man those are good times."

"I'm coming out there when we lick the Japs and I'll buy the gas," I told him.

"Deal," Smitty said. "You'll like dad. That man knows how to do anything."

"Like the way you fixed that machine gun on that first night," I told him. "Guess you're just like your dad."

"Dad would say, 'you gotta do what you gotta do'," said Smitty.

"I was a little worried about you when you left our hole," I told him. "But I should have figured you'd be okay."

"Yeah, sorry about that," Smitty said. "I was listening for that Browning and when it stopped, I knew that blasted feed was messed up again. Finicky. I hated to leave you alone."

"But the right call, Smitty," I told him.

"My machine gun team was on the right side of that bulge in the line," he told me. "I was a belt feeder all night. We prepped the field pretty well but they still got through."

"Our hole was on the left side of the same bulge," I told him. "So I know a little about what happened. Your guys come out okay?"

"My buddy Randy bought it," Smitty told me softly. "Took one in the chest. Corpsmen got to him pretty quick, but there was nothing they could do."

"Randy a Cornhusker, too?" I asked him.

"Town east of us called Roscoe," he told me. "Played against each other in football. We signed up the same day."

"You going to write his parents?" I asked him.

"Guess I'll have to," he said. "And he's got a girl. Randy was trying to memorize some sonnets for her. Shakespeare. He had a little book. Something about a 'lark at the break of day arising.' I thought it was nice. Randy liked it. I'll send it to her."

"That's a fine idea," I told him. "You got a girl back home, too?"

"There's one I like. Rebecca," he said. "But I don't want to write her. Don't want to get her hopes up in case I don't make it back." It was the fatalism Marines carried, a dead weight that only got heavier. The odds shifted against them the longer they were in the field. It was one of the unspoken reasons they looked out for each other. It seemed like nothing could guard against the random lightning bolt, the millisecond journey a bullet or piece of shrapnel might make to find another good kid. Now I knew it was something you couldn't plan or foresee. It was something that would simply *happen*. And the world would move on without you. It made you believe in the next minute of your life, and the one after that, and the whole heaping pile of time that awaited—but for the projectile screaming through the air bent on your destruction.

Smitty and I quietly got to our feet, looked all around, and stepped onto the trail. I was cognizant of the fact that, while we had Haggerty assigned as bait, our position in trail might very well place us in the same role. Smitty took the point of our little two-man patrol, and I followed him back a few steps, circling around from time to time to walk backward and scan our rear. Once in a while I told him to hold up so we could just listen to the sounds of the jungle.

Smitty had a good ear. There were monkeys swinging in the trees, and what looked like quetzal birds with their long tails. Once I saw the furry ball of a sloth way up high. But Smitty didn't react to things that were supposed to be there. Like me, he was waiting for the sudden and the unexpected. We took a dozen steps, then stopped to listen. Smitty had his hand up, and I walked up to him so we could confer.

I took one last look behind us, and then heard him say, "Bushes moving at our two o'clock. Something big."

I could see some vegetation shake, and it was such an unnatural movement that I convinced myself it was being caused by a human being. Smitty was carrying one of the big old Springfields Puller loves. I was perfectly content with my carbine. We each brought our rifles up, ready to take down the threat, when a wild boar burst out of the vegetation, gave us a good look, then scampered around us and headed north down the trail. The natural order was restored, and we continued south.

I was in the process of checking our rear when Smitty and I both heard rapid footfalls in front of us. Someone was running toward Haggerty and our patrol. We both started running down the trail to catch up, and I decided I had to warn our people.

"Haggerty. Behind you!" I shouted into the jungle, wondering how many Japanese stragglers or snipers I'd alerted to our presence.

Smitty and I kept running, sliding down muddy rivulets and bashing through saplings. I could hear shouting now, and I was glad Barnes and the squad seemed to have turned themselves around. They needed to backtrack towards Haggerty. We got closer and I could hear the sounds of two people grunting as punches landed. Smitty and I got up to Haggerty and he was lying in the middle of the trail, winded but conscious. He had an impressive welt over his left eye.

"Fucker snuck up on me," he told us. "Thanks for the warning."

"You sure it was him?" I asked.

"No doubt," he said. "I got my knife into the calf of his left leg. He let out a howl and headed into the bush. There should be a good blood trail." I congratulated Haggerty on getting in some licks, and Barnes had a corpsman treating his eye with Merthiolate and gauze. The young man was muttering something about Haggerty needing a stitch.

"Just butterfly the thing and let's move," said Haggerty. "There's some blood over there, Jonas."

Barnes and his squad mates were ready to head off the

trail into the jungle.

"At least he seems to be heading back toward the river," he observed, and I liked the sound of that if weren't for the knowledge Flynn was likely headed toward Puller, his new objective. Barnes assigned Smitty to keep an eye on us old-timers and he had us positioned in the middle of the procession again. I was not sure he liked the idea his two non-Marine responsibilities might get slugged by our fugitive—or worse. We bushwhacked off the trail for a good hour, and Barnes reported the blood spoor on the vegetation was getting more pronounced. Haggerty was delighted at the prospect we'd find Flynn curled up dead somewhere. I still wanted to get him properly incarcerated and charged, our purpose for being out in this green hell.

I look back on that single-minded young lawyer I used to be, the one who revered the neat strictures of the law, and I wanted to slap him in the face and shake him by the shoulders.

'Damn you Pratt,' I want to tell him. 'It's the law of the jungle. Don't you see?'

If we could take him alive, it would satisfy my misaligned worship of law and order...But Flynn was dangerous. I couldn't allow the man to hurt more people. That needed to be the prevailing sentiment. And it would prevail throughout the rest of the war as my obeisance to the law confronted the savage truth of armed conflict.

Another hour went by and we saw where the blood stopped at the river's edge. Smitty made a pertinent observation.

"If he stays in the river a bit, it'll be hard to figure where he comes out," he said.

"He could be going upriver or down river," I added.

"We can't be sure."

Barnes decided to cross the river, and he divided the squad up into two search parties, each tasked with trying to pick up the blood trail on the other side. Each team would look for fifteen minutes, then, regardless of what we'd found, we'd come back to our spot on the east side of the Lunga before we'd come up with the next idea. Smitty, Haggerty and I were chosen to man our little outpost on the river and we settled in for a few minutes. Haggerty managed to grab a nap and I could tell by looking at the bump near his eye he was uncomfortable. The stalwart Smitty found some aspirin in his first-aid pouch, and some clean water in his canteen. The normally grumpy Haggerty seemed grateful for the attention.

Thirty minutes went by and Barnes returned with half the squad. "Nothing to the south," he reported. One of his corporals came back into our spot by the river and told us he'd found blood by the river leading to the northeast—in the direction of Henderson Field. It was time to pick up the pace and see if we could catch up with the injured Flynn.

"Should have stabbed his other leg, too," Haggerty said, and we were all a bit encouraged we'd be able to end our manhunt satisfactorily. Barnes's man found the blood spoor on the side of the trail, and we moved into the jungle, now on the east side of the Lunga. Barnes called his men around him in a circle and went down on one knee to reinforce the objective.

"You know why we're here," he explained. "Guy we're chasing is a bad one, and Mr. Pratt and Mr. Haggerty need to take him into custody. In this jungle, remember you are going to hear him before you see him. So, listen for footfalls, heavy breathing, vegetation rustling. Thanks to Mr. Haggerty, he's wounded. So he shouldn't be able to outrun us. But he's got some stamina all right." A young rifleman raised his hand. It's another teenager, a kid named Griswold from Connecticut.

"Gris?" asked Barnes.

"Rules of engagement?" asked the young man, and I found the question simple and astute. What were we going to do with this lunatic when we actually caught him?

Barnes looked at me.

"We want to take him alive, gentlemen," I told the squad, and Haggerty had to look away. "But we have to assume he is armed and dangerous. If you think you're threatened, or the guy is threatening one of your buddies, you can shoot to kill. I want you to use discretion. If we can take him in, that would be preferred." I get nods of agreement all around.

"I think the Japs have pretty much cleared out of here but we might find a straggler," said Barnes. "Same rules apply. If we can take one in, I am sure intel would appreciate it. But if the enemy has a knife, a gun, a dirty look, you are obliged to take him down. One dead Jap might mean saving one or more of our guys. I want to move aggressively through this patch, so get ready to hustle."

They were clipping their haversacks onto their web harnesses, and snapping closed their ammo pouches or taking a last bite out of a candy bar. Barnes was telling them to bury their cigarette butts and a couple of guys on a nature call were emerging from the bushes buckling their pants. Barnes asked his radioman to tell the CP 'Kingpin' was moving toward the line and to pass the word. The day signal would be "Honus Wagner." We didn't want friendly fire. Finally, he arranged us in a broad line with himself and two of his young roughnecks in the middle. Haggerty and I were to his right and the rest of the squad fanned out. Like Puller said aboard *Bridger* when we were trying to capture our serial killer, it reminded me of driving deer.

"You guys on the ends stay up with us," said Barnes, prodding our flankers.

We moved into the bush and we were all tromping through saplings or waste-high brush. On a couple of occasions, we had to go through on hands and knees. We finally got to an area of head-high grass and I could see our boys to the right and left moving with dispatch toward a stand of trees a couple of hundred yards off.

That's when two things happened at once, which tended to confuse the next quarter hour of our morning walk. First, there was somebody shooting at us from ahead and right. Barnes yelled "sniper" as loud as he could. At the same time, I saw Flynn performing a limping run across our front from left to right. He was drawing the sniper fire, and a bullet buzzed past him and over our heads.

"Flynn coming to the right," I yelled to the Marines to my right and then I hugged the ground. There was another rifle crack, and a bullet pinged into the ground next to me. Barnes had a BAR and he fired it into the trees. Haggerty got his Thompson into the fight, and that got everyone enthused about killing the sniper, our current problem, which moved Flynn down on our agenda. My worries turned toward my compadres to my right, and while Barnes and company had the sniper occupied, I decided to move to my right to see if I could back up our guys in that direction. I was constantly worrying about friendly fire.

"Pratt coming your way," I told the Marine to my right, who turned out to be Smitty. He was wondering if he should get his Aught-Three into the fight against the sniper. But he'd been trained by Puller, and he'd had enough discipline to wait until he could get a clear shot. I got to him and we decided to move farther to our right and see if we could find Flynn. I got a look at the trees up ahead and I saw a Japanese sniper fall out of a big tree called a Kollo, as I later learned. Barnes and his BAR were credited with the kill.

I shouted back in Barnes's direction and told him Flynn had gone to the right. I could hear our squad coming my way. Smitty and I kept moving and formed up with two other members of the squad.

"I saw the fucker," one kid said. "Kind of a green blur, but he's moving north and east."

Barnes, Haggerty and the rest of our party caught up to us and soon we found more of Flynn's blood trail. Barnes was counting heads. He was relieved he didn't have a man out there in the grass with Flynn on the loose. He didn't like us bunching up and he told us to "fan the fuck out!"

That's when Smitty saw some movement across the grass and heading for the trees. The whole squad broke ranks and ran after the undulations in the vegetation. I was recalling our earlier sighting of the boar when, sure enough, we saw Flynn hopping on one leg through the tree line, and up a rise toward our perimeter. We rushed into the trees and out into the open and I could see the enemy dead from the previous days' carnage. The stench was unbearable, and the flies were everywhere. Flynn was supernaturally quick on that bum leg but I could see fresh blood on the trail. Barnes was yelling for the sentries to stop our fugitive, but the young riflemen just looked at us, uncomprehending, as they parted the concertina wire to let Flynn through. Our squad was getting close, though, and I could tell Flynn was heading straight for Puller's command post. There were Marines everywhere looking at this spectacle, unable to put together we wanted the bastard stopped.

Smitty, destined for Cornhusker glory, got right up to Flynn as our killer approached Puller's encampment. Inexplicably, in the heat of the chase, Haggerty and I weren't far behind. That's when I saw Flynn pull out two hand grenades from the big cargo pockets of his utility pants. I heard Smitty yell "grenade!" at the very top of his young, virile lungs—lungs that had known the free, unfettered air of the Nebraska Plains, lungs that would help score a bushel of future Cornhusker touchdowns, lungs that would carry him through a long life and a comfortable old age. Smitty tackled Flynn right on Puller's CP doorstep. The grenades left Flynn's hands and fetched up in front of a small clutch of young, disbelieving Marines, who were watching this performance and wondering how it would all turn out.

Smitty stood up, leapt through the air, and landed on the grenades, clutching them underneath him. He took the full blast of both with his perfect Nebraska body. My young friend was blown into the air. Both legs and an arm were separated from his torso and there was a spinning spray of blood. Barnes came up, followed by five more of his squad. They landed on Flynn and had him handcuffed behind his back with chains around his legs and neck. He was subdued, and the remains of Smitty were flung off the side of the trail like so much bloody trash.

I got up to Flynn. He was on his back smiling up at me, and I kicked him in his fat, gap-toothed face. I wanted to scream and puke and cry. And I couldn't do any of those things in front of these men—just boys really—who had probably seen worse.

I took out my .45, which was cocked and locked. I

pointed it down into Walsh's hideous, grinning face, and I fully intended to murder the man right there. He was immobilized by handcuffs and chains but I knew if he somehow got loose, he'd kill again. It was time for me to stop this monster for good. I was pointing my pistol at him and he was telling me to "pull the fucking trigger, fancy pants." All I needed to do was brush off the safety and squeeze.

I felt a hand on my elbow and it was Haggerty.

"Jonas don't..." he said into my ear. "You're better than this."

He moved my gun hand down. I could feel my heart pounding, my breath hot. I couldn't see through the tears flooding my eyes, and I was utterly lost in despair as I saw the bloody green twill that used to be Smitty, that wonderful son of Nebraska.

Haggerty aimed his pistol at Walsh's laughing, maniacal face.

"Nate, stop," I said, putting my hand on his arm and moving his gun down.

I pointed my own pistol between Walsh's gruesome bloodshot eyes and pulled the trigger.

The report from the weapon flushed the birds out of the trees, and the bullet made a jagged hole in Flynn's forehead, covered in blood, brain and powder burns. His mouth was frozen in an upturned smile, mocking the small crowd of stunned Marines forming a circle around these two dead bodies. I couldn't find the words...normally my tools, my comfort and my refuge. Now, there was nothing left to say.

Chapter Nineteen
Black Cat

I have thirty-years of tears running down my face, and Margie is crying, too. It's mid-December. It's only three o'clock in the afternoon, but it's nearly the shortest day of the year. The sky is a slate gray, and there's a bitter cold rain beating against the panes of our old house. We are sitting on the couch in the living room, listening to the wind whistle down the chimney. My wife is holding me like you'd hold a frightened boy.

"He was a perfect," I told her. "He was sharing his life, and he volunteered to get that son of a bitch Flynn. He didn't think about the danger. It was just something he had to do. A walk out in the jungle away from that bloody ridge. What could go wrong? Smitty was gone in an instant." I snapped my fingers, and Margie left my side and came back with two big bourbons over ice.

"Did you ever reach out to his family?" she asked.

"We exchanged a couple of letters, and I sent money to his high school so they could put a loving cup in their trophy case with his name on it. 'Reginald Howard Smith.' With 'Smitty' in quotes... plus his gridiron record. Born June 1924. Died October 1942. Henderson Field Guadalcanal.' He received the Congressional Medal of Honor, and the school told me they'd draped it over his loving cup. He was like a lot of other good kids. He just happened to be the kid I served with during my brief and inconsequential tour in combat. God, there are days I wish it had been me."

I was shaking and she put her arm around me.

Haggerty and I could pack up and leave that horrible place. But those kids weren't so lucky. Island after island. Assault after assault. They kept fighting and dying, and *Bridger* and I kept pouring young Americans into the hell of the Pacific war.

Bulldozers were shoving wrecked airplanes off to the side of the airfield, fuel-fed fires were slowly being extinguished, and the wounded were lying on stretchers outside medical tents, waiting their turn. They were burned, blackened, bandaged...and some were missing limbs or had their heads swathed completely so you couldn't see their eyes. In their blindness they only had a simple trust their fellow Marines would see to their needs.

Off on a small rise to the east of the airfield there was a cemetery where burial parties were disposing of the American dead. Chaplains were ministering to the spiritual needs of this tight-knit band, who were attending to their inner wounds after the havoc they had witnessed. And I realized Smitty's story might be exceptional, but not unusual. These men would do anything for each other. I saw Vandegrift's deputy, General Rupertus.

"Colonel Puller told me you and Haggerty were instrumental in turning the enemy back at the salient," he said

"We were just two more guns, general," I told him. "These kids are the heroes."

"Well, you'll be mentioned in the colonel's report," he told me, and I wished I'd had the guts to tell him where he could stick his report. But I didn't. I saluted instead, and I hated myself for it.

"Our command post has a message for you from *Bridger*. You can talk to my yeoman."

"Surprised they got a message through," I told him.

"They had to route it through Pearl, then back to us," said Rupertus. "Captain Kelly is being ordered to Brisbane with a ship full of wounded. They leave this afternoon."

"Guess we will have to catch up with them by and by," I told him. "I'll figure out where we can pitch in here, general."

"Not so fast," he said. "General Vandegrift has ordered a sea plane up from New Hebrides. One of our Black Cat Catalina flying boats. Those PBYs are slow but well-armed. They're coming up to get you and they'll help you find *Bridger* if she's already under way."

"Premium service, general," I thanked him.

There was a water tank that hadn't been ruptured and Marines were standing in line to take showers fully clothed to get rid of some of the dirt and blood that clung to everything. Haggerty and I were soaking wet when we found a hastily arranged field tent that was trying to serve some captured Japanese rice and fresh-baked bread. There was nothing else to eat. But there was some coffee from God knows where and we managed to each get a cup. We were sitting on a log watching the earnest strivings of a Marine base coming back to life after three nights of hell.

"How's your face?" I finally asked Haggerty.

"Beautiful as ever," he told me.

We sipped our coffee and the bruise on his face shifted from a dark purple to a new shade of green with mustard accents. Soon we saw a huge flying boat enter a downwind leg for an approach to the field. It was big and slow and it made a textbook touchdown in the first quarter of the runway. I was impressed. We walked up to the airplane after it shut down and we waited for the crew to emerge from one of the observation blisters in the waist. I noted the Black Cat had two machine-gun barrels protruding from a nose turret, twin .50s port and starboard jutting from the observation pods, and two torpedoes and four bombs attached to the underside of the wings. This lumbering seaplane was also a warrior.

I met the pilot, Lieutenant Tucker, and he made introductions all around. He had an observer who served as a gunner, a co-pilot, a bombardier who served as a navigator/radioman, and a nose gunner.

"We saw *Bridger* when we left," he told me. "She's got a good head of steam up and she's heading southwest. We'll have you back aboard before you know it." Little did I realize getting back aboard would offer another trial by fire. For the remainder of the war I would never be able to fully rest or lower my guard. It would be another hard lesson.

The PBY crew had brought C-rations, cigarettes, cans of vegetables, ham and turkey, plus mail. In no time they'd formed a brigade to offload these supplies and get them into a bunker. A personage no less than General Vandegrift was handing out mail and reminding the headquarters companies to save some cigarettes for the Marines in the line.

We finally got aboard and we were ordered into the mid-section of the airplane for takeoff. We could move back to the observation blisters after we climbed out. Soon the Black Cat's engines were screaming, her fuselage was shaking, the brakes were released and we were galloping down Henderson Field's gravel runway.

"I feel a little guilty leaving them," said Haggerty.

"Me, too," I told him. Little did I realize the guilt would

never fully depart this heart of mine. I was a survivor, and it would be my cross to bear.

A young seaman came back to join us. He handed us a document with aircraft identification silhouettes. "Lieutenant Tucker would like you guys to help with spotting if you wouldn't mind," he told us. "Looking for Zekes, Kates, Bettys. Anything at all."

"Submarines?" I asked him.

"Especially submarines," he responded. He flipped the page over and there were silhouettes of Japanese I-boats. He handed us each a pair of binoculars and we got to work. The wind looked like it was blowing out of the southeast. That meant the center of the system was off to our northeast and far enough away to create only a light rolling sea. We were on top of the cloud deck and the choppy air dissipated. We were charging along smoothly, our twin Wrights humming. A couple of hours went by and the crew shared some sandwiches. Lunch concluded, we received two pieces of information that frightened us to our bones.

The young seaman came back and told us, first, the flight deck could see smoke on the horizon and it was probably from *Bridger's* exhaust stack. Second, they might have spotted a periscope running in parallel with our ship. "Lieutenant would like a word," he said. I moved forward to speak to the flight crew.

"Definitely *Bridger* down there," Tucker said. "But our nose gunner said he saw a periscope wake off to her north. We're going to go down to have a good look."

I have to shout over the engines: "Do you know if we've got any subs operating this far south?"

"We asked before we left New Hebrides," said Tucker. "All our subs are up in The Slot between the Canal and

Rabaul. If there is a sub down this far, it's gotta be a Jap."

Maybe they'd heard *Bridger* was down here, I reflected. Bagging a troopship would offer the Japanese big advantages in keeping Marines out of the islands they've taken. Tucker pulled back on the twin throttles and lowered the Black Cat's nose. The engines changed their tune, and the needle on the airspeed indicator touched a hundred and ninety knots as we lost altitude.

"You've seen what we've got for armament," Tucker told me. "But we've also got a big .50 cal we call a tunnel gun. Shoots aft out the bottom. Maybe one of you guys can operate that." I moved aft and discussed the tunnel gun with Haggerty who was delighted to have a gun he could shoot. I went back up to the flight deck and tried to offer some context for our young pilot.

"Subs only make about fourteen knots on the surface, and five submerged," I told him. "*Bridger* can outrun them."

"What if there's more than one?" asked Tucker, and the question chilled me. "What if one sub is chasing *Bridger* into the path of number two? They're sneaky that way."

"Mind if I stay up here for the show?"

"There's a folding seat you can take," said the co-pilot, another big kid in a Navy that's filled with them. I had my binoculars working and I could see my beautiful ship make turns toward Australia. The co-pilot handed me a headset and I could hear the crew through the ship's interphone. They were busy and I was grateful for this distraction. Yes, we'd lost Smitty, that marvelous young man from Ogallala. But there was still work to do and I couldn't dwell on it. There would be plenty of time to grieve.

"Anything yet, Barney?" Tucker asked, and the nose gunner responded. "Still looking...wait. Yes. At your eleven o'clock. I see a periscope wake."

"Taking her down to the deck," said Tucker. Mike, see if you can raise *Bridger* and tell them we've got a submerged bogie at her three o'clock, possible range four thousand yards." Mike, who also functioned as bombardier, was working the frequencies and we finally heard him make contact with someone in *Bridger's* radio shack. I imagined all hell breaking loose aboard, and thought to myself, 'They'll turn south and commence zigzagging, maybe get the after five-inchers ready.' Five minutes went by and *Bridger* responded to my telepathic suggestion. I yearned to be on her bridge deck right now as she faced this peril.

Tucker continued the descent and Barney the nose gunner emitted a highly professional "holy shit." I tried to see what he was seeing and I couldn't believe it at first. The Japanese submarine was surfacing, when she'd be at her best speed. She was trying to take on *Bridger* in broad daylight— and she was figuring *Bridger* was lightly armed. They weren't half wrong. I don't think they thought about a Black Cat coming out of nowhere.

"Barney charge your guns," said Tucker. "We're going to make a strafing run right up her tailpipe. With any luck her deck crew won't know what hit them. Somebody tell the tunnel gun to get ready." The Black Cat came in from the north at an altitude of fifty feet. "Mike we'll come back around and set up for a fish. Get ready. Barney, light her up."

Our nose gunner was pressing the attack and I could see tracer rounds winging by the submarine's conning tower. A couple of the sub's crewmen were trying to get a deck gun ready, and Barney shot them up pretty thoroughly. Tucker flew the big sea plane over the stricken sub, as more crew were coming up on deck. I could hear our waist gunners and the tunnel gun get into the action. We banked to the right and Tucker set up for a big righthand circle that would have us coming back at the sub at a right angle, aiming straight for her broadside.

"Barney, keep the guns working while Mike pickles the fish," said Tucker. He took over communicating with *Bridger's* radio shack.

"*Bridger. Bridger.* This is U.S. Navy PBY three thousand yards to your north, now engaging enemy submarine. We have delivered machinegun fire and we'll have a torpedo in the water in ten seconds."

"Aye-aye, PBY," returned *Bridger*, "Grateful for any assistance." I have to put in my two cents.

"Lieutenant Tucker, advise *Bridger* to be on the lookout for additional submarines at her twelve o'clock," I told him and he made it so. Better to be safe than sorry. That's when Barney the gunner chimed in with a spirited "Fuck."

"Our fish is away," he told us. "But they just fired a pair of bow torpedoes!"

I could feel a hot numbness between my eyes, as I strained to see two torpedo wakes streak south toward my ship. *Bridger* had brought her after five-inch deck guns into action and I could see a pair of shell splashes bracket the enemy submarine. There were a couple of machine cannons ripping up the water and I was glad our weapons training was being put to good use.

"Tell *Bridger* to take evasive action," I shouted at Tucker. "Turn west and order the engine room all ahead flank. Now."

"*Bridger* this is PBY. You've got two enemy torpedoes in the water coming toward you. Suggest immediate evasive action to the west, All-Ahead Flank." It occurred to me the team on *Bridger's* bridge deck might not appreciate these suggestions from the peanut gallery. But so be it. I could see more than they could right now. Haggerty came up to the flight deck and offered an encouraging word.

"Our torpedo just hit that Jap sub amidships." Tucker repeated the news for his crew and I heard a war-whoop through my headset. *Bridger* came back on the line with a "nice shooting" pat on the back, and then verification that our first fear may have been realized.

"PBY this is *Bridger*. We've spotted a periscope two thousand yards to our south and wonder if you can investigate." I told Haggerty to go aft and see if he could see sub number one sinking. It would be nice to confirm that before we departed to take on sub two.

He came forward again. "Bow is sticking up in the air. It's definitely hit."

I communicated this information to Tucker and he advanced the power to gain altitude. We wheeled around *Bridger's* bow as she powered to the southwest. I could see two torpedo wakes streak a hundred yards off her stern and I could start breathing again. I had my binoculars out and I was scanning the ocean to the south of my ship. Barney up in the nose once again reported a sighting.

"Periscope moving in an easterly direction," he reported, and I took that as a good sign. The second sub was throwing in the towel. We were at an altitude of two thousand feet and we performed a tight left orbit around the spot where Barney thought he saw the periscope.

"Nope," he told us. "It's down."

"But you say it was definitely heading east," I queried.

"Definitely east," he repeated. That meant the opposite of *Bridger's* direction of travel. I told Tucker *Bridger* would be widening the distance pretty quickly, but we should give her another half hour of westerly heading before we attempted a landing and a passenger transfer at sea. Tucker encapsulated the message appropriately and conveyed it to *Bridger*. We received an acknowledgement and I told our fine pilot I'd just assumed he had enough gas to fly westbound a few more minutes.

"We're good on fuel, Commander," he reported. "Worry not."

I told Barney and Mike nice shooting and the general atmosphere aboard our Black Cat brightened. A half hour went by and the sun was declining in the west. I could tell *Bridger* had backed off the speed, and I imagined the bosuns were getting the captain's gig over the side to come get us. The sun bathed my ship in a golden light as Tucker came up on her stern and made a victory pass close down her starboard side and circled back for a touchdown as the ship stopped in the middle of a bright blue ocean.

The gig was in the water and moving as we settled down, cut the engines and popped open the twin observation pods. I was standing in the opening when the first person I saw was our own Sal Marchionda, who was leading a bunch of very rough Master at Arms boys from Donahue's office. They were obviously expecting to find Flynn. I had to explain *Bridger's* killer was no longer with us. Puller's men had thrown his body in a slit trench with a pile of Japanese dead.

"Gotta scoot," said Lieutenant Tucker as we shook hands all around. I gave a special pat on the back to Barney and Mike and told them they were invited aboard *Bridger* any time.

The bosuns brought the gig up to the big double-wide door on C Deck and *Bridger* had her brow deployed to help us aboard. Haggerty and I were dressed in web gear and green utilities, with our rifles slung over our shoulders. The mud of Guadalcanal was on our boots, but I thought it fitting we would be getting our ship a little dirty. I made my way up and forward to my quarters on the bridge deck. I could feel *Bridger* pick up speed for our mission to Brisbane, and I was delighted to see Captain Kelly in front of my cabin door.

"Good work, Jonas," he told me. "But it looks like you've gone all Marine on us."

"A field expedient, sir," I told him.

"Your replacements did a credible job in your absence...but let's just say I am glad you're back in charge," he told me, turning to go back to his cabin.

"Our prisoner expired during the fight on Guadalcanal," I told him, not technically inaccurate.

"Good news, Jonas," he said quietly but firmly. "He won't be able to cause any more mischief." I would let that be the coda to this barbaric tale. Flynn caused more than mischief. But I knew my inner lawyer would never let Flynn out of my sight. He would inhabit my dreams and make me question myself again and again. Somehow, I managed to put it aside for the good of our ship. There was plenty of work to do, and work would be my salvation.

I went to my cabin, unloaded my weapons and stripped off my utilities. I got into a hot shower and watched the dirt go down the scupper. One of the chiefs had put my pressed summer khakis in my closet. I got my epaulets, bars, and service ribbons fastened, straightened up the "gig line" between my shirt buttons and my fly, and stepped out into the companionway. I walked forward to the bridge, and I took comfort in the fact that everyone was paying attention to their duties.

Timothy Cole

Someone said: "Commander on the bridge!" and I responded with a leisurely "At ease, gentlemen." It was as good a welcome as any, as Bryant vacated my elevated chair, and handed me that day's fitness reports for my review.

"Request permission to maintain the lookouts and the gun crews," he asked me.

"Make it so," I responded, as I cast my gaze towards the far horizon.

Ship of Tears

Epilogue

After *Bridger's* brief trip to Australia (following our PBY drop off at sea), we were sent back to San Francisco, then back to the South Pacific. We did that three more times before we took up our duties ferrying Eisenhower's armies from Boston to Liverpool in the runup to Operation Overlord. During this period, and against our better judgement, we acquiesced to taking *Bridger* into the high Arctic latitudes to get war materiel into the hands of our Soviet allies. It was during the Murmansk run when our Soviet friends, aided and abetted by our own Lend-Lease overseers, kidnapped our entire crew and tried to steal our ship. It was not *Bridger's* first misadventure.

From the frigid waters of Scandinavia's northern capes, to our dangerous dash through France to rescue kidnapped Jewish kids, to the perilous cul de sac of the Adriatic... I would encounter thieves, spies, misfits and charlatans who would do *Bridger* harm. My job was to stand in their way. Chesty Puller, Smitty, even General Vandegrift showed me that fighting this world war left no room for self-doubt. Parsing legal concepts was best left for the courtroom. Out in the many theaters of war where *Bridger* sailed, it was kill or be killed...and I learned that lesson the hard way on Guadalcanal.

But there is an important, and I daresay more wholesome, coda to the story of *Bridger's* lone wolf, the evil Gerry Flynn. My beautiful spouse Margie was behind it. One June morning, on my way down the stairs dressed for a day at the office—stacks of yellow pad under my arm now ready for the typist—she handed me an airline ticket and informed me we are headed for Nebraska.

"Ogallala in the summer," she said. "Pack light."

I had an inkling of what she was up to, and I could only stand up straight and pay attention. Margie brooked no argument when she was in charge. We were heading out, together, to see the land that raised and nurtured my fine friend Smitty.

She'd booked us from Rochester to Chicago to North Platte, Nebraska. She'd arranged a rental car, and it was late that afternoon when we got to Ogallala. We checked into a small hotel on the main street and we found a little bar that served a decent pasta and meatball supper. We were early to bed after our long day of travel, and the next morning we drove to the high school. She wanted to be there when the bell rang, to see those fresh-faced, optimistic kids ready to tackle the big wide world. We found the trophy case in the lobby by the entrance to the auditorium. Smitty's loving cup was right in the center, next to the silver bowls, strutting trophies and brightly colored ribbons celebrating decades of Ogallala glory. Smitty's Medal of Honor was a little dusty, the pale-blue ribbon a bit faded, but someone had kept his loving cup shined. There was a photograph of that fine young man, taken before his trip across the seas. He was in his Marine dress blues and white cap, looking straight into the camera with a determined glint in his eye. His spectacles were clean and in good repair. There was another shot of Smitty taken on Guadalcanal. His utilities were ripped and dirty and the bridge of his glasses were taped together. But he was smiling. He was safe. He was with his buddies. The missing limbs, the bloody utilities...they were off in some unimaginable tomorrow.

The kids were trying to make it to class and the crowds in the hallways were starting to thin. We were joined by a gray-haired matron who wanted to know if we needed help. Margie explained our connection to the loving cup and the school, and soon we were in front of the principal, Mr. Trant. He took us on a tour and we visited a history class taught by Mr. Wheeler. I talked about Smitty, leaving out the scary bits. We pulled out an atlas and tried to find the Solomons to discuss why our leaders thought this piece of ground was important. We discussed lines of communication, supply routes, freedom of navigation, relationships with our all-important allies—and all the capabilities of our big ship and her talented crew. I gave them some of the strategic detail that offered the relevance of these far-off places to our own freedoms.

After class, a beautiful brown-haired girl named Theresa came up to me and told me Smitty was her dad's uncle. We learned her father now ran Ogallala Truck and Tractor. She gave us directions and soon we were standing in a big Quonset hut filled with threshers, combines, disc harrows and articulating hay rakes. Margie and I were admiring the Farmalls, John Deeres, and International Harvesters when a young man approached. It was Theresa's dad, Stan. I explained our mission. I'd served with Smitty, Ogallala's medal of honor winner, and I just wanted to take a look at the place where Smitty had lived, to see the things he saw.

I was suddenly struck by the sheer brilliance of my dear Margie. She wanted me to come out here to create new memories, to replace the vision of Smitty's lifeless body with the tangible reality of tiny Ogallala, bright with energy and promise. She wanted me to change my story, that horrific tape that kept looping through this old lawyer's careworn brain.

Stan was delighted I'd remembered Smitty had soloed in that Stinson when the boy was only fourteen. He led us out back to an adjoining hangar, where the Smith's Stinson was kept in a corner, restored to perfection and prized like the family pet. There was a wall with photos showing all the Smiths and their close friends who'd flown in the little Stinson, and Stan showed us a picture of a young Smitty standing in front of the airplane with his father, holding his pilot's license.

There was a big Cessna 180 taildragger sharing this space with the little Stinson and Stan suggested we go up to see a little of the Nebraska countryside, where Smitty and his friends had hiked and hunted.

"Any excuse to fly," Stan said.

He slid open the hangar doors, pre-flighted the machine and buckled us in. Margie wanted me to take the right seat up front and I was afraid to show how tickled I was. Stan shouted "clear prop!" and made sure his controls were "free and correct." Soon we were whipping down a grass strip and the tail came up. We levitated off the ground and I was struck by all the sky and space these Nebraskans called home. We flew low over the rolling countryside for a lap around Lake McConnaughy, a man-made impoundment dug out in 1935 that was still filling when Smitty shipped out in early '42. We were wearing headsets to block out the din from the airplane's throbbing Lycoming engine, and Stan told us all about Ogallala's heritage as a fuel and watering hole for the trans-continental railroad, and its history as a cattle transshipment point. Ogallala saw a constant flow of cowboys, buffalo hunters, saloon keepers, and riffraff who peopled this budding corner of Nebraska. We circled the swamps and sloughs where Smitty shot ducks with his dad, and we flew low over the rolling grasslands where Smitty sought fellowship with his hunting pals. Stan concluded our impromptu air tour with a low pass over the Ogallala gridiron, where Reginald Howard Smith—"Smitty" to his friends—held the line.

Stan and his wife invited us to their home for dinner that night, and this being Nebraska, they invited friends and neighbors who all came with a dish to pass. They wanted to get a good look at the man who was with Smitty the day he died, and I wound up amplifying on some of the history that *Bridger* and her crew had lived throughout the war. Margie and I made our way back to our little hotel late at night. It had been an exhausting day and we had a flight out of North Platte the next morning. As we lay on that double bed with the worn-out springs, Margie took my hand, patted my old head, and said, "Thank you, Jonas Pratt."

"Why are you thanking me?" I asked her. "I should be thanking you. You brought us out here... so I could finally put the war to rest."

"So have you?" she asks. "Put it to rest, I mean..."

"You'll find out in the next installment," I told her. And she rolled over to turn out the light

Ship of Tears

The END

Timothy Cole

Notes and Acknowledgements

Ship of Tears is inspired by the real-life hometown heroes of New York's Finger Lakes who served in our nation's military. This region of long, deep lakes and vineyard-studded hillsides is bounded by Binghamton to the southeast, Syracuse to the northeast, Rochester to the northwest, and Hornell to the southwest. Many areas lay claim to being "God's Country," but the Finger Lakes may have had an inside track regarding any intercession from the Almighty. Aside from heart-lifting beauty, the area has fostered a fearless, focused people who have always responded during times of national emergency— from The American Revolution to Operation Enduring Freedom.

Our family friend Warren Fribley was an American airman imprisoned in a German POW camp. My school friend John Post's mother Rosemary was an Army nurse in Europe. My favorite high school history teacher, Milton Wheeler, flew P-38 Lightning's in the South Pacific. My English teacher, Gary Madigan, was a U.S. Army Ranger in Vietnam. Joe Meade, Jr., served aboard the aircraft carrier *Ticonderoga* in World War II and received a commendation for valor after she was struck by Kamikaze off Formosa. Air Force-veteran Art Wilder was a Cornell-trained engineer who scratch built flying replicas of aircraft designed by Glenn Curtiss, a worthy son of the Finger Lakes who manufactured the ubiquitous Jenny and used the pristine waters of Keuka Lake to perfect the seaplane. Curtiss's shop in Hammondsport created the U.S. Navy's first aircraft, the A-1 Triad.

Too many to count let alone name, I can only offer a salute to friends and acquaintances who answered the call. It's a long list. Bath pharmacist Fay Dildine and classmate Pete Langendorfer both enjoyed long careers in the Air Force. Many locals joined the Army: Bob Gelder, Stephen Wightman, Gilbert "Gib" Marchionda, and Drs. Bryan Braman and Vrooman Higby. My dad served as a medic in the U.S. Army in a pre-conflict Korea. My cousin William Cole was aboard the *Nautilus* when it made the first sub-sea transit of the North Pole in 1957. His brother Tom served on Navy cruisers (and he's always obliged me when I've dragooned him into reading one of my manuscripts.) Bath's Larry Naron began his career in the nuclear power industry after serving in the submarine *George C. Marshall.* There are more names of sons and daughters of the Finger Lakes found on memorials in the communities sprinkled around this special place.

Inspiration for *Ship of Tears* was provided by my grandfather, Robert E. Cole, who was the damage control officer, then the executive officer aboard the *U.S.S. West Point*, converted into a troopship in 1941 from the ocean liner *America*. Commander Cole received a citation from

Admiral Chester Nimitz for his work in managing damage control response aboard his ship. A relaxed, congenial, Harvard-trained attorney, he turned himself into a marine engineer to accomplish this formidable, yet vital task. The manual he wrote on the subject came into my possession and was especially useful in creating the mighty *Bridger*, for which I confess some artistic license. I thought about using *West Point* as the scene of the crime in *Ship of Tears*, but I had to blend so many details to make the ship fit the plot that inventing a new troopship was the only way to avoid offending *West Point's* many knowledgeable admirers. After the war, *West Point* was turned back into an ocean liner and passed through several owners before she foundered on the rocks in the Azores as she was being towed to a new owner in the Mediterranean—a sad end to a ship with a magnificent history. I will never know if my grandfather would have approved of my project to turn *West Point* into a fictional set piece. But every novel must have a central character, and here it's the ship itself.

Plus, as we all know, every good story needs a hero; someone who is interesting, responsible, knowledgeable, and, to round things out, not without some manageable, less-than-fatal flaw. Jonas Pratt's fealty to the law is the trait that gets him into the most trouble when he faces a lawless war. But his respect, appreciation, and deep sense of caring for his crew is what sets him apart. These qualities, and his love of the outdoors, were the best parts of my grandfather. His wife Gertrude was an equal partner, companion, and wife. She is my "Margie" in this tale, and it was important to get her loyal, loving perspective involved when helping Jonas through his post-traumatic stress. She is his caregiver, sounding board, fellow gourmand—and a crack wing shot who also knows how to tie a dry fly. In a novel populated by men, Margie's voice adds a smart, and comforting, female dimension.

"Robert E." was also very practical. He told me once, (I was eight or nine), "Now remember. When you see a submarine periscope, you either head straight at it, or straight away. Never present your broadside." It still seems like good advice.

It is to this exceptional man, the individuals I mentioned—and the many more left unmentioned—that I tip my hat and to whom I dedicate this work. I am thinking of all of you as I send *Bridger* across the seas—next, to expose the dastardly Soviets in *The Murmansk Affair*. Then war-torn France in *Night Train to Buchenwald* as Jonas Pratt saves Jewish kids from a Vichy concentration camp. After that, to the Balkans, seething with intrigue, in *Sea of Secrets. The Last Kamikaze* is working through its twists and turns. Throughout the many voyages of the *James F. Bridger*, I hope the talents and the triumphs of Jonas Pratt carry the day for you, as he does for me.

I have thanked many people over my years as a novelist, and your enthusiasm for the voyages of the

James F. Bridger are gratefully received and appreciated. Here are special mentions: Mike and Susan Burke always encourage me with two thumbs up (and a neatly served gin and tonic); My pal Eric Burns was an early reader and awarded a thumbs up; Alison Murdoch is forever keen to be one of my valued beta readers; and Maggie Aftanis has previewed and devoured all the books in the Jonas Pratt series. She now calls Jonas "our guy." As usual, I am indebted to my dear friend Bonnie Barney of Penn Yan, who has helped me more than she'll ever know. Steve Marchionda loaned me his last name for my esteemed can-do character, "Sal."

As ever, my Polaris, the guide star by which I navigate, remains my loyal and loving Sarah.

Ship of Tears

U.S.S. West Point shed her escorts and sailed the seas alone, relying on her speed as her main defense. She carried 350,000 service members during World War II, and in August 1944 broke her own record by carrying over nine thousand souls. Credit: Naval History and Heritage Command.

ABOUT THE AUTHOR

TIMOTHY COLE

Timothy Cole's forty-year career as a journalist, editor, and author has taken him aboard America's nuclear Navy, to ozone depletion studies at the South Pole, and to the flight deck of a B-1 bomber. He is an instrument-rated private pilot and holds a 50-ton captain's license from the U.S. Coast Guard with a Merchant Mariner Credential. Currently, Tim serves as the chief content officer of Belvoir Media Group and is the publisher of *Practical Sailor* magazine. In prior roles he served as an editor at leading marine magazines and was the science/technology/aerospace editor of *Popular Mechanics*, where he covered Naval flight operations, underwater salvage technology, and the discovery of the *Titanic*.

Nurturing a lifelong fascination with ships and the sea, Tim and his wife Sarah Smedley live on the southern tip of Manhattan, where they regularly visit the South Street Seaport and Fraunces Tavern, crossroads of America's maritime history. Tim is working on *The Murmansk Affair*, which will take *Bridger* into the high latitudes of the Barents Sea to deliver war materiel to the Soviet Union, America's pugnacious and inscrutable World War II ally. Also in the works: *Night Train to Buchenwald* and the rescue of Jewish children from the Vichy concentration camp at Drancy.

Tim is the author of the Dasha Petrov mystery series, and his novel *The Sea Glass Murders* was a finalist for Connecticut book of the year.